The Last Time We Were Here

Jaime noticed with a little flutter that his eyes had dropped to the necklace at her throat.

A subtle change flicked over his face, but what the change meant, she couldn't tell. He reached out and took the little silver *J* in his hand. His touch against her throat felt familiar to her, weirdly familiar, not like Evan's hand, but like someone known well to her, nevertheless.

"Where did you get this?"

She caught her breath. "Oh, it's something I've had for a long time." She tried for a casual tone. "An old boyfriend gave it to me."

"I don't know why it looks so familiar to me. Maybe I've just seen one similar when I was picking out jewelry for Francesca."

"Probably." Jaime nodded, afraid to breathe.

Dane seemed to relax a little. "When you wear it," he teased. "Does it make you think of the old boyfriend?"

"I—I was just kidding about the old boyfriend." Jaime, caught in her own choice of words, was thrown off-guard. Before she could continue, Francesca was at her side, linking her arm through Jaime's.

"Isn't that pretty, Dane? Can you believe she found that on one of our antiquing mornings?"

Jaime held her breath. Would Dane believe the fib? He dropped his hand and let the necklace rest against her throat again. His face relaxed as he shook his head in bewilderment. "I must have seen something like it somewhere. It's pretty, so simple, but sometimes the simplest things are the most meaningful. It actually is something I would have bought for a girlfriend."

Yes. It is something you would give to a girlfriend, and a long time ago you did. When your name was Donnie, you gave it to me.

THE LAST TIME WE WERE HERE

Joan Conning Afman

A Wings ePress, Inc.

Paranormal Romance Novel

Wings ePress, Inc.

Edited by: Patricia Evans
Copy Edited by: Karen Babcock
Senior Editor: Karen Babcock
Executive Editor: Marilyn Kapp
Cover Artist: Tricia FitzGerald

All rights reserved

Wings ePress Books
http://www.wings-press.com

Copyright © 2009 by Joan Afman
ISBN: 978-1-59705-590-1

Published In the United States Of America

Wings ePress Inc.
3000 N. Rock Road
Newton, KS 67114

Dedication

To my mother, Marjorie Billings Conning, who always told me, "I think you could *write.*" Here's to you, Mom.

Prologue

June 14, 1961
The tenth reunion Mill Pond High School, class of '51
Lakeside Inn,
Mill Pond, Massachusetts

"Not *me!* Not *me!*" Kathy screamed as the gunmen advanced across the well-polished dance floor of the elegantly restored old hotel, but she was the first to fall in a hail of bullets. Forrest Brown, brandishing his hunting rifle, and "Balls" Brass, firing indiscriminately with a pistol, attacked just as they had long planned to do on this evening. And Kathy Kelly had helped them plan it.

Paul Peller and John Crenshaw rushed the shooters in vain; they collapsed not ten feet from the table where the horrified classmates who had been noisily celebrating their tenth reunion sat. Sylvia, their class president, took a bullet in the forehead, and Francie, their prom queen, went down, swaying gracefully as a dancer. Janie Carlson Rance sat frozen and watched all the others fall in their ballet of death, all The Nine, as they had been called, the most popular kids in the class of fifty-one, and the four spouses or significant others. Donnie Barrett seized Janie's hand and attempted to pull her down under the table, but it was too late. Forrest had them in his sights, and the last thing Janie saw was Donnie's face covered in blood and tears.

One

At last the moving van pulled away with a series loud groans. Jaime collapsed into the new Hitchcock rocker the movers had left conveniently in the center of the high-ceilinged living room and set her coffee mug down with a resolute thump on a nearby occasional table. Jaime smiled at her husband, Evan, who sat on the sofa and wiped the sweat from his forehead with a handkerchief. "Well, we're moved in. I'm glad this part of it is over."

"And I so appreciate all your hard work."

It really is a beautiful house. Jaime gazed around the room. She'd had it wallpapered in a pale yellow print, "morning sunshine," and it did indeed reflect the shy morning light that peeked through the tall, elegant windows.

"Well, here we are." Jaime stretched her arms, trying to relieve her aching muscles. "Mill Pond, Massachusetts, middle of nowhere."

Evan stuffed the handkerchief back into his jeans pocket. "Look, Jaime." His voice oozed patience. "I know you didn't want to leave Atlanta, I know you gave up a promising career, and I admit this was a selfish move on my part, and I want you to know that I realize—I owe you, kid. We'll make it work, I promise."

"I just hope this is worth it for your sake I was about to be promoted to sportswear buyer for all three stores. Where am I going to find a job in fashion in these parts?"

"Boston—"

"Too far to commute."

"Springfield—"

She snorted. "There's no store there that begins to compare with Jordan's. I don't want to start all over again, any more than you would want to."

He sighed and stood up "I can make such a difference here. I never would have made super in Atlanta, as you well know. In spite of getting my doctorate and teaching part time at Emory, it's so political there that I never would have been more than head of the English department."

She nodded. "I know, Evan, but—"

"I'll have three districts here, Mill Pond, Sandville, and Westlake. I feel called to do this. They need me here to bring them all together into one modern school system. I have the vision to do it."

"*Called,* like a clergyman?"

He ignored that but added, "and it will be a much better place for the boys to grow up. Small town atmosphere, running in and out of each other's houses without having to take a bus somewhere, ice-skating on that little pond down by the mill—"

"Snow, ugh. Ice, yuk. I'm a southern girl, Evan. I don't know why I ever agreed to this." She looked around at her living room. "It is a beautiful house, though," she admitted with obvious reluctance. "Much nicer that we could ever have afforded in Atlanta."

"Come on, Jaime, I know you'll grow to love it here. You're a strong woman who's adapted to other difficult circumstances in your life." He stood up. "I have to shower and change. I have a meeting with the three principals in half an hour."

~ * ~

Jaime puttered around, putting things away as she heard Evan's deliberate movements upstairs, the water running, then his footsteps coming back down the stairs.

"Come on, walk out with me," he coaxed, taking her arm.

Reluctantly, she got up and went outside with him.

"It feels like home, doesn't it, Jaime?" he asked as they stood on the sidewalk, holding hands, gazing at the intricate Victorian façade of their newly purchased house.

She nodded and ran her hand over the old-fashioned mailbox, which she had already painted with the name. It did have a home-like feel to it— The small town with its one main street lined with necessary shops; the Mom and Pop grocery; the hardware store; the drug store, not a chain, but locally owned still; the local beauty shop, Main Street Manes; and the rest. And here was their beautiful new house, a true jewel among other Victorian gems lining Oak Street.

"It'll be a good place for Jack and Josh to grow up," Evan said. He grinned at her and placed a hand on her belly. "As well as for whoever is coming along next."

"Well, there's nobody living in there yet." She laughed. "But there might be soon. I'll keep you posted."

"You'd better!" He leaned over to kiss her on the mouth, right in front of anyone who may be looking out their windows at them.

~ * ~

Later, Jaime let herself relax against the rich, burnished wood of the rocker, closing her eyes. She had to admit there were advantages to this move, even though she'd had to give up her own blossoming career. Evan was so gung-ho and so happy, and he was right, it would be a great place for their children to grow up. If they stayed long enough, they would have the same friends all through their school years, from kindergarten through high school, and that was a wonderful gift to give children, that sense of place and belonging. She'd been grateful to her parents for providing that for her, and she had to agree with Evan, she did have an eerie sense of it feeling like home here.

It was almost as if she already knew the town with its antique-looking streetlights, the winding streets off Main leading down to the river where the old woolen mill, now silent and brooding, covered with vines, slumped, hunched over and useless. And outside of Mill Pond, just before the acres of light woodland began, was the P & B Lumber Company—"Everything you need to build or repair." It all seemed so familiar to her, as if she had lived here before, but that was just déjà vu, the trick the mind plays on you, or memories from novels she had read that were set in small towns like this.

The doorbell rang and startled her.

The woman, one side or the other of fifty, thin and wispy-haired, dressed in shorts and a striped tee-shirt, held a steaming casserole, her hands protected by colorful potholders. She had interesting, almond-shaped amber eyes that held Jaime's for a moment before she spoke.

"Hi!" She projected an aura of cheeriness. "I'm Jane-Michelle Taylor, next door in the green house." She nodded her head in the direction she meant. "Welcome to the neighborhood."

It was so small-town, so bucolic, but so comforting in its cheerful directness, that Jaime could not help but smile back at her. Did people really still bring casseroles to new neighbors? Shades of the 1950s. She accepted the dish, mitts and all.

"Come in. I'm Jaime Reid. My husband, Evan, is the new—"

"Oh, we all know that already!" Jane Michelle flashed a toothy grin. She looked around the room. "This is such a beautiful house. If it had ever been for sale when we were buying, we would have bought this one. I've always loved it. I used to roller-skate by it when I was a little girl and fantasize about living here."

Again the feeling of déjà vu swept over Jaime, and she leaned against the kitchen counter to steady herself. In her mind she saw the girl, green corduroy overalls and long braids flying, skating along the sidewalk and staring with longing eyes at the house, *her* house.

Jane-Michelle accepted her offer of coffee, and they sat together on the sofa, which the movers had placed in front of the two tall windows flanking the street. Jaime had pushed the coffee table into place in front of the sofa. She tapped the arm of the sofa. "I'm not sure I'm leaving the sofa here."

Jane-Michelle gestured across the room. "I think I'd put it over there, facing the fireplace, and let this side of the room be the more formal one."

"Just what I thought!" Jaime followed her gesture. "And I don't really want the television in here. There's a den off the kitchen we'll use for that."

They went on companionably, sharing thoughts and learning about each other's lives.

"Main Street Manes is your mom's?" Jaime asked in surprise, as Jane-Michelle told her about her humble upbringing in the shabby house down by the river, and her mother, Willow, who had somehow got the money and energy together to go to beauty school and eventually borrowed the money to open her own shop. "Her real name is *Willow?*"

Jane-Michelle smiled and nodded. "Isn't that *awful?* I'm sure glad I didn't get saddled with that! Jane-Michelle is old fashioned and complicated enough."

"Your name is lovely," Jaime objected. "Actually, I think Willow is pretty, too."

"For a dog," Jane-Michelle said. "There's actually a golden retriever in that pink house..." She waved a finger in the direction of a salmon-colored, three-story house with a turret across the street. "...named Willow. My mother was planting some flowers in the yard for me once, and one of the neighbors called to her from their yard. The dog came running!"

Jaime laughed. "What about your father?"

Jane-Michelle's friendly, open face shut down instantly. She shrugged and pretended to examine a small figurine on the coffee table. "We don't talk about him.

Embarrassed, Jaime retreated. "I'll need a haircut soon. For sure I'll make an appointment with your mother."

"Just walk in. No appointment necessary. Of course you don't have any choice of where you get your hair done in Mill Pond—unless you want to trek into Springfield. Then you can make an appointment."

Amid their laughter, the phone rang. As Jaime, an apologetic expression on her face, got up to answer it, Jane-Michelle, with gestures readily understood by all women, fluttered her fingers at Jaime and bowed herself out of the house.

"I think I made my first friend here." Jaime described Jane-Michelle's visit. "Her mother runs the only hair salon in town."

"I knew you'd make friends fast." Evan sounded pleased. "In spite of your dependence on concerts, art galleries, power lunches, and big-town shopping. There are things to be said for small-town life, especially for the kids."

"I can see that. And how did your meeting with the board go?" She couldn't deny the enthusiasm in his voice, which she suddenly realized she hadn't heard for a long time in Atlanta, and because she loved him, she was glad. Yes, she would miss the galleries, the excitement of the city, the clubs they occasionally frequented with friends out in Buckhead, but she would adjust. And they still had friends there. She could fly back for weekend visits, letting the kids have all-boy weekends with their dad.

She checked back in to what Evan was saying. "And we're going to hire more special ed teachers, more art and music people, and set up some activities where kids from all three towns can get together. Hopefully we can eliminate or at least dampen down the rivalry between the kids of all three schools, especially at the high school level."

"That's good, really good, Evan." Jaime thought he'd made an excellent start. "All three schools serve all the grades in the their own towns, K-12, isn't that right?"

"Right, and as cozy an arrangement that might have been in the past, the elementary kids need their own school, and the high schoolers definitely need their own turf. And...," he said, excitement rising in his voice, "there's a real possibility that in a few years we might start a building drive for a new, state-of-the-art regional high school that would serve all three towns. Just think, Jaime, what that would mean for this region."

He went on. She half-listened, half-drifted, thinking about Jane-Michelle, how comfortable she had instantly felt with her, and how different life would be now, here in Mill Pond. *No more keeping up with the Joneses. We* are *the Joneses.*

As if on cue, when she hung up with Evan, the boys came tumbling down the winding staircase. For two small boys, they made all the noise five-year-old twins could manage to make, which was considerable. She clapped her hands over her ears. "Inside voices, boys!"

"We want lunch!" Josh announced. "What's this?" He lifted the foil from one corner of the casserole, bent down. and sniffed.

"Chicken and biscuits, by the smell," Jaime smiled at her son and ruffled his hair. "We're going to have to get you guys haircuts before school starts."

"Yuk!" Jack said. "Grilled cheese!"

"Peanut butter and jelly!" Josh demanded.

"And then we want our bikes," Jack insisted. "Where are they?"

"In the cellar, I think. I'll go look for them after I make your sandwiches." She set about pulling the ingredients from the refrigerator and putting the sandwiches together, cutting off the crusts and cutting the bread into quarters, as the boys preferred. She poured glasses of milk and set them up at the table, from the forties, she guessed, that had been left in the house by the former occupants. Truth be told, the whimsical side of her nature really liked the old table and thought they just might keep it—on the other hand, she wrinkled her nose as she glanced at the stained old porcelain sink that had not responded to any of the cleaners she had tried. That definitely had to be replaced, and soon. She'd already spoken to Evan about it, and he'd promised to drive out to that lumber company, P & B Lumber, down on the river road to see what they had or could order for them.

While the boys ate, and giggled, and poked each other, Jaime wandered into the living room. She pulled aside one of the heavy green damask drapes—they *really* had to go—and stared with a strange, growing sense of unease at the green house next door.

Jane-Michelle. It was a pretty name, a combination she had never heard before, but it seemed vaguely familiar, as if she *had* known someone by that name. And that house—she could just picture the living room, old dark furniture, a well-worn rug with a pattern of flowers and leaves, two teen-aged girls sitting on the floor by the fireplace, one of them writing something in a small, brown book... Jaime shook her head as the vision faded, but as she let the drapery fall back across the window, she looked around and realized with a shock that the living room she'd imagined was not Jane-Michelle's; it was hers, the way this room had looked a long time ago.

"Mom! The bikes!"

Jaime turned to see Jack standing with his hands on his hips. He tapped his toe impatiently. He looked so much like Evan that it made her smile.

"Okay, let's go downstairs and look for them," She led them down the rickety, cobweb-lined staircase that led to the unfinished basement—the kind that once housed an actual coal bin and a root cellar.

"Here they are!" Josh and his twin jumped on their bikes and began to pedal around the large, open space.

"Man, it's spooky down here." Jack screeched to a stop after several turns around the floor. "How do we get the bikes out of here?"

"There's a door over here," She led the boys across the floor to the far end of the cellar, where the cement floor gave way to dirt. A shabby door—its dark green paint mostly worn down to ancient wood—opened with a series of creaks and groans to the driveway.

"Here you go." She held the door open for them. "Stay close to home, please, guys until we get to know the neighborhood better."

They were gone with whoops and shouts, and after making sure they were staying within bounds, Jaime closed the door and turned back to survey the cellar. It would take a lot of time, work, and money, but a nice rec room could be created down here eventually. She smiled as she noticed a metal shelf unit stacked with old-fashioned glass canning jars—the kind her grandmother had used.

"These jars *are* antiques and might be worth something. I've noticed several antique shops around that might be interested." She pivoted slowly around, taking note of the ample space and strong structure. Her eyes went to the rugged wooden beams that crisscrossed the ceiling. *I like those. They can stay when we rehab.*

"What's that?" Something wedged into the corner of two intersecting beams caught her eye. It looked like—what? A book? What was a book doing up there? She looked around for something to stand on and spied an old ladder on the other side of the room. Jaime dragged it over, balanced it as well as she could against one of the side walls, and climbed up, going step by step to make sure the ladder held. It did, and she was able by the fourth rung to reach up and pry the book loose.

"Ugh!" It was covered with grime, and a large brown spider she disturbed crawled indignantly over her hand. She flicked the spider into the air, dropped the book, and scrambled back down the ladder.

It looked like someone's diary, well-worn and filled with undisciplined scrawls. She flipped through it; the names meant nothing to her: Sylvia, Francie, Janie. *Oh, my goodness! There was a mention of Willow! That had to be Jane-Michelle's mother. Well, I guess this might make interesting reading after all, when I have the time.*

The diary was sparsely written, and seemed to span a number of years, yet it was only three-quarters filled. She turned to the last page.

It's all set, Saturday, June 14th, the tenth reunion of the class of '51. Forrest and Balls have the guns, and I will call them from the Inn and tell them exactly where we're sitting. I wish I had a gun, too. I'd blow off snobby Sylvia's head with real joy. And all the rest of them too—Francie, Paul, Barb, Donnie, Janie, yes, and even Suki who's supposed to be my best friend. Some best friend. Every time she can get away and do something without me, she does. I hate them all so much—too good for everyone else, their noses in the air, their parties where no one else is included, their secret conversations, where nobody else knows what they're talking about.

Forrest told me, "I've waited forever to pay back that snotty Sylvia for the way she's treated me. Even if she agreed to marry me and bear my kids, it wouldn't change my mind. I want the bitch gone forever."

We've had to wait ten years for our revenge, but it'll be worth it, just to see the looks on their faces when they realize what's happening. Saturday night they will all be dead.

Jaime collapsed onto the lowest step of the stairway. "Oh! Oh, my God!" she whispered. "I never made that connection. This is where that first Columbine-type massacre happened forty-some years ago!"

She narrowed her eyes, thinking. Her husband had conveniently forgotten to mention that little fact.

Two

"So this is Mill Pond, as in the Mill Pond massacre of '61?" Jaime asked as they lingered over coffee and French toast, made with homemade bread from Pam's, the local bakery on Main Street.

"I guess it is, yes," Evan mumbled, concentrating his attention on an article in the *Springfield Register* and not looking at her.

"Evan..." She caught at his hand, which forced him to look up and meet her gaze. "You knew that, didn't you? Why in the world would you want to be superintendent in a school district with a reputation like this? Plus the fact that this is now the place where our kids will be *from.* Did you ever think of that? That's the first thing people will think of when they say they're from Mill Pond."

"Oh, that was fifty years ago." Evan gave an off-hand shrug and folded the newspaper. He pointed to the article he had been reading and handed her the paper. "There's an article here about the new, brilliant, innovative superintendent of schools in the tri-town area, in case you're interested."

She took the paper, but continued to look at him. "Evan, why *here?*"

"I don't know, Jaime." He shook his head "As soon as I saw the ad in *Today's Educator,* I knew I had apply for it. I knew I wanted that job. I told you—I felt *called.* I knew I was supposed to come here."

"But why didn't you level with me about its history?"

He stood up, stretched, and gazed at her with an apologetic look. "I knew it would be hard enough getting you out of Atlanta. You had your career there, your friends from childhood, your parents—" He shrugged, as if the rest were obvious. "I might as well level with you about what else I found out."

"What?" She didn't know whether she wanted to hear the answer or not.

"Well, Dane Summers, the Mill Pond principal, told me that the Brown family, once lived in this house."

"So?"

"Forrest Brown, as in one of the shooters at the sixty-one massacre, that's who."

That got her attention. She put down the forkful of French toast that she was just about to put in her mouth and stared at him. "How did you find that out? I've asked several people, and nobody will even talk about it. They say something like 'Oh, let's leave the past in the past', and change the subject."

"Dane told me. His wife grew up here. Her name is Francesca. I think you'll like her a lot."

Evan began to raise his coffee mug to his lips, then hesitated, and gazed out the window, where several birds perched on a branch of the maple tree and twittered a conversation among themselves. "Dane said Forrest's parents lived here briefly when Forrest and his sister Willow were kids."

"Willow, Jane-Michelle's mother." Jaime nodded

"Did you happen to ask your new friend, Jane-Michelle?"

"I did. Same thing. Got very nervous and changed the subject."

"That's weird." Evan shifted his gaze from the window to her. "I tried to look it up on the Internet, and there is no mention of it at all. Like it never happened."

"*Very* weird." Jaime had lost her appetite. She pushed the plate of barely touched French toast away, put her elbows on the table, folded her hands, and leaned her chin into them.

"How about the school board? You did bring it up with them, didn't you?"

"Same thing. Long time ago. We've been on top of that for years and years. Never happen again. No one will discuss it at all."

"I thought the Browns were a poor family," Jaime said. "How could they afford an expensive place like this?"

"Well, I'm not sure they owned it," Evan began to pull on his ear lobe, as he often did when he was thinking something through. "This was a poorer neighborhood then. It was all rehabbed about twenty years ago. I think they rented."

Jaime glanced toward the staircase, where sounds of small boys began to echo from the upstairs regions. "Dane told you all this? It's more than I managed to pull out of anyone."

"I also talked to the guy at the lumber company. Ryan something—Barrett, I think, as in P & B Lumber. I stopped in to ask about a replacement sink for the kitchen..." He gestured toward the stained porcelain sink. "Ryan told me they had done a ton of work for the Potters, who sold the house to us."

The twins tumbled into the room, their sandy hair so like Evan's sticking up in unruly tufts just the way his did before he showered and tamed it with gel in the morning.

"You guys will be starting kindergarten next week," Evan said, as Josh climbed up into the chair next to him. "Are you excited about it?"

Ignoring his father, Josh traced one of the decorative tiles on the enameled kitchen table. "Why is this table *pink?* And why isn't it wood? I never seen a table like this one."

"You never *saw* a table like this one," his father corrected him.

"That's what I said," Josh replied. "Don't you ever listen?"

"It's old." Jaime smiled. "It came with the house. I painted it pink, and I sort of like it. And don't talk back to your father like that."

"How old?" Jack asked. "More than eleven years old?"

"Yes," Jaime told him. "Probably forty or fifty years old. Older than Daddy and I are."

"Wow," Jack exclaimed. "That's *old*!"

"I don't like it." Josh stuck out his tongue. "I like *new* stuff."

A frown crossed Evan's face. "You can't be rude to your teachers like this when you go to school. You have to learn to be polite, even when you don't like something." He shifted his glance to Jaime. "I think it's good you're going to be home to spend more time with them."

Jaime shrugged, not looking at him. "You know what they say, Evan. Teachers' kids and preachers' kids are the worst behaved."

"Well, there's no excuse for that." He gave the boys a pretend-glare, but his voice was stern. "I want to see better behavior from you two, starting now."

He got up and took his dishes over to the sink. He leaned against the counter. Jaime felt him watching her as she cut up French toast for the boys and drenched it in maple syrup. "You're a wonderful mother, you know, but you're too easy on them."

"I know. Part of the problem was that I was working all the time in Atlanta, and someone else took care of them. But I'm home now, and we'll work on it."

Evan shifted his weight from one foot to the other. "I'm meeting with the principal and teachers at the Mill Pond School later this morning. I can be home about one, and I take the kids to the park and buy them hot dogs for lunch if there are things you want to get done."

"Thanks." She fiddled with her hair. "Actually, I could use a haircut. I thought I might drop in on Willow."

He raised his eyebrows and nodded. "Well, she *was* Forrest's sister. Maybe you can get something out of her, without trying too hard, of course."

She grinned. "I won't be obvious, if that's what you're driving at. She's probably pretty sensitive about the past and her brother's part in it."

"I'm going to go out and toss the football around with the boys for a while. I don't think the past here has anything to do with the present, so try and relax and enjoy your new home."

"Easy for you to say," she called after him as he headed outside with the boys. "You're the one who wanted to come here, not me."

Feeling slightly unsettled and rebuffed, Jaime perused the article he had given her and then set it aside. He had felt called to come here, to run this particular school system? Why? It was eerie; she had felt that she already knew this town, was familiar with these elegant old houses on Oak Street. Evan had driven her past the consolidated school where he would have his office. Just looking at the old brick edifice had given her the shivers.

She glanced at the diary, resting on the kitchen counter. She had meant to show it to Evan, but hadn't. Well, maybe she'd just read it first. He had his secrets; she could have hers. She started with the first entry. If her calculations were right, this would be the end of the senior year.

February 3, 1951

This ought to be rich! Forrest is going to ask Sylvia to the Valentine's Day Dance, knowing of course that she wouldn't be caught dead with him and that she already has a date with Paul. He hates her guts for the way she treats him and everyone else, as if they just don't measure up to her elevated status. This will make it all worse, as she's bound to be nasty when he asks her. Balls is going to ask Francie, who goes around with her nose in the air ever since she got to be prom queen last year—just to get the same reaction from her—but he's already promised to take Willow, Forrest's sister, whom nobody else would dream of asking anyway. Me—I'm going with my cousin Jack from Pittsfield, but I made him swear not to tell anyone he's my cousin. We'll be sitting with The Nine, and it should be an interesting evening!

She closed the diary written in green ink. It seemed to span ten years, from the time of the Valentine's Day Dance in 1951 to just before the tenth reunion in '61. What on earth had happened to bring on the slaughter that had happened ten years later?

Three

Mill Pond's proverbial main street *was* Main Street. It ran north to south with scarcely a curve, unusual for New England towns, where the local roads were often as twisted as cow paths.

Jaime parked the car and strolled up the street, which was only a few blocks long, crossed at the crosswalk, and surveyed the shops on the other side. She passed Willow's beauty shop, which was called, generically, Main Street Manes. The sign in the window, hand-lettered, read 'No appointment necessary. Friendly service.'

I hope so, thought Jaime wryly. *There's nothing worse than having someone antagonistic hovering over you with a razor blade and scissors.*

She stopped to look at the offerings in Gifts of Grace, Grace Gray, Proprietor: Unique handmade Gifts by Local Artisans. *Maybe they would take a couple of paintings on commission. I can paint local scenes, barns, piney woods, and horses as well as I can paint Southern mansions and salt marshes.* She passed by the hardware store and noted that they carried paints, oils and acrylics, watercolor pads and canvas, and that was good to know. O'Brien's Shoes came next and a small department store, which, by the displays in its windows, seemed to carry some of everything.

Suddenly she stopped short. In an alcove between two building was a doorway and a stairway leading to a suite of offices on the second floor. The name of the law firm, James and Johnson was lettered in gold, and in small letters underneath it stated that the firm was originally Crenshaw and Crenshaw. Why did that name ring a bell?

She sighed, and headed back toward Willow's shop She thought wistfully of Maurice's French Twist, where after her hair was styled and colored most discreetly by one of the best European hair experts, she would be offered a glass of wine (and good wine at that! None of these drugstore brands!) and have a manicure and a facial, if she wished. Classical music played in the background, the chairs were butter-soft white leather...

Oh well. She sighed. No use thinking about all that. That life was gone like a dream.

A stout, middle-aged woman in a pink smock greeted Jaime as she entered the shop. "Well, hello!" she said in a hearty voice, as she wiped her hands on a small white towel and then tossed it into a basket of used cloths. "You must be Jaime Reid, the new super's wife. Jane-Michelle told us she met you, and we've been hoping you'd show up sooner or later."

"How about sooner? Are you Willow?" Jaime offered her hand and a smile.

"Oh, no! I'm Linda Cane, one of the beauticians here. I also do manicures. And you look like you could use one."

Jaime laughed. "As soon as I get through stripping and painting. We bought the old Porter house, and there's a ton of work to be done in there."

"Oh, I bet!" Linda agreed. She turned toward the back of the shop and gestured. "Willow's in the back. I'm just finishing up Mrs.

Norwell, but Willow's free to do your hair if you want. I'll tell her you're here." She flashed Jaime a smile and motioned toward several vacant chairs. "Just have a seat for a few secs." She fluttered away like an oversized pink butterfly, light on her feet in spite of her weight.

The shop was small, painted shell pink with pink checked curtains drawn to the sides and fastened with mammoth floppy bows flanking the front window. A few shelves, placed high and out of reach of the stylists' working supplies, held a variety of country china, sugar bowls and creamers, tea pots, vases, coffee cups and saucers, and decorative plates upright on stands. Several framed prints, amateur watercolors, boasted rural scenes painted in the manner of Grandma Moses, simple but charming.

A shock of instant recognition ran through her as Willow came toward her. How could this woman she had never seen before seem so familiar? Then, with relief, she realized that Willow was Jane-Michelle's mother. Of course she seemed familiar!

Willow was an older version of Jane-Michelle: medium height, gray streaks in her sandy hair, same cheerful smile. Only the eyes were different; Willow's were a pale, almost watery blue, where Jane-Michelle had those unusual-shaped brown eyes. Willow had to be in her late sixties or even early seventies in order to be Jane-Michelle's mother. There was a hint of faded prettiness, but the lines etched in her face spoke of a hard life, frustration, and sadness.

~ * ~

But there was something else, something that put Jaime in such a weird mood that it was difficult to keep up with and supply answers to Willow's chatter, as she sat in the chair, hair freshly washed and smelling of apples, draped with a pink cloth and feeling like a lamb prepared for the slaughter, rather than a pampered client, as she had at Maurice's.

"Now what shall we do?" Willow asked, running her fingers through Jaime's shoulder-length hair and regarding her in the mirror.

"I—I thought I might go shorter." Jaime threaded her fingers through her hair. "The boys are just starting school, and I'm working on the house, so something easier to take care of might be better."

Willow nodded. "I see you have it colored. It's a beautiful shade. I can match that if you want, or—" She paused, biting her lip thoughtfully. "You could just let it go natural, and I could sell you shampoo and a rinse to bring out the golden highlights." She laughed. "This is the country, after all, Mrs. Reid. You won't be going to too many balls here!"

She flushed. "*Jaime*, please. I already consider Jane-Michelle a friend, and I hope you will be, too."

"Do you, now?" Willow asked softly, as if more to herself than to Jaime. Then, briskly, she continued. "All right, Jaime, shorter, layered, a little fringed on the ends?" She cupped her hands under Jaime's hair and pantomimed a shorter style. "This will be easier to keep up with, I think."

Willow was obviously very good at what she did. Jaime watched as she snipped and shaved a few strands at a time. In short order, Willow transformed the shoulder-length bob into a shorter, more contemporary style. As she sat under Willow's capable hands, enjoying her touch and the feel of the comb on her scalp—why did it feel so marvelous when someone else did your hair?—she pondered as to how to bring up the subject of the Mill Pond massacre.

After a period of silence, in which Jaime closed her eyes and let her mind wander, Willow spoke, her voice quiet, as if she didn't want it to carry to the other stations. "Do you know..." Not meeting Jaime's eyes, Willow continued her snipping "...that I once lived in that house, the one you bought, when I was a child?"

Jaime snapped awake. "Jane-Michelle said something. Oh, she said she'd always loved that house and they would have bought it if it had ever been for sale."

"So she would have, and she and Glenn bought the house next door, but we rented there—the Porter house—when I was a little girl. My parents and my brother, Forrest, and I. You're familiar with the name Forrest Brown?" She put her hand under Jaime's chin and tilted her head to look at herself in the mirror. "Is this short enough? I could go shorter. It would look good on you."

Maybe she's just testing me to find out what I've already heard.

"Yes, I think so. I mean, shorter." She nodded at Willow's questioning look. "And yes, I've heard about Forrest. Somewhat."

"When... all that happened, we had been long gone from that house. My father died in a barroom brawl, and that seemed to have a disastrous effect on Forrest. My mother, God bless her, worked her tush off, taking in laundry and cleaning houses, and with my working in high school, we were able to buy that little shack down by the river, where we lived when... it happened."

"By *it,* you mean the school shootings?" She held her breath. Was Willow actually going to talk about it?

"Forrest was my older brother, you know," Willow went on, as she carefully snipped around the edges of Jaime's hair. "He had a lot of problems as a child, and later, fitting in at school." She gave a short, humorless laugh. "We both had trouble fitting in, when it comes to that. I was never much of a social success either." She dusted the back of Jaime's neck with a clean white cloth and handed her an ivory-handled hand mirror. "Take a look at the back. Would you like me to even it off or cut it a little shorter?"

Jaime took the mirror and inspected the back, turning her head this way and that to get the best view. Willow had shaped the back to her head, leaving the ends fringed, and layered the top for fullness. Jaime smiled with pleasure, fluffing the sides. "It's wonderful! I think you've taken ten years off!" Indeed, she did look younger, more casual and carefree.

"Short hair often does that." Willow nodded. She began to untie the cape from around Jaime's neck and to dust her off with a soft whisk broom.

Jaime hoped she could learn more about Forrest. "You said you were younger than Forrest. Was he living at home, when all that happened?" She couldn't bring herself to name the school shootings, or call it a massacre, when she knew Willow's brother had been one of the shooters. When Willow stared at her without answering, she tried again. "Were you close, you and Forrest?"

The animation went out of Willow's face, and she stared at Jaime as if she had asked her a very personal question about her sex life, something that was absolutely none of her business. Willow closed up just like shutting a book. Having completed the hair cut, she dispensed with all feelings of intimacy along with it, as if she had never said anything about her life. Her professional demeanor returned just as if she had never shared any personal information with Jaime. Now she was just another customer.

"If you will just wait at the counter a second. I will go in the back and get the shampoo and rinse that I mentioned before, that will give you shine and highlights." She went off with a brisk step.

"Yes, of course." Jaime went to wait at the counter. Her eyes followed Willow around the shop, but she knew that whatever confidentiality she and Willow had shared was over, for the moment anyway. It was odd the way the woman had simply closed off, after seeming willing to disclose information about her childhood and family. Maybe there were boundaries past which you simply did not go.

Jaime paid for the haircut, the shampoo, and the rinse. She appreciated the fact that it was so much less than she had ever paid in Atlanta. All at once the pink shop closed in on her as if she were trapped in a pink cardboard box, and she couldn't wait to leave all the pink and the cute country touches behind and breathe fresh air again.

Four

"How old is this school anyway?" Jaime asked, looking around at the old-fashioned desks, with the round depression in the right-hand corner where the bottles of ink used to be placed. The desks were actually bolted to the floor. The room was airy and neat, the windows bright and clean, but it seemed to her hopelessly archaic. And her boys would be going to school *here?*

"It was built in the thirties," Evan replied. "I know it seems way out of date, Jaime, but the teachers are great. It's a young and energetic faculty, and we're going to use federal grant money to modernize the classrooms."

"Computers? Movable desks and chairs?"

He laughed. "You bet. Now be the good super's wife and tell them all how charming it is."

The outside *was* charming. They had parked in back of the faded brick building, which was set well back from the street and boasted a huge amount of well-tended lawn. There were trees and even a flowerbed, home to fall flowers like asters and black-eyed Susans and some spiky purple things she didn't know the name of. At the back of the parking lot there were several bicycle racks for the students' bikes. Behind them, a small hill rose with a fenced-in field stretching back to woods. She would not have been surprised to have seen a cow or two.

A pretty, young woman in blue slacks and a white sweater approached them

"This is Mrs. Gleason," Evan said, "Josh and Jack's kindergarten teacher. They're going to love her."

Jaime thought that that indeed they would, if first impressions were to be believed. Sandra Gleason was petite, almost child-sized herself, with straight blonde hair and a pert, freckled face.

"And I'm so honored to be the first one to teach the new superintendent's children." She beamed at Jaime.

"Maybe not. They're a handful."

~ * ~

The reception in Evan and Jaime's honor was held in the cafeteria. The lunch tables were arranged around the sides of the large, sunny room, bordered on one side by a bank of windows that looked out on the meadow in back. Clearly, this room was an addition made to the old building. Although no alcohol was served, there were two kinds of punch and a wide assortment of tasty appetizers and desserts laid out on several tables covered with tablecloths in autumn colors—orange, yellow, coppery red. Many parents had shown up as well, some with their children, who milled around, pushing and poking each other and giggling among themselves. For a small town, it was a wonderful turnout.

Names and faces blurred as Jaime met one teacher after another and was reassured in her own mind by their obvious energy and enthusiasm. And, as Evan had promised, it was a young faculty for the most part. He introduced her to the fifth grade teacher, Matt Thompson, who was a balding gent in his early forties. He wore a lime green vest and an orange tie, and even he radiated a good nature and a youthful outlook.

"Does he always dress so weirdly?" whispered Jaime, as someone else claimed Matt's attention.

Evan laughed. "Yes. It's his signature. The children like it. " He took her hand as they walked away. "I want you to meet Dane Summers, the principal." They skirted the crowd around the table and headed toward a small group of people standing near the door. Jaime's eyes flicked over the faces, trying to guess which of the several men would be Dane, and all of a sudden, she knew. A pair of dark eyes met hers, and a shock of recognition hit her, almost like a physical wave of energy. She gasped, and stopped in her tracks.

"What is it?" Even looked down at her, concerned.

"I know him!" Jaime stared back at the man whose eyes were locked with hers. "He's—he—" But no name came to mind. Only the words to an old song from the fifties filled her mind: *You may see a stranger... across a crowded room.* And what was that from? One of the popular musicals that ran on Broadway for years, maybe, but she didn't know which one, or how she even knew those words.

"You can't possibly know him." Evan sounded amused. "That's Dane Summers, and he's lived here all his life, went to UConn on a basketball scholarship, then switched to education. Great guy! C'mon."

Dane's eyes held hers as they approached, and the little group dispersed, leaving only the three of them. His smile, flashing very white in a tanned face, disconcerted her even further, as she read the questions in his eyes, too.

He reached for her hand, and closed both of his around hers. "Jaime Reid! I'm so pleased to meet you—but I feel somehow that I've met you before. Where could that have been? At an educational conference somewhere, maybe?"

Evan laughed. "You two! Maybe you knew each other in another life sometime. Jaime believes in all that reincarnation nonsense, you know."

"Do you?" He looked down at her from what seemed to be a great height, even though he was only an inch or so taller than Evan.

Disconcerted, she fumbled for an answer. "Well, it goes a long way toward explaining some of the strange things that happen, doesn't it?"

"Like feeling you already know someone?" he asked.

"That—and other things." She sensed Evan getting restless. "But to answer your other question, no, I'm not in the educational business. I have an art degree, and I never go to conferences with Evan. I had a career as a retail fashion buyer in Atlanta—but now I just stay home with the kids. I'm working on the house we bought. It needs a lot of interior work, and I can paint, plaster and wallpaper."

"My wife, Francesca, wasn't able to come tonight," Dane said, "but she'd be very interested in trading past-life theories with you."

"Really?" Jaime gazed up at him. She realized he was still holding her hand in both of his. She withdrew it and tucked it in around Evan's arm.

Dane continued. "She actually believes that some of us lived here before and were involved in—you know, all that unpleasantness in sixty-one and that we've all returned to the scene of the crime to keep it from happening again."

A shock rolled all through her body, almost as something she had always known and dreaded had risen to the surface.

Evan laughed. "Well, that's an interesting theory, Dane, but it's not going to happen again on my watch. We need to spend a few minutes together, and go over some of the changes we want to make in the school." He looked at Jaime. "Just half an hour or so, sweetheart. Can you socialize without me for a bit?"

Sandy Gleason rejoined the group. "Of course she can!" She turned to Jaime. "I want to get to know you and talk about your kids and our kindergarten program anyway, I think you'll be quite excited about what we're going to do here. It involves a lot of ecology, green-awareness, we call it, and all the teachers participate in the program."

Jaime watched Evan and Dane walk down the hall toward the principal's office, as Sandy took her arm and guided her to her classroom.

~ * ~

The first thing Jaime noticed was the row of standing easels at the back of the room.

"Oh! I was hoping they would get some art. I do what I can at home, but they're very active little boys and would much rather be running around."

Sandy laughed. "We're very into art, that is …as much as we can be, in as much as we don't have any certified art teachers. I hear you're an artist. Maybe you'd come and paint with the kids some day, or even give them a little lesson. Would you?"

"Well, I could do that," Jaime agreed, "but usually the teachers don't appreciate their program being interfered with. I was told that more than once in Atlanta, when I offered to come paint with the students."

Sandy smiled at her. "Well, we'd be more than glad to have you here. Promise me you'll think about it."

Jaime nodded, then thinking that the conversation was going well, she ventured the question she really wanted to ask. Off-handedly, looking around the room with a casual air, she asked, "Do you know Dane's wife, Francesca?"

"Of course. This is a small town, Mrs. Reid."

"Jaime, please. What do you and the rest of the teachers think about Francesca Summer's reincarnation ideas—?" She managed a skeptical little laugh, as she added, "and that we're all called back here in a different life to mend things and prevent them from happening again?"

Sandy stiffened and got very busy arranging things on her desk and shuffling through a pile of papers. After a pause during which neither said anything, the silence became uncomfortable. Sandy glanced up at her and remarked, "You have the cutest little Southern drawl, Jaime. Did you grow up in Atlanta?"

Jaime sighed. "Why won't anyone talk about what happened here? It's history; I remember hearing about it when I was in high school. We even had some training sessions about what to do in case someone broke into our classroom with weapons." She spread her hands, imploring. "Why won't anyone talk about it? I can't even find anything on the Internet. It's like it's been wiped out of everyone's minds."

Sandy stared down at her desk and fiddled again with a pile of picture books before she answered. "People *want* it wiped from their minds. This is a *very* small town, Jaime, and so many people are interrelated. Jane-Michelle, for example, who lives in the green house next to yours, is Willow Brown's daughter, and Willow was Forrest's sister. Ryan Barrett, owner of the P & B Lumber, is the son of Donnie and Francie Barrett, who were killed that night. Dane and Francesca grew up here, and Francesca has some very weird ideas. But you see, if we dwell on all that, if Willow and Jane-Michelle keep getting linked with what Forrest did—not to mention the Brasses, and the Kellys, and the Crenshaws—well, it's a small town, and we all have to get along together. Talking about this just stirs up the hornets' nest, so to speak. So we just prefer to pretend it never happened." She met Jaime's eyes, and her soft voice held a definite warning. "Just leave it alone, please."

Evan, a pleased expression on his face, appeared in the classroom doorway. Jaime judged that his conversation with Dane had gone very well.

"Come in, Dr. Reid," Sandy said with obvious relief, motioning him to join them. "Let me show you and Jaime some of the new activity books we will be using this year."

It looks like I'm not going to get anything out of her, either. I really need to talk to Francesca Summers, because this is really getting to me. I need to know what happened that night—and why.

Five

Wearing jeans and an old tee-shirt, her hair covered with a scarf tied in a knot behind her head, Jaime plunged into the job of clearing out small odds and ends left behind by the Porters and, she guessed, the tenants who had lived there over the years. Already she'd found a man's watch, the face cracked and clouded, the strap frayed and mouse-chewed, in a far corner of an old corner cabinet in the kitchen as well as a Dick and Jane primary reader from the forties and a very old doll, her face scarred and scratched, her once-pretty pink dress in tatters. The watch and the doll looked beyond salvation, so she had no compunction about tossing them into the trash. The primer however, she dusted off and looked through with amusement at the colorful pictures of Dick, Jane, and Sally, and their pets, Spot and Puff. She laid it on the counter; maybe the boys would get a kick out of looking at it as they learned to read, and Evan would certainly be interested.

Dane Summers' tanned, handsome, face flashed up before her, his engaging grin and dark eyes so familiar that she couldn't get them out of her thoughts. And the things he had said so casually about his wife, Francesca's *beliefs*. He had hit the nail on the head with Jaime, as some of the experiences she'd had led her thoughts often in the same direction. Reincarnation—was it possible, was it true? Was this what life was all about, coming back time after time until you'd learned the lessons you were supposed to learn? And just who was it in charge who decided what you needed to learn?

Evan had little use for organized religion. He did believe in *something* but had trouble articulating just what that was. Religion, he said, was nothing more than "crowd control."

"What do you mean by that?" she'd asked, perplexed.

He'd been on his way out the door to play golf on a Sunday morning and good-naturedly sloughed off her request for him to go to church with her and the boys. "If you read your history," he tossed back at her, "you'll see that every king, every tribal leader, every pharaoh has told his people the same thing. *'I have had a revelation of the all-powerful invisible God, and he has given me a set of laws that you must obey, and he has commanded me to enforce them.'*"

He'd smiled back at her. "I'm not into telling anyone else what to believe, Jaime. Go to whatever church you want to and take the boys. They can decide for themselves when they're older. It's just not for me."

So she had joined the local Presbyterian church, pledged a weekly donation to their budget, worked on church dinners (to which Evan cheerfully accompanied her), even taught Sunday School for a year or two. She had hoped to achieve that deep conviction of faith that so many people had, but she was still just coasting along, as far as all that was concerned.

But there were two events that she *knew* happened, because they happened to her, and she wasn't asleep or meditating or using drugs. She was wide awake, tending to her children, when these strange happenings began to change her thinking on the nature of reality, and life itself.

She wiped her brow, as she finished scrubbing out the last of the kitchen cabinets. The kitchen now smelled of bleach, and the trash was full of filthy paper towels. They had been eating on paper plates for the two weeks they had been in the house, because she had refused to put china plates in those cabinets until they had been cleaned and relined with fresh shelf paper.

As she continued with the task, measuring and cutting the flowered shelf paper and fitting it onto the shelves, she thought again about those two incidents and what they might mean. The boys had been two and a half, not yet toilet trained. She had Josh belted onto the changing table and realized she was out of diapers and had to go get a new box. "You be a good boy, now." She scooted into the laundry room off the kitchen to get more diapers. She was only gone thirty seconds or so, but when she came back, Josh was twisted into a strange position, as if he were trying to see something above and beyond his right shoulder.

She tugged gently on his legs. "C'mon, Josh, straighten out so I can put your diaper on."

He didn't move, however, and said something that sounded like "Gottsybama."

"What?" Jaime was totally mystified. Josh seemed to be trying to peer out the kitchen window, so she walked the few steps to it and looked out into the yard. No one there, not even a dog that might have engaged his attention.

She'd looked at him more closely then and saw his eyes moving back and forth—as if he were reading something! Well, this was obviously not possible, since he was only two and a half, but intrigued, she followed his gaze to see what it might be. There, on the wall, which was the corner of an alcove where she'd placed the changing table, was a newspaper article featuring a diet she was trying to follow. The opposite side of the page was what Josh was—to her absolute amazement—ostensibly *reading*. Incredulous, she noticed the headline: *Can Barack Obama pull it out for the Democrats?"*

Gottsybama. Got to see Obama?

Josh gave a little sigh and straightened out of his own accord, but Jaime, unable to process what she had just seen, stood staring down at him.

But it had happened. She was there, and she knew it happened. And it had begun to change her mind about the meaning of life and who human beings really were, way down at the soul level. Was that why mothers instinctively loved their children so much, because they had known them and loved them before, in other times and other places?

The second incident, this time involving Jack, had not been nearly so dramatic, but it had rocked her nevertheless. It was a year later. Jack was three and a half and had adamantly refused to take a nap, even though Josh was fast asleep upstairs. Jaime, tired herself, lay on the sofa, Jack playing with his blocks nearby. Jaime watched her son making buildings and wondered if he would grow up to be an architect. Were his talents surfacing already, the way hers had, with an insatiable desire to draw and paint, even as a toddler?

He glanced up and saw her watching him. Something changed in his face, and he scuttled over to the sofa where she lay and dropped to the floor beside her. To Jaime's amusement, he began to brush her hair back from her face with his hand, as she had often had done with him and Josh. It felt so good, the little hand against her skin, and she smiled at him without speaking.

Jack was the one who spoke in a casual, conversational tone. "You know, the last time we were here, *you* were *my* baby."

It took a few seconds for her to process what he had said, but with amazing presence of mind, she attempted to continue the conversation. "What was my name?"

But the moment was over. Jack went back to his blocks and didn't answer her. The more she thought about it, the more confused she became. Sure, he could just have said that, as if she were a doll—but the words themselves! Why would a three-year old use the phrase *the last time we were here*, and how would he have any idea of what that meant?

Jaime glanced at her watch. The cabinets were now as clean as they would ever get, and she could begin to unpack the china and organize the kitchen. She knew Evan would be glad to eat a civilized dinner on china plates again, but he had been very good about not complaining.

The boys would be home from school soon and hungry for lunch. She climbed down from the stepstool and turned toward the refrigerator. There, in mid-air, against the white background of the refrigerator, hung an image of Dane Summers' face.

"Oh my God! My God!" She gasped, suppressing a scream. The image faded, slowly, his eyes boring into hers, his smile so familiar that she staggered against the counter, holding onto it for support.

"*I know him. I* know *I know him, and he's trying to tell me something. I need to talk to Francesca.* Jaime reached for the phone. Then she heard her boys, laughing and yelling, tramping up the sidewalk and onto the porch. The door to the foyer creaked open, then slammed, and Josh and Jack burst into the kitchen, waving their papers from school for her to see.

Francesca would have to wait, but not for long.

Six

Saturday after the beginning of school dawned in New England bright and blue. The maple outside the kitchen window was just starting to hint at the color that would blaze over the tree.

Jaime wanted to ask Evan if he thought Francesca Summers would be open to meeting her for lunch, but even as the words formed in her mouth, the phone rang.

Evan answered it in the den and she could hear his muffled voice, but not the conversation. When he emerged, he was grinning. "Dane. He asked me to play golf with him at the Country Club, and Francesca said why don't we come over for an informal get-together later this afternoon. I said we'd love to. Is that okay with you?"

"More than okay," Jaime said. "But what about Jack and Josh? We don't know any baby-sitters yet."

"Oh, we're supposed to bring them," She could tell his mind was already on the golf course. "Do you know what box my clubs are in?"

"In the den, where you just were. Do they have kids?"

"Does who have kids?" Evan asked absently, heading for the small room in back of the kitchen they had designated the den.

"Dane and Francesca! The couple we're going to visit tonight."

"Yeah," he called back. "Two boys, like us. One is older than Josh and Jack by a year or two, the other just a little younger."

He talked to Josh as he moved around the den and looked into boxes that had not been assigned permanent places yet. Jaime heard a long and satisfied "Aaaah," then heard his footsteps sounding on the steps as he ran upstairs to change his clothes.

The boys, who usually played so well together, had squabbled from the time they got up that morning, resulting in a shoving match, until she finally separated them. She had sat Josh down in the den watching *Nemo* and put Jack at the kitchen table, where he watched cartoons on the small kitchen TV.

Now in the relative peace that ensued, she busied herself in the kitchen, finding places for various pot and pans and serving pieces, and wondered idly why such an old house had no pantry. Maybe one corner of the large room could be made into one, near where that back stairway led up to the attic.

In her pleasure at Francesca's invitation, and looking forward to the evening ahead, she'd forgotten to tell Evan about her vision of Dane's face hanging in the air, and as the morning wore on, it seemed less and less important. It was probably just a premonition of their get-together later that afternoon anyway, but she couldn't banish the image of his handsome face, his engaging grin. It was so familiar to her—but how could it be?

She had offered to bring potato salad to Francesca's. Now where was that recipe that her mother used to make, the one with red potatoes and olives that Evan liked so much? Searching among her cookbooks, she found the diary she had hastily stuck in among them while cleaning off the counters. She glanced at Jack. He seemed glued to the TV as he absently chewed goldfish crackers and sipped milk from his special mug that had a frog in the bottom, which you could only see once the milk was gone.

Standing there at the kitchen counter, she opened the diary. She didn't know why she hadn't read any more of it since she'd found it. She hadn't exactly forgotten it—it had crossed her mind now and then. But with working on the house, getting the kids ready for school, and listening to Evan enthuse about his new job—well, she just hadn't gotten around to it.

Now she had a few minutes. She turned the diary over in her hand, looking at the well-worn cover and wondering who had written it. Written it, and hidden it in this old house. She opened it at random.

February 25th, 1951

Boy, were we lucky last night. Forrest nearly started a fire in the attic of the old Porter house, where we snuck in and had a few smokes last night. Balls grabbed a ratty quilt and smothered it before it burned anything but an old newspaper, but it could have spread in a hurry among all those dried-out things up there. It's easy to break into the cellar, and then we go way up to the attic, which is nice and cozy and has some left-over chairs and cots to flop on. We took Willow with us, as she's still crying over Janie's latest snub.

Why she even cares about Janie Carlson is more than I can understand. But—Willow seems to think she's a movie star of sorts, and just idolizes her. It's true that Janie is cute, and popular, and has great taste in clothes, and has some art talent too, but she's just another girl. Another human being like the rest of us, although The Nine don't seem to realize that.

Anyway, at the basketball game Friday night, Janie was sitting alone, so Willow took a chance and went over and sat down beside her. When Janie didn't speak to her, Willow said something... "Are you saving this seat for anyone?" ...and Janie didn't even answer her, just got up and moved, and left Willow sitting there, feeling like crap. I keep trying to tell Willow that when Donnie Barrett's out there on the floor, Janie doesn't have a mind for anything else. She can't keep her eyes off him, and it's so obvious. She'll never get him, though, and I, for one, am really glad there's something she can't have.

~ * ~

"I hope you don't mind paper plates," Francesca said as she handed Jaime one of the tall, red laminated paper cups. "Help yourself to wine on the picnic table there, or beer in the cooler. That's all I'm serving." She laughed. "Unless you want lemonade." Francesca was small, compactly built, dark-haired, and pretty, with a freckled face and sharp, intelligent eyes.

"This is fine, and we've been eating off paper plates for weeks now. I just got the cabinets cleaned out and painted and the china put away."

"Well, with the kids running around," Francesca explained, "it's just too much of a temptation for something to get broken."

"And for someone to fall on a broken piece of china and get cut." Jaime cast an eye at the four young boys chasing each other around the yard.

"And for someone to have to drive that kid to the emergency room in Springfield," Francesca said.

"And for some poor doctor to have to leave his own backyard barbeque party and rush to the hospital to take care of him." Jaime enjoyed getting into the verbal game.

"And for me to run into said doctor's wife at the next charity event and have her tell me I should have used paper plates—"

"Therefore paper plates." They both nodded, laughing.

"It's a big job, moving into an old house like that." Francesca wiped her hands on her jeans. "Have you found anything left behind in the nooks and crannies?"

How odd she would ask that. Jaime told her about the watch, the doll, and the Dick and Jane primer. "Oh, and what looks like an old diary in the cellar. It was jammed up among some beams near the ceiling."

Francesca gasped and wheeled around to stare at Jaime. "You found the *diary*? Kathy Kelly's diary?"

"Is that whose it was?" Jaime was bewildered. "Why?" She sat on one of the redwood picnic benches.

Francesca stopped puttering around and joined Jaime on the bench. She poured herself some of the white wine from the bottle into a red cup, and took a sip.

"Oh, that's good! I mean, the wine." She gave a short laugh. "Well, scuttlebutt has it, and I have absolutely no proof of this, that one of the girls, Kathy Kelly, from the sixty-one massacre, wanted to be a writer and kept a diary. No one has ever found it, but Willow Brown, who was a friend of hers, says she knows she had one, and wrote about *everybody*. Not real flattering stuff, either."

Jaime took a sip from her own cup. "I haven't read too much of it yet, but it does mention people named Sylvia, Janie, Donnie—and yes, Willow. So it has to be Kathy's doesn't it? But... weren't the Browns long out of there before Willow was a teenager?"

"Oh, yes," Francesca agreed. "I wasn't saying I knew the diary was there. I was just saying there supposedly was one, and I for one, would give just about anything to read it. Will you let me read it? I would die to get inside her head."

"We can read it together some afternoon." How strange Francesca's wording was. "There aren't a lot of entries in there. Willow told me a little bit, but then cut me off at the knees when I started asking her questions, and Jane-Michelle wouldn't say a word either. And Sandy Gleason said it was too small a town, and there would be too many bad feelings if people talked about it."

"There's something to that, but my mother's younger sister was there that night, and I've heard just enough from her and my mom to want to find out the whole story, and why Rob Brass and Forrest Brown did it."

"I'm just the new kid on the block, literally." She tossed Francesca a smile. "But I'm fascinated by the story, too. I'd love to help you try to piece it all together, if I can."

Francesca lowered her voice and leaned over toward Jaime. Jaime saw Evan and Dane approaching across the lawn and sensed Francesca did not wish her voice to carry.

"There's another reason for finding out what really happened, why the guys did it." Her voice was almost a whisper. "There are some people around here, and I'm one of them, who think it's not over. That it's going to happen again."

"Hey! The grill is ready, and I could put the steaks on now," Dane announced. With cans of beer in hand, the men joined their wives. "What have you two been gabbing about?"

"Babies, diaper services, meatloaf recipes, and *Desperate Housewives*." Francesca jumped up. "I'll get the steaks. They're marinating in the fridge." She went off in the direction of the kitchen. The four little boys chased after her, with a chorus of "we're hungry" in assorted voices.

"Steaks *and* hotdogs," Jaime heard her say as she disappeared into the house with her entourage.

Jaime, feeling as though she had been punched in the stomach, met Evan's eyes, hoping the shock of what Francesca had said didn't show on her face.

Evan gave her a speculative look that said he knew her all too well. "*Desperate Housewives*? I'll bet."

Seven

Jaime relished the comfortable, warm friendship that bloomed between her and Francesca Summers as they spent what time they could spare, given the busy beginning of the school year, poring over the old diary. A good relationship had developed, as well, it seemed, between Evan and Dane, who both had an obsessive interest in golf, as well as educational policies. All fall, on every fair-weather Saturday, they headed for the golf course.

She told Evan what Francesca had said about the diary supposedly written by Kathy Kelly.

Evan listened. "Well, maybe it is, and maybe it isn't. It won't hurt anything if you and Francesca want to try to figure it out, but please try to avoid stirring up the natives. You already know they don't like to talk about it."

"I keep finding things. I cleaned out the bookcase in the den yesterday, and look what had fallen down behind one of the loose boards."

"I can't wait. What is this thing? A toy gun?" He took the miniature pistol, discolored and rusted, from her and turned it over and over, examining it.

"It's a cigarette lighter. Popular in the fifties. You pull the trigger to make it light."

"Great," he pronounced, disgust in his voice. "Just the thing to use around kids. Well, keep it away from the boys. You know we don't want them playing with guns, even toys."

"I know. I couldn't agree more. I'll throw it out."

He took it back from her and dropped it into his pocket. "I'll throw it into the river when I cross the bridge into Sandville." He sighed. "I sure didn't want problems this early in the school year, but I seem to be getting them anyway from the board." He ran his fingers through his sandy hair in a gesture of frustration that she knew well.

Jaime put her hand on his arm. "What kind of problems?"

Evan hesitated before answering. "Nothing I can't handle—I think. Some people are concerned about their taxes going up, and two brothers—one from Sandville and the other representing the board from Westlake, seem to be Neanderthals from the stone age, as far as education is concerned. No need to replace the furniture bolted to the floor—it was good enough for them, why spend the money? No need for sissy subjects like art and music and theater."

She snorted. "What do they want?" A shooting range?"

"As a matter of fact, that's *just* what they want, in back of the school in Westlake. 'Make men of the boys, teach the girls to protect themselves.'"

She laughed. "I know you're not going to let that get through."

"I suggested an archery range. They laughed at me." He kissed her again. "I really have to get going now, beard the lions in the den. See you for dinner."

~ * ~

The painter had done a great job in the den. In her visual language, the two walls not pine-paneled were coated in an off-white color that was something between cream and custard. She had scrubbed and sanded the built-in bookcases and tacked the errant board where she'd found the lighter back in place. She'd had the salesman at the hardware store mix up a color for her that had been named 'October Bronze' on the color slip. It was burnt sienna in her lexicon, but close enough, for her needs. She pried the lid off the can, stirred the paint with the stick they had supplied, and noted the color with satisfaction. Even the first brush strokes of the lively color seemed to brighten the room like a shaft of sunshine. She set to painting with enthusiasm and lost all track of time until she heard the twins running up the sidewalk. There was more noise coming into the house than just two little boys.

~ * ~

Jaime emerged from the den to find Jack and Josh, waving their colorful collection of school papers as usual, accompanied by the Summers boys and Francesca.

"I hoped you might have time for coffee and conversation." Francesca grinned at her. "I hope this isn't a bad time."

"Not at all. I need to take a break anyway. I'll put some sandwiches together. Go see what I did in the den."

The boys crowded around her, demanding juice box drinks. She gave them to them and shoed them out onto the porch to play with some of the bigger toys she kept out there for them while she made lunch.

"I love that color, the bookcases, I mean," Francesca announced, coming back into the kitchen and seating herself at the pink enameled kitchen table. "Isn't this table a piece of work! Are you going to keep it?"

"I think so." She lathered peanut butter and jelly on slices of white bread. "I think it has character, but Josh is so funny. Every time he sits down here he says, 'I hate this table. Tables shouldn't be pink.'"

Francesca chuckled. "Not a great remark from an artist's kid. "Look, can I help you with anything?"

Jaime piled the sandwiches on a paper plate and handed it and a basket of pretzels to Francesca. "You can give this to the wild cowboys out on the porch, and I'll add to the salad I've already put together."

Deftly she sliced chicken breast from last night's dinner into the bowl of lettuce, cucumbers and tomatoes and added a handful of walnuts and dried cranberries. She set out three bottles of dressings and set the table—*with china plates!* all before Francesca made a reappearance.

Jaime smiled at her guest. "Coffee, tea, or diet soda?"

"Water, please."

Jaime poured herself a mug of coffee, feeling the need for an uplift after her morning of painting.

"Francesca," Jaime began, spearing a piece of chicken but holding it just above her dish, "who are the two brothers on the board who are, as Evan put it, Neanderthals from the stone age, who might be giving him a hard time?"

"Hmm," Francesca mumbled. She waved a finger at Jaime, indicating she would answer as soon as she finished eating. "Rad and Ferris Bauer, I'll bet. Dane's about at the end of his rope with those two also. Nothing to be done about it, though, except to vote against them. They do represent a certain segment of all three towns that think everything is just fine the way it is."

"Rad and Ferris? What kind of names are those?"

"What kind of name was Forrest?" Francesca laughed. "A lot of people say 'what kind of name is Dane?' My own mother quipped, that all it means is a person from Denmark."

Amid their laughter, the boys came racing back into the kitchen, surrounding the table.

Josh wrinkled his nose. "I hate this table. It's *pink.*"

"Yuk, pink is for *girls*," Kevin, Francesca's older son added.

"Can we watch a movie in the den?" Jack asked. "And have some cookies?"

"I just painted the bookcases in there, and they're not dry yet," Jaime told her son. "But you may have cookies and take them up to your room." She tore open a package of Oreos and put eight cookies on a plate. "Two for each of you. If you play nicely and don't wreck the bedroom, we'll all go to the park playground in a little while. Okay?" The boys scrambled off toward the bedroom, Kevin, as the oldest, elected to carry the plate of cookies.

"Don't count on their not wrecking the bedroom, but while they're playing, I'd like to run some ideas about Kathy Kelly's diary past you."

"Evan doesn't believe it's of any consequence." Jaime leaned her elbows on the table.

"Oh, I wouldn't be too sure about that." Francesca's dark eyes sparkled amid the freckles. "I'm convinced that the more we can understand what happened then will help us to keep it from happening again."

Jaime shrugged. "Willow would be the best source, since she's Forrest's sister, but she wouldn't talk to me about it. She brought up the subject, actually, but then she closed up like a clam, and looked at me as if we hadn't been talking about that at all."

"No. Pardon me for saying this." She put her hand on Jaime's arm. "*Nobody* is going to say much to you and Evan, because you're not—well, natives. People are ashamed and embarrassed by what happened here—what, almost fifty years ago. They don't like to talk about it, or even admit it ever happened."

"What did you want to run past me, then?"

Upstairs a door slammed, and they both glanced up as the sound of running feet in the hall above filtered down to them.

"We ought to be very methodical about this. Let's go through the diary, make notes on who she mentions and anything about them. Let's see if any of the traits match with us, and anyone else we might know. Let's see if we can find out who we *were*."

Jaime nodded. "Excellent idea. And, I think we should check the old bookstores and antique shops for anything that might give us more clues. Not just the one on Main Street, probably *not* that one, but some of those I've noticed on Route 10, going down toward Granby, and others in the outlying towns that you know of."

"Oh, there are dozens. Antiques are a cottage industry around here."

"I'm surprised you haven't already done that. But it's a great idea, and I have the perfect excuse for our poking around in them."

"What?" Francesca reached for a cookie. "Hmmm, these are good."

"Evan wants old maps and antique prints with clipper ships for his den. We can go look for them and search for whatever else without anyone catching on."

"Perfect! Well," she said after a moment, glancing upwards. "There's a lot of silence up there. I suppose we'd better see what they're up to and go to the playground so they can work off all that energy."

Jaime rose, leading the way to the stairs. Contentment ran through her body in a current of pleasure, as when she'd eaten something rich and chocolate, or set her eyes on an artwork, a painting, or a sculpture that moved her senses. Life was going well in Mill Pond, and she had to admit to herself that she liked her new life. In spite of his opposition, Evan felt a growing sense of mission and accomplishment, and she loved her old house more each day. The kids were happy and doing well in school—and well, if their furniture was bolted to the floor, so what? Evan and Dane, would, in time, take care of that. And she had a friend, an intelligent, lively, interesting woman who had already engaged her in a fascinating pursuit.

~ * ~

Jaime and Francesca both froze at the bottom of the stairs as what sounded like a shot rang out and a scream of agony from one of the boys pierced the air.

Jack lay curled up on the floor, clutching his leg. Bloodstains were already spreading out into the fabric of his jeans, and blood oozed from the wound and seeped into the carpet. Josh and the younger Summers boy, Kyle, sat on the lower bunk bed, their eyes wide and their mouths open. Kevin raised the pistol and aimed it at Jaime.

"Bang! Bang!" He pulled the trigger.

Eight

"Where did they get the gun?"

"There's a crawl space off one of the guest bedrooms that has been used as a storage area." Jaime's voice shook as Seth Foster, a veteran cop—tall and thin with hair graying around a bald spot—asked questions of the four adults. A younger policeman took notes.

Jack had suffered only a flesh wound; the bullet had not hit the bone. He had been whisked to the emergency room at high speed with horns blaring and lights flashing—all of which he remembered with glee, now that he was no longer in pain. He had crutches, which he would not need for very long, and was lapping up the attention. Jaime suspected that Josh was even a little jealous!

The four boys were watching TV in the den—Jack with his leg bandaged and his new crutches leaning against the bookcase—and had been told to stay there and not get into anything.

"And you didn't investigate to see what was in there?"

"I did!" Jaime protested. "I threw out stacks of magazines, some old clothing, and other odds and ends that I found in there—but it goes way back along the side of the room, and I didn't crawl in there."

"She's found lots of things as we go through the house." Evan defended her and held her hand tightly. "This is a big place. We're cleaning out and painting as we go."

"I'm not saying it's her fault," the cop said. "Lots of people have lived here over the years, and stuff is bound to accumulate and fall through the cracks. What else have you found?"

Jaime went through her list; the watch, the doll, the pistol-shaped lighter, and everything else she could remember, except the diary. She didn't want that taken away from her. "A lot of it I just threw out."

"Well, you're lucky there was only one bullet in the gun." Foster's expression was grim.

Dane and Francesca sat rigidly on the edge of their chairs as the interrogation proceeded. Francesca, tears in her eyes, kept her head down and stared at her fingers, twisting almost of their own accord in her lap. When, at times, she looked up, imploring Jaime with her eyes, Jaime could not look at her. Yes, she knew it was an accident—*but her kid shot my kid!* went round and round in her brain. She didn't know if she could ever get past it.

Foster turned his questions on Dane and Francesca.

"Do you have guns in your home?"

"Oh, heavens, no!" Francesca paled to the point that her freckles hardly showed.

"I think you know that we're all very concerned about safety." Evan's voice had a steel edge. "For Pete's sake, Officer Foster, I'm superintendent of schools and Dane's principal of Mill Pond School. You can't possibly think we're negligent parents!"

"An accident is an accident." Dane's tone mirrored that of the other men. "We're incredibly sorry it happened, but that's what an accident is, an accident."

Foster nodded at his subordinate, who snapped his pad shut. "I know that. There's no blame here. A lot of people around here own guns, and that's no crime either. Just—clean out the rest of the place before the kids find something else they shouldn't. Okay?"

"We'll help." Francesca's tears spilled over. She wiped them away with her hand. "We'll do anything to help—-I just feel so awful about this."

"We both do," Dane said as he put his arm around his wife, who, sobbing, leaned into him.

The cop confided, "We called Willow Brown down to the station to see if she could identify the gun as belonging to her father or brother, Forrest, but she couldn't."

Dane nodded. "She was just a kid when her family lived here, and not for very long at that."

Foster nodded. "Mmmmmm." Then, looking out the kitchen window, he observed, "You know, I have a vested interest in keeping this community violence-free. My brother was Marc Foster, who was murdered in the sixty-one massacre. I don't ever want to have to go through something like that again."

"I'm sorry, so sorry—" Jaime began, but Foster waved his hand to cut her off. The officers stood.

Foster glared at Evan and Dane in turn. "You guys keep a sharp eye on things, you hear? A sharp eye and a firm hand." The words came out tough as nails, but his face reflected the pain he felt.

"You were damned lucky. Next time—you might not be so lucky."

Jaime folded, closing in on herself. "I know."

"That's why there can't be a next time." Evan's voice was as hard as Foster's. The two men regarded each other almost as antagonists attempting to stare each other down.

But it wasn't antagonism. It was resolve, on both sides.

~ * ~

"How about the attic?" Evan asked, a day or so after the four adults had thoroughly examined every cabinet, cupboard, bookcase, and hidden recess or alcove in the big Victorian house.

"No." Why did his question make her feel defensive? Did Evan believe what happened had been her fault, her lack of foresight? "The boys can't possibly get up there, Evan. There's a pull cord they can't even reach, and stairs that fold down—impossible for them. And the stairs from the kitchen have a locked door on the first landing."

"I know. I'm asking if *you've* checked it out."

"I looked up through the opening. There's an old Christmas tree and a lot of dust. That's all I saw." She heard the resentment in her own voice.

He put his arms around her. "Don't be grumpy. Nobody's blaming you, Jaime. Francesca couldn't feel worse. I hope this won't affect your friendship. It's awful that it happened, but Jack is going to be okay."

"I know." She leaned her body against his, loving the reassurance that flowed through her as she felt his strength.

Evan sighed and pulled away. "I hate to end this intimate moment, but I do pay the bills around here, and I have to go to work in order to do that."

"Right." She began to pick up the breakfast dishes from the table. "How are those two guys on the board—the ones with the funny names?"

"Rad and Ferris Bauer? They're being Rad and Ferris, opposing everything, agitating every meeting for their firing range—which," Evan pronounced, as he placed the coffee mugs in the dishwasher, "they ain't gonna get. Not on my watch!"

~ * ~

Jack's wound healed, the crutches were discarded after just a couple of weeks, and Jaime's world slowly returned to normal. The police had hushed up what had happened so that there had been no TV or newspaper stories about their son's accidental shooting. Jaime was gratified that the local authorities had put a lid on the story of their own volition; this was not something they wanted the world to know had happened in their town. For the first time, Jaime really understood how the massacre of fifty years ago had been buried in the town itself.

It was hard to see Francesca. Jaime knew she was being unreasonable, but every time she thought about Francesca, or ran into her in town, the same refrain ran through her mind, like one of those songs you can't get out of your head. *Her kid shot my kid... her kid shot my kid... her kidto the first two-page shot my kid.*

Try as she might, she couldn't get over it. Jaime ran into her almost everywhere, the market, the drugstore, even the beauty shop when she went to Willow's to get a trim. As it happened, or didn't happen, Willow was not available to tend to her, and she had to settle for a loquacious, orange-haired beautician who gave her a passable haircut but never let her get a word in edgewise. She paid, tipped the girl, and left, her senses numbed by the incessant chatter about nothing. As she left, Francesca came in, her arms full of packages, and they literally bumped into each other. One of the bags fell to the floor, and everyone turned to stare as the sound of something breaking rang out through the shop.

"O—h! Fr—Francesca!" Jaime stuttered. "I'm so sorry. What was that? I'll—I'll replace it. How are you?"

"Fine, we're all fine." Francesca seemed just as flustered. She dropped her packages into one of the chairs intended for waiting clients. "That was just a new teapot for my china set. Kyle made earthworm tea last week, and I couldn't drink out of it anymore."

Jaime tried to control herself, but the thought of Kyle's offering his mother earthworm tea, most likely in one of her delicate floral teacups, was too funny to be able to control herself. She doubled over with laughter, and Francesca began to laugh with her.

Jaime gasped. "Was it hot?" She couldn't stop laughing. "Did he actually boil them?

Tears streamed down Francesca's cheeks. "Yes, it was hot—and very, very *brown.*"

Suddenly Jaime was aware of the sudden silence that had fallen over the shop. She looked around and saw every eye fixed on the two of them. The dam inside her gave way, and what antagonism she still felt for Francesca melted like a spring thaw. She grabbed her arm. "C'mon outside, Francesca. We need to talk."

Nine

"I thought this might be a good place to look." Francesca pulled into the driveway of what looked like an ordinary, turn-of-the-century house, white with green shutters, a picket fence with a gate opening onto the sidewalk that led to the front steps. The sign, in an approximately Old English style of lettering, proclaimed that this was *Lily's Little Antique Loft,* and it pointed would-be antique hunters to the red barn in back of the house.

"It's not little, it's not a loft, but there definitely is a Lily." Jaime cast an appreciative eye at the picturesque old barn, thinking it might be a good subject to paint, as they walked in the direction the arrow pointed.

They had passed the *Welcome to Connecticut* sign, which also told them the name of the current governor and informed them that this was the home state of the NCAA basketball champions of the University of Connecticut, both men's and women's teams.

"That's a lot of information to process all at once. It's enough for me to know we're in another state, without actually going very far."

Francesca laughed. "Eight miles. But you can't live in Connecticut without being obsessed by the UConn teams. Everybody's UConn crazy here. Dane went to school here, at Storrs, you know, on a basketball scholarship, and he wouldn't miss a game, either in person or on TV, for anything." She bit her lower lip. "*Almost* anything."

Lily was herself almost an antique, being tiny and white haired, but not in the least frail. Her blue eyes sparkled like some of her antique glassware as she asked just what it was they were interested in. "Or you can just poke around on your own," she added in her chirping, bird-like voice.

"I'm looking for some antique maps or old prints of clipper ships and turbulent oceans, that kind of thing, for my husband's den," Jaime told her.

Lily pointed to one corner of the barn, empty now of its cattle stalls, but still looking very much like a barn with saddles and harnesses hanging from the walls, and the merchandise displayed on wide, rough planks and shelves. There still was a loft, and Jaime noted that Lily had a desk and file cabinets up there, evidently used as office space.

"Over there and almost anywhere else. Just poke around, and if you find something you like, give me a call. I'll be right upstairs." Lily strode with a surprisingly strong step toward the stairs, then turned back toward them. "Coffee." She pointed to a table in the corner. "Help yourselves."

Jaime found several seagoing-type prints with a sepia cast and frayed edges and put them aside. Sipping the hot coffee, she wandered around the barn, shuffling through piles of old sheet music and magazines, looking for anything that might be of interest. She did find a frame she thought might complement one of the prints, and when she put the print against the glass, it did please her eye. She laid it on the counter near the cash register for later purchase and kept hunting. When she found a dusty, leather-covered album, her heart quickened.

Francesca showed up at her elbow just as she carefully peeled back the first page, which was glued to the cover. "I see you found something, maybe."

"Maybe." Jaime turned over the first page, which was blank, to the first faded two-page spread and found an arrangement of snapshots, with a typed index card inserted with them. Jaime and Francesca peered at the smudged typing.

"Our Class trip to Washington, D.C.," Jaime read. "I wonder what year this was?"

"And what high school?"

"It looks like the right era." Jaime flipped through the pages. "Look at the peasant blouses and broomstick skirts. That's just what my mother wore!"

A few pages later, whoever had taken the pictures had caught the back of a boy wearing a school jacket, the name white against the dark fabric.

"Granby." Francesca sighed. "Not what we're looking for." She looked at her watch. "We should be getting back before the kids get home."

Francesca waited while Jaime bought the antique print and frame at the counter. When she produced her credit card, Lily looked at it and raised her eyebrows. "Oh, you're the new superintendent's wife up there in the tri-towns. I should have known by your sweet little accent."

Jaime decided to take a chance. "Do you ever get any old diaries or high school yearbooks? I'm really interested in comparing how things were in my mother's day, fifty years ago or so, and today. It's a fascination of mine."

"Is it, really?" Lily didn't bother to hide the sarcasm in her tone. "You wouldn't be hunting for the diary Kathy Kelly supposedly left behind, would you?"

Jaime and Francesca exchanged astonished glances.

"No!" That was the truth. She wasn't searching for Kathy's diary.

"Listen to me." Lily's face was grim, and her voice suddenly dropped several degrees. "Leave well enough alone. If I did have Kathy Kelly's diary, it would never see the light of day again, believe me."

"But why—?"

"There are rocks better not looked under." Lily handed back her credit card and a bag with her print and frame wrapped in newspaper in it.

"Enjoy the print." Lily's blue eyes glared like ice, the sparkle gone. "But please don't come back here again."

Beside her, Francesca gasped. Jaime felt her face grow crimson as she stared at the old woman, her mouth open in astonishment.

As they clambered back into Francesca's SUV, Jaime still squirmed with embarrassment. "I just don't get it. That's the first time I've ever been thrown out of an antique shop." She attempted to lighten things up. "Maybe we're just not old enough to be antiques?"

Francesca laughed as she plugged the key into the ignition and started up the car. "We weren't exactly thrown out—just invited not to come back. And I can't help but wonder why."

"Is she related to someone? What's her last name?"

Francesca thought a minute. "Smith. But I don't know what her maiden name was if she was married, and I don't know whether she was or not."

"That would be interesting to find out. I'm taking the boys to the library for story hour tomorrow. I'll sneak away and see what I can look up, old marriages and obits, and so forth."

~ * ~

Using the available computers while the boys listened to one of the librarians read, Jaime quickly found what she was looking for. An article on antique shops mentioned Lily's Little Antique Loft on route 10. It had been opened by Lily Paris Smith in 1993 two years after the death of Arthur Smith.

An obituary notice for Arthur Smith noted that he was survived by his wife, the former Lily Brass, and they had no children. They had two nephews, Todd and Brett, and one nephew, Robert, who had predeceased him.

Well, that's why Lily didn't want any discussion of Kathy's diary. There are family ties there. She was related in some way to Balls Brass, one of the killers.

Ten

One frosty day in November, after the boys had been sent off to school, the phone rang. It was Jane-Michelle, asking if she could stop over for a quick cup of coffee.

"Of course! I'd love that." Jamie's heart lifted at the thought that Jane-Michelle might be interested in a friendship after all.

After Jane Michelle's arrival, Jaime poured the coffee into a flowered English teapot that had belonged to her Grandmother, and set the matching sugar bowl and creamer, cups, and saucers on the tray with it. "Let's go in here." She led the way into the living room, which looked much different from when Jane-Michelle had seen it their first day in the house.

"What a nice job you've done!" Jane-Michelle looked around. The walls had been done in the palest of soft yellows. The sofa, upholstered in an ivory brocade with hints of soft, floral tones, flanked the fireplace, along with two old-fashioned side chairs and the Hitchcock rocker. This left the rest of the room free for a small, marble-topped Victorian table and two chairs that Jaime placed in front of the tall windows looking out onto the porch and the yard, another pair of chairs and a side table for conversation, and an entertainment center—actually, it was a Japanese cabinet called a *tansu* that Jaime had found in another antique store she and Francesca had investigated. It held the flat screen TV; the DVD player; a smaller, older TV that still played videos; and a collection of films on video and DVD.

"You have so much space. This room actually makes my living room look small."

"We need the space. We'll have to do some entertaining sooner or later. I was thinking of a cocktail party. You'll come, won't you?"

"I'll think about it. I'm not much of a party person," was all Jane-Michelle said, as they sat at the table and Jaime poured coffee for both of them. She changed the subject abruptly.

"I wanted to say, for my mother and me, how very sorry we are about the gun's being left in the house," Jane-Michelle began without preamble.

Jaime shivered. "The police said Willow couldn't identify it. It's certainly not your fault it was here. You couldn't have known." *Am I being two-faced here? I was mad at Francesca because her kid shot my kid, but I don't blame Jane-Michelle's family for leaving the gun in the house? Well, maybe my anger is all burned out. I hope so.*

Jane-Michelle held her cup with both hands to her lips for what seemed to be a long time before she answered. "No, Mom couldn't positively identify the gun, but odds are that it did belong to her father, who stashed it away in the crawl space. Again, we're so sorry."

"But her father did own a gun?"

"Probably. He did hunt, and of course my Uncle Forrest had a gun, a hunting rifle. He was very odd, lived out in the woods in a hut he built himself, and when he left home after high school, my mom hardly ever saw him. So it certainly wasn't *his* gun."

"How about Rob Brass?"

Jane-Michelle put down her cup and spread her hands in question. "How could it be his? Rob and Forrest weren't friends until high school, when they were both sort of— outcasts." Her voice dropped on the last word. "My mom wasn't popular either, but things weren't quite as bad for her, though she did have her own problems."

Jaime wanted to probe further, but she was afraid that Jane-Michelle might shut down completely if she did, so she kept her silence and waited.

Jane-Michelle stared fixedly out the window. "You know, high school is tough here. There are only about sixty in the graduating class, and everyone has known everyone else since kindergarten, since all the grades through high school are in the same building. It's almost like a caste system. You have your place in the line-up, and you'd better not try to get out of it."

Jaime gestured toward the green house where Jane-Michelle lived. "But you seem to have done all right."

"I'm okay, thanks to my mother's grit and Glenn, the guy I married. I went to college, which my mom never had a chance to do, and I met Glenn there. He's a medic in Iraq, which is why you haven't met him."

"And no kids?"

Jane-Michelle met her eyes. "All my life I've been whispered about, pointed out, known as *Forrest Brown's* niece, Willow's daughter." She said the name with loathing. "Do you think I would subject my kids to that, being social outcasts because of who their ancestors were?"

"You could move," Jaime pointed out. "Springfield or farther out west, one of the sweet little towns in the Berkshires."

Jane-Michelle was silent for a moment. "Maybe I'm too stubborn to run away. And I never had that big urge to have kids anyway. I majored in elementary ed, taught for a year, and hated it." She shrugged. "While Glenn is away I use up my time volunteering, trying to help others. Glenn says I'm trying to atone for the sins of the past, and maybe he's right." She gave a short, bitter laugh. "But I'll never change the minds of people in this town, no matter what I do. I'm still Forrest Brown's niece, guilty by association."

Jaime paused a moment before she spoke. "Francesca and I went antiquing the other day. We found some old prints for Evan's study. Lily's Little Loft—ever hear of that?"

"I know where it is, yes. Lord, is she still alive? She used to be a friend of my grandmother's. Then there was some sort of falling out when my mother was a teenager, and nobody saw her after that."

Jaime decided to take a chance. "We were looking for the diary that Kathy Kelly supposedly left behind. Do you know anything about that?"

Jane-Michelle's thin, pretty face, etched with its lines of sadness, suddenly went blank. Her voice cooled by twenty degrees. "Jaime, leave it alone. Nobody wants Kathy's diary found, if it ever existed."

"Francesca says your mother *knows* Kathy was keeping a diary," Jaime pointed out. As Jane-Michelle jumped to her feet, her face hard, she knew she'd pushed things too far.

"Leave it alone! Do you think this town wants to know all those ugly details?" She brushed her straight, sandy hair away from her face and glared at Jaime, the light dimmed in her almond eyes. "Don't you *see?* The students in Mill Pond High now are the grandchildren of the class of sixty-one, and their parents are our leading citizens, people who care about this town and make it thrive, people who are working with your husband to make our educational system better. Make that diary public, and all those old, ugly feelings will surface again."

She put her coffee cup down with a force that made Jaime jump. She glared at Jaime. "I'm *almost* sorry I came over. *Leave it alone, Jaime, I'm warning you!"*

Jaime, feeling a hollow in the pit of her stomach, watched Jane-Michelle hurry down the sidewalk and head across the lawn toward her own house, almost running. *Good grief. People in this town would hang me up by the toes if they knew I actually have the diary. Francesca and I have gone through it, just to see what it says, but maybe it's time to sit down and really take it seriously.* She let the ivory drapes fall back across the window and watched Jane-Michelle's retreat. She shivered, and it wasn't just because the first soft snow of the season had begun to fall.

Eleven

"I've only been in this job for five months, and already I've got problems." Evan cut up his French toast into neat little sections before eating it, as he had always done. He did this even before putting syrup on it. He gave her a wry smile. "The Bauer brothers, my loyal opposition, so to speak."

"What do they want you to do?" She was preoccupied these days with how she was going to decorate the house for the holidays. She forced herself to brush away the visions of door wreaths and strings of blue lights across the front of the house, in order to pay attention to what he was saying.

"It's more like what they *don't* want me to do." He dug into his toast, now that it was neatly organized and covered with just the right amount of syrup.

"They *don't* see a need for art teachers or music teachers in the schools, and even though the rest of the board has overruled them and approved the hiring of three art and music teachers for each town, they are still ranting against the idea."

Jaime shook her head in commiseration. "What do you mean *ranting?* Do you mean literally *ranting?*"

"Literally. Rad banged his shoe against the table last Thursday, and Ferris shouts—really *shouts*—his opinions, as if the rest of us were all hard of hearing. He said we were 'elite' and wanted to turn the kids into 'citified sissies'."

Jaime laughed. She reached over and stroked the side of her husband's face. "You're getting lines under your eyes that you never had before, Evan. Do you regret taking on this school system?"

"Not at all. I enjoy the challenge. I've just had trouble sleeping, that's all. Dane and I are playing indoor tennis this afternoon. That will help me relax." He stood, carried his dishes over to the sink, and turned back to her. "And, Mrs. Cat-eyes, what are you going to do today?"

She smiled, liking the pet names he called her because of the color of her eyes, green with gold flecks surrounding the irises. Many people had commented they had never seen eyes like hers, and frankly, when she looked at herself in the mirror, she had to admit that neither had she.

"I'm going to tackle the attic. I should have done it before, but it was too hot up there. Now that the weather has cooled down, I think I can stand all that dust and not suffocate."

"Good girl! But please don't find any more guns up there."

Jaime shuddered. "Believe me, I'll try not to!"

He shrugged into a copper-colored suede jacket, leaned over to give her a kiss, and was out the door. He wore a shirt and tie and sports coat to board meetings, which were open to the public, but dressed casually when he worked from his office, which was in Mill Pond High School, at the opposite end of the long main hall from Dane's office. She watched him go and smiled.

~ * ~

Jaime pulled on the frayed rope that brought down the rickety stairs to the attic. Why hadn't the Porters ever built a proper staircase, as the space above was ample and could have been rehabbed into a couple of spare bedrooms? There already was a back door, hardly ever used, that led to the narrow staircase off the den, which went up to the second floor. They could have the space divided into two good-sized bedrooms with built-in beds and storage spaces, bookcases, and closets, and rent them out to a couple of college students. *Great idea.* She almost patted herself on the back. *Be sure and run it past Evan later.*

It took her several trips up and down the makeshift staircase to get her cleaning supplies into the attic. At last, armed with mop and broom, buckets of water, dusting cloths, and cleansers, she stood and surveyed the empty space. Well, almost empty, except for the ancient Christmas tree, just a skeleton of tired branches, its needles under it, fallen like rain, brown and withered all around it. *Such a fire hazard. Why in the world would anyone stick it up here and just leave it for someone else to clean out?* She had no answer for that. As she dragged it toward the hatchway, she noticed the charred marks on the withered trunk. It *had* caught on fire at one time or another. Probably the lights had burned it. Lucky the whole house hadn't gone up in flames.

She set to work cleaning up the needles, and when that was done she dragged the tree over to the trap door and let it slide down the stairs to the second floor. She was soon covered in dust and grime as she toured the space, stopping to pick up items that had obviously been there for years. Here was a once-colorful scarf, the kind of thing girls in the fifties had worn over their hair and tied under their chins. Babushkas, they'd been called. This one was faded beyond belief, frayed at the edges, and had disintegrated in several places.

"Ugh!" She lifted the scarf by a corner with two fingers and dropped it gingerly into the trash bucket. She picked up an open matchbook packet that was under the scarf and, seeing it empty, dropped that into the trash also.

And what were these? Oh, for God's sake—condoms? Old, shriveled, grimy, disgusting! She used a paper towel to pick them up and wrap them in it as she discarded them. She got her broom and swept the floor, ending up with a tidy pile of dirt, insects, buttons, safety pins, bobby pins (did anyone use bobby pins anymore?), a once-white sock, and a tiny pile of bones, which had probably once been a mouse. Nearly gagging, she kept on sweeping, mopping and scouring until the space was clean and she had dusted everything in sight, including the two windows at the far ends of the room. She paused as she sprayed glass cleaner on the panes and wiped them until they shone. This window, at the west end of the house, looked different from the other. As she looked closer, she saw that some of the panes had been replaced, but the repair had been clumsily done, obviously an amateur job. Well, maybe a bird had flown into the panes by mistake, They did that sometimes.

Finally, she was done, except for a rusted white enamel cupboard that, barely able to stand, listed crazily in one of the corners of the attic. Jaime had left that for last, fully expecting it to be filled with old, rotting objects of one kind or another—who knew, perhaps even old containers of food or soda pop. The front panel was divided into two long doors, each side with a simple metal handle, and a small drawer at the bottom of the cabinet. Jaime tugged on one and then the other; they were both stuck. Sighing, she went back down the ladder to the garage, where she found one of Evan's wrenches, and returned to the attic. She pushed the wrench under the left door handle and inserted the sharp end into the crack between the doors. It didn't take much effort. The door sprung open. To her surprise, and relative relief, there was nothing in the cabinet. It wasn't even particularly dirty. But it wasn't in good enough shape to leave there, either. She would have Evan haul it out to the curb later, when he brought down the Christmas tree.

"Well, that's that." She looked around the attic with satisfaction. She glanced at her watch. She had planned that well, she congratulated herself. In just twenty minutes or so, the boys would be home. She needed to take all the cleaning supplies downstairs and start lunch for Josh and Jack.

Her eyes lit on the cabinet again, and this time she noticed the small drawer at the bottom. *Might as well check that out.* She crossed the room toward it. The drawer slid open easily. An envelope, yellow with age, lay askew on the bottom. Jaime reached in and picked it up, turning it over a few times. It was not addressed and unstamped. She ran a finger over a watery pattern with pale blue edges outlining the irregular shape. Tears? Someone had cried over this envelope, or whatever letter had been inside it?

To her amazement, two folded sheets of lined paper were inside the envelope. She drew them out, and unfolded them. She experienced a vague sense of voyeurism—and yet, how could it hurt? Whoever had written this long ago was most likely dead.

As Jaime began to read the letter, she was absolutely certain that the writer of the letter was still very much alive.

Dearest Janie,

I shouldn't call you dearest, should I, since we aren't even friends, and I guess we never will be. You will never know how much I admired you, and how much I wanted to be friends with you. But—you've gone away to college, and I've only run into you twice in the two years you've been gone.

I graduated last year, Janie, a lot you care, I know. I've been going to beauty school, cosmetology, they call it. Maybe someday you'll come back and get a haircut from me. Hah—fat chance.

But that's not why I'm writing you this letter—if I ever mail it. I don't know if I have the guts to do it or not. I'm sitting up here in the attic of the Porter House, trying to decide what to do. We used to live here, briefly, before my father died, and I always loved this house. Forrest, Balls, and I, and sometimes Kathy Kelly, sneak up here to smoke and drink and fool around. Balls and I sometimes come up here, just he and I, and do something else.

Did you know that I have a watercolor painting you did in art class and threw away? Forrest dug it out and gave it to me. It's of that cute house your family still lives in, with the picket fence and the roses. If I ever have a shop of my own, I'm going to frame it and put it on the wall.

And if I have a little girl, I'm going to name her Jane-Michelle after you.

The letter gave Jaime the chills, as well as a feeling of deep empathy for the writer of it. She ran her hands up and down her arms, and tried to soothe the prickly feeling. There wasn't any doubt who wrote the undated letter. She was sure the writer would not want the letter back, reminding her of an humiliating era in her life. Jaime tore it into tiny pieces and added it to the trash bag. Willow might not be willing to tell her anything now, but she had left her a message from the past anyway.

Twelve

Jaime poured coffee for both Francesca and herself. "We finally have a whole morning to go over this. No husbands, no kids, nothing that has to be done immediately." She placed the soiled diary on the table. "Willow's letter has really piqued my interest now."

Francesca took a sip before she spoke. "We've been over the whole thing a dozen times." She pulled the book toward her and opened it. "But if we're supposed to be finding something out from it, I don't know what it is. So... let's start at the beginning and take notes. Here's the first entry, dated January 1, 1950."

"The middle of their junior year. Kathy is starting the diary, and it's the first mention of all The Nine, as they called them."

Francesca handed the diary back to Jaime. "Read it out loud. I'll write down the names and anything else that might seem important."

"Okay, here goes."

January 1, 1950

Hello Diary, this is your first entry from the future best-selling author, Kathleen Louise Kelly. Right now, however, I'm just a nobody junior at a dinky nowhere school in the no-

account town of Mill Pond in the western hills of Massachusetts. We are so unimportant in the life of this town that we don't even have a separate high school. Our class, all sixty-nine of us (hey! That's an interesting number, isn't it?) have to go to a school that starts with kindergarten and worms its way up to the senior class—us, that will be, next year.

Balls and Forrest swear they are going to kill them all. "Them" are the ones who think they're too good for the rest of us. I will go ahead and list them here: Barbara Paris—! I hate that bitch! She thinks she's so pretty, always stealing glances at herself in any mirror that she happens to pass. Got the best guy in the class, too, Paul Peller, basketball star. Never saw anyone as good-looking as Paul, but he's got eyes for no one but Barb. Then there's Sylvia Mason. Creeps, what a snob! She's about six-feet tall and absolutely gorgeous, in her own eyes anyway. She's forever telling people she's Norwegian as if that's some kind of blue-ribbon status or something. She's class president, and Balls hates her more than anyone else. Whenever he tries to make a suggestion during class meetings, she always pretends to write it down, and then says to him, "and your name is—?" It cracks everyone up, everyone except Balls, who just hates her more. Even Miss Kowalski, our class advisor, just stands there and smirks. Damn them all!

Jaime looked up. "Got that so far? Barbara, Sylvia, Paul, and Kathy herself. And Balls and Forrest, of course."

"Yep. Go on."

"Then there's this whole saga of Willow and Janie at the basketball game. I'll pick it up where there's some new info here."

I saw Willow run out of the auditorium, and I went home after her, down to that miserable shack down by the river. I had to make some excuse to Suki, like I didn't feel well and thought I might puke if I hung around, which is true, I did feel like puking, but that was because of Janie. If she had ever seen Willow crying and crying—for hours, before I could calm her down, it might just have melted her hard heart, but I doubt it. But, I digress. (Don't they say that in novels a lot?)

Donnie. He's on varsity basketball with Paul and Marc. Cat-eyed Janie is nuts about him, and always has been, I think, since second grade or so. But he doesn't want to get tied down and plays the field a lot. He and Marc have this stupid thing going on the court. Whenever they think they can work together to make a good play, one of them will yell "Geronimo!" Coach has told them not to do it, but they do anyway, and how can he kick them off the team, when he wouldn't have a team without them?

"Janie, Donnie and Marc." Francesca scribbled on her pad. "Who's left?"

"Francie and Suki. And she does mention them. Listen up."

I think the only reason Marc is part of The Nine is that he's super friends with Donnie and plays basketball. He sometimes takes Janie or Suki to a dance or a movie, but everyone thinks he's not really interested in girls. He's really funny, though. One time in Mr. McMartin's class—the old fart fell asleep at his desk after giving us an assignment—Marc snuck up to the desk and cut his necktie off, right below the knot. When Mr.

M. woke up, he couldn't control the class, and couldn't understand why they wouldn't stop laughing.

And the only reason freckle-faced Francie is part of it is that she made cheerleading, and Sylvia seems to hang out with her sometimes, God only knows why. Francie flunked social studies, of all things, last year, and is repeating it. Suki is such a snob that she's a natural for that group, but I don't know why she's such a snob. Her family isn't anything special, but she just has that attitude—you know? She and I have been best friends since forever, but I don't really like her. I just hang on so I can be one of The jerk-off Nine, too. And I am.

"Francie, Suki and Kathy... that's nine. Hey, Jaime, are you all right?"

Her head reeling, Jaime dropped the diary into her lap and sat back against the sofa cushions. She saw it like a movie in her head. Janie, pert and immaculate in her plaid skirt and cashmere sweater set—Willow, pale-faced and overweight, her limp hair straggling around her face, wearing her second-hand clothing She approached Janie and sat beside her, hope and adoration lighting up her plain, washed-out features—and Janie, giving a little start of surprise but not even deigning to glance at Willow, got up and climbed the bleachers to join Barbara and Sylvia. Janie didn't even glance back. The vision faded, and Jaime shook her head. "Yeah, I'm okay. I just got a little dizzy for a moment."

Francesca took a deep breath. "Okay, I'm just going to lay this on you. Do you believe at all in reincarnation?"

"Well, as I've told you, I've had a lot of strange things happen. I told you about what the kids said when they were little. I just don't know where a three-year-old would get a phrase like 'the last time we were here.'"

Francesca nodded. "Unless—they *had* been here before. By 'here' I don't mean Mill Pond necessarily. I mean on earth."

Jaime put a finger to her lips. "I don't think anything's impossible. What are you getting at?"

"Do you think you were Janie? I'm asking you this, because I think we could have been 'The Nine' in Kathy's diary, and we could have all come back to try to prevent another massacre, like the one in sixty-one, from happening again.

Jaime stared at her. "I—I could have been. And just for the sake of playing out the game, do you think you were Francie?"

"Well, the similarity in names is there, but I don't think I sound too much like Francie. However, when I was born, my mother said she was going to name me 'Jessica', and the minute she saw me she thought I should be 'Francesca'. The name had never even occurred to her before then."

"She had freckles, and you do, too," Jaime pointed out.

"Dane sounds like Donnie, his personality and all. Dark and good-looking with a killer smile, and a basketball star."

"That's a possibility, and when I first saw him at that school reception, I had an instant feeling of recognition."

"Well, you can't have him in this life, either," Francesca joked. "He's mine."

"If we're going to take this seriously, Evan doesn't seem to be one of them, does he?"

"No he doesn't. But sometimes, people come in from 'outside' the main group, so to speak, to help. Maybe Evan is like that."

"Evan doesn't think there's anything meaningful about the diary. I wanted to go through it with you first, and see what we could get from it. Evan thinks the reincarnation stuff is a lot of hooey anyway."

"No point bringing it up then, What do you think should be our next step? What's the next entry?"

Jaime flipped through several empty pages to the next entry.

Sept. 12, 1950

I snuck out last night and met Balls and Forrest down by the river. They had beer, don't know where they got it, and I don't care. Balls wants to do something to make Sylvia miserable without her knowing it. Because I'm in with that snotty group, I said I'd try to figure something out for him. I can't go to October Bash with Forrest, although I'd like to, because of my connection with "the group", so I'm going blind-date with one of the hoity-toity college guys from UMass that Sylvia knows. God! It will be awful, boring as hell, but I have to sacrifice for our ultimate goal. Forrest hates Janie because she's so mean to Willow. He tried to get her, Willow, to come with us, but her mother and Aunt Lily—

"Aunt Lily!" they both exclaimed at once. "How did we miss that before?"

"Go on, Jaime. What else does it say?"

...Aunt Lily were there, measuring her for her homemade prom dress. She's going with Balls, not happy about it, but who else would take her? Balls says if he can ruin the prom for Sylvia it would make his year!

"It ends there." Jaime flipped a page over. "Now, we know Aunt Lily was a friend of Willow's mother, but it doesn't seem to have any more significance than that. It's just another tie-in."

"Willow. She's the one with all the answers, if she'd only let us in on what she knows. She was actually there."

They stared at each other.

"Do you think she'd tell us anything?"

Francesca pondered. "I'll make a hair appointment for Saturday. You come with me and notice everything you can, and then we'll go to lunch and compare notes. I'll see what I can get out of Willow."

"You just had your hair cut. Isn't it a little suspicious for you to go back so soon?"

Francesca ran her fingers through her honey-colored hair. "I've been thinking of having it colored. I noticed some gray showing up in it, and I'm not ready for that yet."

"You hair is beautiful! Why would you want to color it anything else?"

Francesca winked at her. "Highlighted, that's all. Just get rid of the gray. So... Saturday, okay? The guys can take care of the kids, go to the park or something?"

Jaime shrugged, then nodded. "Okay, but I doubt you'll get anything out of Willow. She's one closed-mouthed lady when it comes to the class of fifty-one."

"So... do you believe in reincarnation? Seriously?"

Jaime swallowed. Mostly she did, but sometimes she thought it probably wasn't so. She tried to be a faithful Presbyterian member, but she just couldn't get past all the theology, all the improbable things that the Bible said were so, all the tenets churchgoers seemed to believe without questioning. She realized that's what 'faith' was, but it simply didn't happen for her.

"I'm inclined to believe in that," she admitted. "You can't deny what happens when you have all the strange experiences, like I've had."

"Well, here's my theory." Francesca hesitated. "And believe me, Jaime, I've done a lot of thinking about this. I think we've reincarnated, and come back, to the scene of the crime, as it were."

"*Who's* reincarnated? *Us?* Are you kidding?"

"I'm the prom queen, Francie, and you're Janie, the cute little snob."

"I'm anything but a snob!" Jaime protested, hurt.

"Look at the similarities in the names," Francesca went on. "I'm Francesca—she was Francie, or Frances, as was popular then. You're Jaime, different in only one letter from Janie."

"Oh, I don't know. This seems like quite a stretch. I was named after my father, James. It's just a quirky coincidence."

"Oh yeah? What's your middle name?"

Jaime hesitated, much too long, then looked Francesca in the eyes and smiled. "Michelle."

"Aha!" Francesca went on. "Just listen, Jaime. I'm blonde, like Francie was, grew up here, was nominated for Prom Queen, and selected, and..." She paused and flushed a little. "Everyone around here knows it, but you probably don't... I was just a bit pregnant when I married Dane."

"Huh." Jaime tried not to show her surprise.

"And they both got basketball scholarships to UConn, but Donnie flunked out, went into the marines, came home to marry Patty, the girl he started dating the summer he graduated, but she was killed in a car accident, so he got Francie pregnant and married her. Just like Dane and me."

"But Dane didn't flunk out of school and go into the Marines, or any other branch of the service, did he?"

Francesca made an impatient gesture. "No! That's the point. The next time you come around you're supposed to do it better."

Jaime bit her lip. "Francesca, I've read over and over in this diary that Janie, according to Kathy, always had a crush on Donnie, but she couldn't have him because he belonged to Patty. She went away to school and married—uh, a guy named Craig something. A teacher."

"Aha!" Francesca pounced. "And Evan's a school superintendent." She smiled at Jaime. "And do you have a thing for Dane, like Janie did for Donnie?"

Jaime laughed. "I'm perfectly happy with Evan, thank you, but as I told you—the first time I saw him at the school reception, I did have this weird feeling that I already knew him."

"See, you did know him. Past life. Only this time you grew up somewhere else, and only re-met him recently, so no long-time unrequited crush. You did it better." She paused and smiled at Jaime. "Saturday. Are we still on?"

Jaime nodded. "Hair and lunch."

"And remember," Francesca said with a mischievous grin, "we were friends once, and we are again. And maybe we can figure out this time just what it is we're doing here."

Thirteen

Willow glanced up, as did the other four operators in her shop, when Jaime and Francesca entered. Willow, a little stouter than when Jaime had been in before, leaned down and whispered something in her customer's ear, then came forward to welcome them. Her smile seemed a little forced, as she greeted Francesca, then Jaime.

"Are we doing anything for you today?"

"No, thanks." Jaime smiled as warmly as she could, just in case she was the person Willow had admired so much a couple of generations ago. "I'm just going to sit here and wait for Francesca."

Willow seemed a bit taken aback by Jaime's sudden surge of friendliness, but she nodded and indicated the coffee pot, cups, and plate of cookies that was available to all who sat and waited.

"Francesca, would it be okay if one of the other girls washes your hair? I just have to finish up Mrs. Henderson, and I'll be ready for you." Willow picked at a strand of Francesca's hair. "You wanted to go a little lighter, maybe?"

"Just to cover up the gray," Francesca said. "Highlights rather than a total cover, I think."

Willow looked puzzled. "I don't see any gray, Francesca."

"Oh, I pull out the hairs as soon as I find them. It's just starting to turn, but I think highlights would hide any new ones that pop up."

Willow nodded, but seemed unconvinced. "Just a few minutes, then. Charlotte!" she called to a tall, slim girl in her mid-twenties, who couldn't have had too many years in the business. "Would you wash Mrs. Summers' hair, please, and I'll be ready for her in about ten minutes."

Charlotte grinned in their direction and held up two fingers, to mean two minutes. In her short skirt, sneakers, and pullover sweater, which showed bright red beneath her pink smock, she looked more like a high school cheerleader than a licensed beautician.

Jaime and Francesca sat down to wait. Jaime kept her voice to a whisper. "Don't forget to ask about Lily."

"That's why we're here! And you keep your eyes and ears open. Maybe you could walk around the shop and look at all the china and pictures, ask some questions. Innocently, of course."

Jaime nodded. "I could do that, and I will. But I tend to get suffocated by all this pink. I may need to go out for air, so don't be alarmed if I disappear."

Charlotte came to escort Francesca back to the sinks, and Jaime helped herself to a mug of coffee and a cookie, which she noted was homemade. She leafed through a magazine and pretended to focus in on an article to read. With her attention not diverted elsewhere, she was able to hone in on snippets of conversation here and there.

"We had to put Aunt Evie in the Lakeview Home. Didn't want to do it, but—"

"Isn't it wonderful Mildred and Tom found each other, after all these years—"

"Johnny has his heart set on going to Montana or someplace like that for college. I just wish he'd stay home and go to UMass. Nothing wrong with UMass—"

Jaime glanced up at Francesca, who was swathed in pink plastic and deep into conversation with Willow. As Jaime watched her, however, Francesca's hand snaked out from under the plastic, dropped to her side, and with one finger began to make circles.

Okay, hint received. She got up and stretched a little, as if she were tired of sitting, and began to stroll about the shop.

Willow's shop, other than being drowned in pink, was divided into two parts, with a center wall separating two operators and their sinks and stalls from the other two. Willow herself had a larger, open area at the back, near the door leading to the office and supply room.

Jaime drifted over to a shelf that held a collection of pretty porcelain vases. They all looked old-fashioned, English, perhaps, and were painted with a variety of pale, delicate flowers. "Oh, these are lovely," she said, turning to Charlotte, who was giving a bowl-cut to a beautiful little blond boy about four years old.

Charlotte half-turned toward her. "That's just part of Willow's *huge* collection. She loves nice things, you know, because of—" She caught herself, broke off, and bent down to the child in her chair, almost as if she didn't want to share any more information about Willow with Jaime.

Jaime walked slowly on, examining several floral watercolor paintings hanging on the wall. She turned back toward Charlotte. "Local artists?"

Charlotte glanced toward the paintings. "Yes. We change them periodically, when someone else comes along and wants to put hers up. Or his. We have had a gentleman or two over the years who've displayed his work here."

"I paint. I have an art degree. Could I show some of my work here?"

Charlotte hesitated. "I suppose so. You'd have to ask Willow. It's her shop." She bent down to the boy again and turned her back to Jaime, discouraging further conversation.

Jaime wandered on. There were more collections of fine china, each displayed with similar items: sugar bowls and creamers on one shelf, plates lined up on individual plate stands on another. Delicate floral teacups and saucers filled another shelf. A cabinet against the back wall held a collection of dolls dressed in frilly clothing to look old-fashioned, even if they weren't. *Interesting, Jaime thought. Willow trying to make up for her deprived childhood with pretty china and expensive dolls she never had.*

The beauty operator at the end of the center wall was a fortyish woman with hair that was almost orange and piled up on her head like the tiers of a wedding cake.

Jaime smiled as the woman turned to look at her. "Don't bother about me, please. I'm just taking up time while waiting for Francesca."

Jaime glanced at the nameplate on the stylist's vanity. The name, in pink script, was spelled Karyle.

"It's pronounced like Carol. I have no idea why my mother spelled it that way. You're the new super's wife, aren't you?" Karyle wiped her hand on her smock and offered her well-manicured hand to Jaime. Her smile was wide and welcoming. "We have two girls in junior high, and we desperately want a new, modern regional high school for the three towns. I know there's a lot of opposition to it, but I hope your husband can get it pushed through."

"Who would oppose that?" But Jaime thought she knew the answer before Karyle spoke.

Karyle made a face. "Those idiots, the Bauer brothers." She glanced at her watch. "My next appointment is late," she complained with a note of irritation in her voice. "She must think I have nothing to do—" She broke off as a heavy-set woman with fly-away gray hair burst through the front door of the shop. "Well, well, here she is now." She got very busy with her towels and combs and other instruments of hair torture, and Jaime strolled on.

Jaime's attention was grabbed by a painting on the back wall, just before she rounded the bend to where Willow held court. She knew instinctively that it was not by the same artist who had painted the others, because the technique was looser, more like her own, and the colors were all a little off, not mere dilutions of the primaries, but interesting mixes. An eerie feeling came over Jaime as she stared at the painting, the sense that she knew this place, had been there before. The painting was of a house, made of fieldstone, with almost a country-inn look about it. A white picket fence covered with pink climbing roses ran along one side, and several white birches stood on the other side. The door and shutters were painted white, and there was a decorative wreath of some kind on the front door. It was charming, but almost too cute. Jaime felt the familiar suffocating feeling overtake her, along with the now familiar disorientation of déjà vu, and she made her way with haste to the front door and out onto the sidewalk.

She took deep breaths of fresh air and forced herself to calm down. She sat down on the wrought iron bench with the green wooden slat seats, and put her face down into her hands. As sometimes happened, it wasn't so much that the scene seemed familiar, or even that the painting style was so much like her own;

before she had fled she had seen the initials in the lower left-hand side of the painting: *J.M.C.,* and the year it was painted, 1951.

Was it possible, she asked herself, that the initials stood for Jane Michelle Carlson?

Francesca came out a few minutes later, looking suitably beautified.

"Did you ask about Lily?"

Francesca acted as if she hadn't heard her. "What did you say?"

Jaime did a double take. "You didn't hear me? Did you ask about Lily?"

Francesca cupped a hand over one ear. "What did you say?" Her voice was so loud several passersby threw her curious glances.

Jaime stared at her. Was this a game? Okay, she'd play. She made a tunnel of her hands and yelled into them, "Did you ask her about Lily?"

Willow came to the door of her shop and threw them both a look of disgust. She flipped over the sign on the outside of the door so that it said *'closed for lunch',* and withdrew inside.

"That's exactly what she told me—nothing. She acted as if she didn't hear me. Boy, it's chilly outside today, isn't it?" She pulled her collar up around her neck.

Jaime glanced back at the firmly closed door. "Chilly inside, too." She and Francesca walked on, giggling like teenagers.

Fourteen

"Well, that's the place, all right," Francesca had parked the car across the street from the old stone house, and she and Jaime sat and looked at it. "Janie Carlson's house. Not the better for wear, unfortunately." A faded red truck sat askew on the lawn, opposite the driveway.

They had driven from the beauty shop south, toward the river, but had taken a sharp turn onto a street called Winslow Place about three miles out of town. The homes there tended to the bungalow style, built in the thirties and forties. Obviously, it had been a trendy neighborhood fifty years ago, but it was definitely low-income now. The old Carlson house had once been a handsome house.

Jaime half-turned in her seat. "Tell me again what Willow said,"

"When I saw you staring at the picture and then run out of the shop, I asked her about it. I've seen that painting of course but never *really* took note of it before. It was just *there,* you know?"

Jaime nodded. "But Willow said it was Janie's family home?"

"That much she did tell me. I don't know who lives here now, though."

Jaime stared across the street at the house. "It must have been really nice in its day, when Janie lived there. And Willow got the painting because Janie threw it away in art class?"

"Apparently, Willow's brother Forrest was in the same art class with Janie, and the assignment was to draw and paint their own homes, as a perspective assignment."

Jaime nodded. "The perspective is a little off, but it's a nice painting, regardless."

Francesca laughed. "I wouldn't know off-perspective from on-perspective. Apparently Janie wasn't satisfied with it, tossed it away and started a new one. Forrest, knowing Willow would treasure anything Janie did, fished it out and took it home."

"Willow told you that much?"

"She did, and didn't seem to mind. What the heck was Forrest doing in an art class, I wonder?"

Jaime tore her eyes from the house and smiled at Francesca. "A lot of very strange people have art talent and need a way to express themselves. There's a museum in Baltimore that has art by all kinds of 'Outsiders', as they call it. It's fascinating, and very different from the usual art gallery kind of place."

Francesca turned up her palms. "I plead ignorance of all that." In silence they stared at the house as if expecting it to speak to them.

"I want to go inside." Jaime looked at Francesca from the corners of her eyes. "Do you think that's crazy?"

Francesca ran her fingers through her new honey-colored, streaked hair. "How do you expect to do that, Jaime? They're not just going to let you walk through."

"It doesn't look like anyone's home. I haven't seen any sign of life in there. Not even a dog. Hmmmmm."

Francesca turned a horrified expression on Jaime. "You can't be thinking of breaking in? Jaime, we can't. Our husbands are prominent in town—they'd never live it down if we got caught."

"I need to go in. I have a mental picture of a bedroom—that one, to the left of the door, upstairs." She pointed to the dormer on the left. "I think that was Janie's. In my mind I see pale green wallpaper with yellow flowers, yellow curtains, an old-fashioned iron bed, painted white—"

"It won't be that way now! Janie Carlson hasn't lived there for forty years!"

Jaime bit her lip, staring at the upstairs window. "There's something in there that I need to get. I know just where it is." She jumped out of the car, closing the door behind her.

"Jaime—don't!"

She leaned into Francesca's window. "Park out in the street. If someone's home, I'll make up a story. If not, and I can get in—just watch, and if a car comes home, honk twice. I'll get out the back door and run through the neighbor's yard back to the road."

"Jaime, no!" Francesca tried to grab her arm, but Jaime ran across the street and up the walk, which was paved with irregular stones, some of them missing, and not well-kept. Some stones were broken, and weeds grew up through the cracks between them.

Jaime slowed down as she approached the door, one of those that protruded slightly from the front of the house, with a triangular roof over it, like a cottage out of Hansel and Gretel. Luckily the earlier snow had melted, so she would leave no footprints.

Jaime knocked at the green-painted door and waited. Nobody answered, so she knocked again and waited. Still no answer. She glanced around at Francesca, who had moved the car to the opposite side of the road, and shook her head. She shivered in her light coat, took a deep breath, turned the door knob, and pushed. The door opened, and Jaime went inside.

It was all too familiar. A chill came over her as she looked around and knew instinctively where all the rooms were: the kitchen, straight ahead down that small hallway, a tiny den behind it for watching TV and a desk for doing homework. There was a quilting frame in one corner, an unfinished quilt draped over it. It looked like whoever lived here quilted. A bathroom off the kitchen. A formal dining room to the left, beyond the stairs. She crossed the living room, not taking note of the furnishings, as in her mind she saw it the way it had been. She ran up the stairs, turned left, and found the bedroom, the smallest of two, but there it was, with a dormer window looking out onto the front lawn.

The old iron bed had been replaced by maple bunk beds, and the room was obviously used by a young boy, or boys. The walls were painted light blue and boasted Disney character stickers here and there. The bunks were covered in matching quilts in reds, blues and yellows. Jaime noted with a quick glance that they were beautifully done. Toys were scattered about: trucks, blocks, lots of dinosaurs, both stuffed and plastic, and a wobbly bookcase with colorful picture books spilling out of it. A large stuffed lion stared at her from the top bunk.

Jaime caught her breath. Would it still be there after all these years? She was the only one who knew about that particular spot, beneath the window. There should be a loose floorboard behind the old fashioned radiator, which was still there, painted dark blue. Jaime dropped to the floor and explored the boards beneath the radiator. Her fingers knew the drill; they found the loose board. It had never been secured. She pried it up, feeling it splinter a little with age as she forced the board up. Her fingers wriggled into the shallow space below. She felt the box and drew it out. It was dusty and misshapen, but it was the box. She lifted the lid, and there it was.

She stuffed the box into her pocket and fled. As she flew down the stairs, she heard Francesca's horn beep twice, and she ran down the hall into the kitchen and out the back door, just as she heard a car putt-putt noisily into the driveway. The bushes hid her as she ran into the neighbor's yard and slowed to a walk. Breathing hard but trying to regain her dignity, unable to believe what she had just done, she crossed the road and jumped back into the car with an ashen-faced Francesca.

They looked back at the family getting out of the battered gray Toyota that pulled into the driveway. A short, thin man, balding, wearing jeans and a black leather jacket, got out of the car, slammed the door, and not looking back, went into the house. His wife got out more slowly. She wore a thin white jacket over a red turtleneck and black jeans. Her blonde hair was tied back with a red scarf. Jaime saw that she had once been pretty, but her face now seemed prematurely lined and tired. She stooped to pick up a six-pack, left behind by her husband, and two plastic grocery bags, and walked slowly up the walk as she carried them toward the house. The children—a boy, just about the same age as Josh and Jack, and a slightly older girl stormed about the yard, whooping and jumping, glad to be out of the prison of the car.

Francesca let out a long breath of relief. "That was close. And they don't look to me like they would have been all that friendly."

The man reappeared in the doorway. He glared at his wife. "Did you leave the back door open?" She shook her head, the ponytail bobbing. He went toward her and grabbed the six-pack from her hand. "Gimme those, slowpoke. You'd let a man die of thirst before you shook your fat ass to get him a drink." His voice was loud, and his tone abusive. Jaime shivered, this time not with cold, but revulsion.

"Who are they? Do you know them?"

Francesca shook her head. "The mailbox said Alden Snyder. I assume that's who he is."

They continued to watch as Alden yelled at his wife and kids from the door.

"Nice guy. I warned you. Do you know how lucky we are in our choice of husbands?" She leaned forward and turned the key in the ignition.

Jaime laid a hand on her arm. "Wait a sec. I need to show you something." She dug the box out of her pocket.

Francesca eyed the small, dirty box with distaste. "What is it?" She gasped. "You didn't take something out of the house, did you?"

"Calm down. It isn't anything of theirs." With great care she lifted the lid and set it on the seat beside her. She lifted out the delicate old necklace, an engraved *J* on a tarnished chain.

Waiting for an answer, Francesca held her breath as her eyes met Jaime's.

"Donnie Barrett gave it to Janie Carlson when he came home from the Marines. They had a few dates, but he never cared about her as much as she liked him, and he dumped her and married Francie."

Francesca's mouth fell open. "How do you know that, and where did you get that?"

Jaime shook her head. "Don't ask me how I know. I just know. I remembered where Janie Carlson put it, and I went right to it, in Janie's bedroom."

"That was in Kathy Kelly's diary?"

"No," Jaime insisted, shaking her head. "I'm telling you, Francesca, I *remembered* where Janie—or I—put it. It was still right there, after all these years."

She looked across the road at the house again. "I can't believe I just did that."

Fifteen

Having been brought up a Southern girl, Jaime felt perpetually cold as winter took hold in snowy New England. Bundled up in sweaters and corduroys, she added long-sleeved turtleneck pullovers and wool socks to her wardrobe, and she bought flannel pajamas to sleep in at night and an electric blanket for the bed.

She admitted that Christmas was a wonder, though, with the snow, icicles hanging from the eaves, the trees glistening with coatings of ice on their branches. Evan strung lights on the small blue spruce in their front yard and across the front of their porch. Jaime bought candles for the windows and an evergreen wreath with a red velvet bow for the front door. She took pictures of their holiday-decorated Victorian house and sent emails to all their friends in Atlanta.

Even the Bauer brothers and Evan's other vocal opponents caught the holiday goodwill fever and ceased their ranting during the holidays.

Jaime missed the social scene that she had enjoyed in Atlanta, however. Only Dane and Francesca issued any invitations, and although Jaime met other women she would have liked to have become better acquainted with, nothing ever came of it. Jane-Michelle waved from the front yard when they saw each other, but that was as far as it went. After the warm and busy community life they had enjoyed in Atlanta, she felt a bit slighted, but Francesca had assured her that New Englanders took their time making friendships, and people in small towns like Mill Pond tended to stay with the friends they already had and not reach out to newcomers. In January, she found herself growing restless.

"Well, how are we supposed to make friends, be part of a social circle?" It had been so easy and natural in Atlanta; she met someone she liked at the gym, at the community swimming pool, at the beauty parlor, and pretty soon she was having lunch and developing a friendship, which might or might not last, depending on a variety of things. But she ran into the same people over and over again, at gatherings at the clubs, and private parties. Jaime began to think she had to make the first overture; a big open cocktail party, maybe.

Evan thought it was a good idea when she broached the subject with him. "It might help to see some of these people in a relaxed setting, not just in the business venue. Let's do it."

"Give me a list of people you want me to invite. I'll make the invitations myself and print them off on the computer."

"By the way," Evan said, changing the subject, "on Thursday evening, we're having an open Tri-town Board Meeting in the high school auditorium to discuss my proposal for the new regional high school. There will be child care, so why don't you bring the boys and come along?"

~ * ~

The next couple days Jaime worked on her invitations, attempting small watercolor paintings of their house from the pictures she had taken. Finally she had one she liked well enough. She put it aside until she had a date for the party and a list of whom to invite. *I've improved a lot since I was Janie.* She smiled a bit and stacked the envelopes and put everything away in a neat pile.

Thursday night was crisp and cold, and the stars twinkled against a velvet sky. Jaime dropped off her bundled-up boys in the care of several pretty, vivacious teenagers and strolled down the hall to the auditorium. It was filling up fast, and as Jaime looked around, she saw almost everyone she did know. There was Willow, sitting with her daughter Jane-Michelle, three or four rows from the front. The twins' pretty young teacher, Sandy Gleason, had taken a seat near the stage, also, and Jaime recognized some of the other teachers she had met the night of the reception. The eccentric, balding fifth grade teacher, Matt Thompson, stood out in a lavender shirt and a bright purple tie.

Looking around for Francesca, Jaime saw her across the room. She was chatting with several other women and deep in an animated conversation. Jaime started toward them, but froze in her tracks as she recognized Alden Snyder and his wife, seated in the back row. Alden looked as surly as he had the other afternoon, and Molly, in a thin blue sweater and her ponytail caught up with a pink scarf, looked frail and tired. Jaime on a sudden whim, changed direction and headed toward the back of the room.

She smiled at the young woman as she slid into the empty seat beside her. She held out her hand. "Hi. I'm Jaime Reid, and I'm new in town. Mind if I join you?"

The girl turned and looked at her, startled. She stared at Jaime's hand, then shook it tentatively. "Molly Snyder." She indicated her husband with a nod of her head, but not looking at him. "This is my husband, Alden."

Alden Snyder favored her with a curt nod and not even the hint of a smile. His pale blue eyes raked over her. Jaime read the resentment on his face, and regretted having worn her cream cashmere sweater set and an expensive silver necklace Evan had given her.

Molly stared straight ahead at the stage, her face empty. Jaime made another attempt. She touched the younger woman's arm. "Molly, do you have children in school here?"

Molly stiffened. She turned to look at Jaime, as if she couldn't believe she was speaking to *her.* Jaime's felt a little pang in her chest. This must have been how Willow felt all those years ago—not ever feeling good enough, not as well dressed, not part of the group. Molly was definitely an outsider, if Jaime read the signs right.

"Elijah's in kindergarten, and Rebecca's in third grade. For the second time. We just moved here last year and the move upset her. She had to repeat."

"You don't need to tell perfect strangers our business!" Alden snapped.

Molly folded her hands in her lap and kept her eyes down. Her voice came out a whisper. "Sorry."

Jaime's heart hardened toward Alden, resenting his mean treatment of his wife, and she decided to plunge ahead. "Where did you move here *from?"*

"Hawk's Lake, Vermont. It's a tiny town up near the Canadian border. There just wasn't enough work for Alden, and—"

"Christ!" Alden exploded. He stood up. "I'm going out for a smoke until they get started up there." He plowed through the people already sitting in the rest of the row, never offering an 'excuse me' as he stumbled over their feet, and disappeared.

"From Hawk's Lake to Mill Pond!" Jaime gave a short laugh. "And what part of town do you live in? We bought that gray Victorian on Oak Street, that the Porters owned. Maybe you know which one that is?"

"No, I don't." Molly's hands were still in her lap, and she twisted them around each other in a sad sort of rhythm. Jaime noticed a dark bruise on one wrist and couldn't help but wonder if Alden had put it there. Molly finally raised her eyes to meet Jaime's. "We live out by the river in an old stone house. We just had a little trailer in Vermont. It was so cold in the winter!"

"I'll bet." Jaime felt a sudden wave of empathy for this young mother who had obviously lived a hard life and had a difficult husband to deal with, to boot. She saw Alden coming back, shoving his way through the crowd. "My twins, Josh and Jack, are in kindergarten, too. We'll have to get our kids together for a play date sometime."

Molly shot her an incredulous look as Alden sat down, reeking of smoke.

The dark green curtains shielding the stage parted, and the twelve members of the Board of Education filed onto the stage and took seats in the row of chairs already there. Evan brought up the rear and took a seat far to the left of the podium. She saw him looking around for her, but she knew she was too far to the rear for him to see her.

A tall, burly man in a blue suit banged a gavel on the wooden podium on the state. "Come to order!' The crowd began to quiet down. Those still standing in the aisles and at the sides found seats, and those who couldn't find one moved to the back of the auditorium.

The room stilled enough for him to be heard. "Good evening. I'm Mack Blake, and I'm chairman of the Boards of Education for Mill Pond, Southlake, and Sandville, Massachusetts. The meeting will now come to order."

There was a murmur of appreciation, but Jaime also heard a couple of low boos. Mack banged his gavel again.

"Madame Secretary, will you please read the minutes from the last meeting?"

A brown wren of a woman stood and walked to the podium. She was small and thin, with drab brown hair, and she wore a cocoa-colored dress. She placed a notebook on the stand and adjusted her brown, horn-rimmed glasses. Her voice was high and unaccented, and she read the minutes in a flat monotone. The audience, however, listened as if she were revealing town secrets and they wouldn't want to miss a word.

"The new superintendent, Evan Reid, laid out the plans for the new regional high school, which would serve all three towns and be called Mountain Central High School."

The murmur rose again and grew louder as the secretary began to recite the statistics concerning the proposed school. When she spoke about the need for additional faculty, including art and music teachers, more physical education teachers, teachers for special education students, and pay raises for the teachers, the noise increased. Finally, her voice was lost in the muttering of the crowd, and she stood aside as Mack strode back to the podium and began to bang on it again.

A man who was sitting left of center in the audience, rose, shaking his fist in the air. "We don't need all this fancy stuff!" His voice was loud enough to be heard over the rustling of the crowd. "And we sure don't need higher taxes to pay for all of that."

"Mr. Lowery, please sit down." Mack waved from the stage. "There will be time for discussion later. That's what this meeting is about."

So that's one of the not-so-loyal opposition. Jaime scanned the faces of the board members, nine men, three women, and Evan. One of the women looked frightened, and one of the men stared at Lowery with a slight sneer on his face. She wondered which two were Rad and Ferris Bauer. The rest of the board showed no emotions at all.

Having calmed the crowd, Mack moved to the side and took his seat again, next to Evan. He leaned over and said something to him. Evan nodded, and pulled at the knot in his tie.

The secretary continued, but just a few sentences later, at the mention of the new state-of-the-art library and the computer labs, another man, tall and skinny with a droopy reddish-gray moustache, stood up and waved his arms in the air.

The secretary took off her glasses, wiped her hand across her eyes and turned to Mack. He got up, heavily, and moved back to the podium, but as he did so, half a dozen other men and a few women, too, stood up in various places in the auditorium, and waved their arms in the air, imitating the first man. To Jaime's surprise, several of the teachers she had met stood also, and joined in the waving motions.

Mack gripped the podium with both hands. "Look, the rules of a meeting are very clear. The secretary reads the minutes, other members of the Board of Ed will present the other reports, the new Superintendent of Schools will speak, and then the floor will be open for discussion. Now, will you please all sit down—Jeff, Susan, Candy, Pete—please! And we'll get on with the business at hand."

A loud protest came from a short woman with coppery hair. "You just don't get it! We don't *want* all these *improvements!* We like our little neighborhood schools. We're a tight little community, and we prefer our tight little schools."

"How are we going to pay for all this?" a tall blond man in a maroon sweater shouted.

"Ruthie, Greg, we can discuss this later—" Jack began, before he was interrupted by a balding man in a blue and rust plaid shirt.

"Let's discuss it now!" He shook his fist at Mack "My kids aren't going to college. They're going to stay right here and run my dairy farms. And Ryan Barrett's sons will take over the lumber mill, and my sister Jen's girls will get training in working at the beauty shops, and her boy can be a mechanic like his dad. What we want—and need—are more shop programs, building things, and electrical and plumbing courses. And a rifle range, like Ferris suggested, so our kids can learn gun safety and how to protect themselves."

A smattering of applause greeted his speech.

It was obvious to Jaime that Mack was making a real effort to sound firm and in charge of the situation. He leaned forward over the podium. "We'll discuss this later. I'm sure when you hear from Dr. Reid what he wants—"

Jaime gasped as Alden Snyder leaped to his feet. "Don't give a goddamn what the super wants!" His chair squeaked loudly against the floor. "We didn't move here for all this fancy new crap. We moved here so our kids could grow up in a small town with red, white, and blue values. We're the ones who pay your salary, and we're—"

"Mr. Snyder, we will be glad to hear your opinion in due order," Mack began, but Alden interrupted again.

"You'll hear my opinions *right now!*"

Jaime froze in her chair as Alden whipped out a revolver from his black leather jacket and fired two shots into the ceiling. Jaime clutched her throat as she struggled to breathe and felt her head grow light as her vision dimmed, and for the first time in her life, she fainted.

Sixteen

"Maybe I made a mistake in wanting to come here." Evan pushed his scrambled eggs around the plate without eating any of them. "This sure isn't what I bargained for when I met with the committee." He gave her a dispirited look, his gray eyes ringed with red from lack of sleep.

"Evan Reid! That's just a tiny minority causing all the uproar. You heard what Mack said, that there would be police there figured he was at the next meeting and no out-of-order disturbances will be tolerated. And Alden Snyder's in jail for a while. You won't have to worry about him."

Evan rolled his eyes and no longer pretended any interest in eating. He sat back in his chair. "I kept looking for you and didn't see you until the end of the meeting. You were sitting near him. Did he say anything leading up to when he fired his gun?"

"I was sitting with his wife, Molly, and trying to talk to her. She looked like such a mousy little thing, but you can tell that once she was pretty. And, no, Alden didn't say much except a few cuss words, but he was really nasty in manner. And, Evan, Molly had a bad blue bruise on her wrist."

He looked at her. "You suspect abuse? You don't know them well enough to assume that. A bruise can be caused by almost anything—even one of the kids holding on too tightly."

She bit her lip. She wanted to tell him what she had seen and heard out at their house, and how she had retrieved the necklace that she knew exactly where to find, but she just couldn't tell him. Not now anyway, after that disaster of a board meeting.

He was still looking at her. "What? What is it? I know you well enough to know there's something you're not saying."

Yeah, you do know me too well, but I can't tell you about this. "Their little boy is in the same class with Josh and Jack. Maybe I could have Molly and the kids over for a play date, especially now that Daddy's out of the picture for a bit."

His eyebrows shot up. "Huh. She doesn't really seem like the type you usually pick for a friend."

Jaime figured he was puzzled by the whole conversation, and she felt herself flush. "Are you saying I'm a *snob*?" She didn't look at him, and she picked at some loose threads in her bathrobe. *Wasn't that what Kathy Kelly had written about Janie Carlson? Janie-the-snob, so condescending.*

"No, no, not at all." Evan reversed their hands, so that his now covered hers. "I didn't mean that. You're not a snob, by any means. But you usually gravitate to women who, well, you know, are educated and culturally minded, like you. Like Francesca."

Jaime was quiet for a moment, then withdrew her hand. "I felt for Molly. I'd guess she doesn't have an easy life. Maybe I'd just like to help her a little."

Evan regarded her with curiosity. "Well, do what you want to, but be careful, Mrs. Cat Eyes, not to get yourself into something you can't get out of. I don't want the twins around Alden Snyder and his restless gun, so get to know her *here,* or on neutral ground, okay?"

She tossed him a wry grin at his use of the familiar nickname. "Absolutely. By the way, Francesca is having a coffee hour for me next week, so I can meet women who are my cultural equals."

"You know I didn't mean it that way." Evan stood up. "Well, I'm going to meet Dane and some of the other board members at the school and see what we can work out to appease the red-neck minority."

"Now who's a snob?" she teased.

~ * ~

Jaime waited all of eleven minutes after Evan left before she called Molly. She bit her thumbnail as the phone rang, and the tired, timid voice answered.

"Hello?"

"Molly," she forged ahead, "this is Jaime Reid. I sat with you at the board meeting the other night—"

The woman sounded frightened. "Look, I had nothing to do with what happened! Just please leave us alone—"

"Molly, I'm not calling about that. I'm not blaming you. I wanted to know if you'd like to get our kids together for a play date."

"What? *What?*" Molly's voice was barely a whisper.

"A play date. At my house. How about tomorrow after school? It's a half-day for the kids. Come for lunch. Elijah can play with Jack and Josh, and we'll make and decorate cookies with Rebecca.

Silence reigned on the other end of the line.

"Molly?"

Molly's tone, when she answered, seemed strained. "Look, Mrs. Reid, I don't think it's very nice of you to make fun of me like this. Why are you doing this? Just to make me feel worse?"

Jaime drew in a whoosh of air. "Molly, I swear to you I'm not trying to make fun of you. I understand that Elijah is in the same class with my twins. I just thought we could get the kids together." She backed off a little, then, afraid of coming on too strong. "Only if you want to, of course."

There was another long silence. Finally Molly said, "Well, Mrs. Reid—"

"*Jaime,* please, Molly. Will you come?"

Her voice sounded lighter, hopeful. "Well... yes. I —We would like that very much. Shall I bring them over right after school, when they get home?"

Jaime smiled into the phone. She hoped her voice would carry the warmth she felt. "Yes, we'll see you then. We're at 37 Oak Street. Is peanut butter and jelly all right for sandwiches? That's all Josh and Jack ever eat for lunch."

"Oh," Molly stumbled an apology. "Elijah's allergic to peanuts. I'll bring egg salad for him. Rebecca eats anything."

Jaime rang off, feeling a mixture of pleasure and foreboding. She hadn't said anything about Alden or asked how Molly was holding up. Should she have, or was it better to ignore the issue of Alden and his outrageous behavior?

She had a couple of hours before the twins came home.

She went into the den, fished Kathy Kelly's diary from its hiding place behind the old family Bible that had belonged to her grandfather Joshua, for whom Josh was named, and curled up in the slip-covered easy chair. She had read it cover to cover, but there were a couple of entries she wanted to check over for possible clues. Francesca was so convinced that she was Francie and Jaime had been Janie—but was that really possible? She still wasn't really sure.

May 30, 1951

The Senior Prom is two weeks from now. Forrest asked Sylvia to be his date, and she practically laughed in his face, as he knew she would. He pretended to cry and wipe his eyes all through Health class, and Sylvia got up and ran out of the room. Of course, she didn't get into trouble! He found out from me what dress she bought for the dance, and the three of us (me, Forrest, Rob) pooled our money (had to steal some of it, as my baby-sitting money wasn't nearly enough, and the best part of that is that I snatched it from Sylvia's purse!), and bought the same dress (a knock-off, natch) for Willow (not telling her, of course, that it was also what Sylvia would be wearing). She will go with Balls, and Forrest will tag along stag, as I can't be seen with him and keep my good standing with The Nine. But maybe I'll dance with him once or twice. I'll laugh it off as a joke. I just can't wait to see Sylvia's reaction when Willow walks in with Balls and Forrest, wearing the same dress! This is going to be good!

Jaime shook her head in disbelief. The girl was so intentionally mean. How was it that The Nine never caught onto her?

Snuck out to see Forrest and Balls after the Yearbook meeting last night. It's real good for my standing with The Nine that I'm yearbook editor, but who else would they get? We got Willow to come, too, and Balls managed to get her drunk, and we all fooled around a little. She was so ecstatic about the prom gown, and the fact she doesn't have to wear her Little Orphan Annie homemade number, that she let him go a little further than she intended to. But I think she enjoyed it! I think maybe she's finally realizing that she can't be Janie Carlson, or even be like her. She just has to be herself. But that's what I appreciate about Willow. She's not petite, she's not extra-cute, she's not artistic and outgoing, but like The Velveteen Rabbit she tries so hard to be real, something Janie Carlson will never be. And real is something I'll probably never be, either.

Feeling as if she'd been slapped in the face, Jaime sat back in the chair and let the diary fall into her lap. She was definitely identifying with Janie, and Kathy's critical words hurt as much as if she and Janie were one and the same. And—were they? Might Francesca's theories be true? Jaime—Janie, the names were almost the same, and Michelle was the middle name for both. Jaime was petite, and cute, so people always had said, and had "cat eyes", just like Janie. And they were both artistic. How much could this be just coincidence? And how about that house, the fact that she'd recognized it from Janie's very amateur watercolor, knew where her old bedroom was located, knew exactly where to find the necklace? There were a lot of questions that needed answers.

She must have dozed off, because before she knew it, her boys burst through the front door and let it slam behind them. She came to with a start, and just had time to replace the diary in its hiding place before they raced, stumbling over each other, into the den.

"Hey! Where's lunch?" Josh demanded.

She folded them into her arms, hugging them both hard, feeling great depths of sorrow for poor, dead Janie Carlson, who had never lived long enough to see her children grown.

Seventeen

Molly was clearly ill at ease. She wore gray sweatpants and a tee shirt featuring Champ, Lake Champlain's local version of Nessie, the Loch Ness monster. Over the shirt she wore a royal blue cardigan from which her arms protruded, thin as sticks. Her lackluster blonde hair was held by a brown barrette at the back of her neck.

"Don't use so much frosting, Becca!"

"Oh, she's fine." Jaime smiled at the seven-year-old girl. She favored her mother, being thin, almost scrawny, with hair that was neither straight nor curly and looked as if it needed to be washed.

Molly was about the right age, although at first she had seemed to be younger, and she and Alden had recently moved to Mill Pond. Could she possibly be one of the class of fifty-one, returned to the scene? But which one could this timid, overwhelmed woman be? She certainly didn't ring any bells from what Jaime had read of The Nine in Kathy's diary.

Jaime watched Rebecca, who was totally absorbed in making designs in colored frosting on the cookies they had baked. Grinning at her mother, she licked a glob of pink icing off one finger.

"I hope to have a girl someday," she confided, meeting Molly's eyes. "You're lucky to have one of each. Not that I don't adore both my boys, but I'd love to have a girl, too."

There was a wistful note in Molly's voice. "You certainly have the space for more kids." She looked around the big, country kitchen. "Our place is so small. Sometimes it feels like we live all on top of each other."

"How many bedrooms does it have?" *Two. I already know that.*

"There are just two small ones. Becca has to share a room with Elijah, which she doesn't seem to mind, but she'll have to have a room of her own in a couple of years. Alden thinks he can enclose the back porch and make a room out of it for her." Having mentioned her husband, Molly looked embarrassed and stared down at the table.

"Molly, how are you holding up?" Jaime hoped she sounded truly empathetic, and not oh, so condescending. *Condescending— like Janie Carlson.*

Molly flushed. She reached over and piled a dozen decorated cookies on a plate. "'Becca, honey, why don't you take these into the den and watch the movie with the boys?"

The girl nodded, took the plate of cookies and headed off toward the den, where sounds of a noisy movie and small boy shouts of enthusiasm could be heard.

Molly's eyes pleaded for understanding. "You know, Alden isn't really *bad* person. He's just very opinionated and fixed on his beliefs. He has a quick temper and doesn't always think before he says or does something."

Molly paused. Jaime nodded and put her hand on the bruise on Molly's wrist. "This?"

"That's what I mean." She drew her hand away and rubbed the bluish area herself. "He doesn't mean it. He loves me and the kids.

It's just that things have been so hard for so long..." Her voice trailed off. "I hoped that when we moved here and he got the job at the lumber company, things would get better. But of course, he'll probably get fired now, when they let him out of jail."

"What did they charge him with?" Jaime got up and brought the coffee pot over to the table, filled Molly's cup, and added just enough to her own to warm it up a bit. She helped herself to a cookie and took a bite.

"Just disturbing the peace." Molly bit her lip. "I guess there are a lot of gun owners around here, and they knew he was just being disruptive, and so were some other people. They gave him a month."

"There are a lot of people who don't want things changed. Evan's finding that out."

Jaime studied her as Molly took a cookie and nibbled at it. The woman was so thin, so drawn, and looked so tired. A week at a spa with healthy food would have her looking ten years younger, and with a new hairstyle and a little make up, she could be really pretty. *Pretty like Barbara. Where did that come from?*

Jaime took the plunge and asked the question that had gnawed at her from the beginning.

"Why did you marry him?"

Molly didn't seem surprised. She tossed Jaime a wry little smile. "Everyone wants to know that."

Jaime waited, hoping Molly would tell her. "Did you go to college?"

Molly shook her head. "I went to the maternity ward. I got pregnant, married Alden against *everyone's* advice, and this is how my life has turned out."

"It's not over." Jaime considered taking another cookie, and then withdrew her hand. "Lots of women go back to school and get a degree later. You could do that."

Molly acted as if she hadn't heard her. "I was so young, so rebellious, so tired of being the 'good girl'. I was on top of the world in high school, head cheerleader, voted prettiest girl in the class. I was spoiled rotten. I had everything, and I threw it all away."

"How did you get involved with Alden?" Jaime glanced at the clock. The movie the kids were watching would soon be over, and she wanted to hear the rest of Molly's story.

"Well, he was one of the wild boys—you know, there are always the guys on the fringe of everything,"

Jaime nodded. She *did* know, all too well. It seemed some things never changed.

Molly went on. "He was always making remarks at me, calling me 'Baby Blue' because of my eyes and the fact that blue was, and still is my favorite color, and I wear it a lot. He asked me out once too often. I was mad at my parents, feeling that I needed to prove my independence—so I accepted a date with him. I got drunk, first time I had ever gotten drunk, we had sex, I got pregnant. End of story."

"You were so young! You could have had an abortion, or given it up for adoption. You threw away your whole future!"

"As I said," Molly related quietly, "I was rebellious and supremely self-confident. I had no idea of what it took to be a wife and a mother. I was sure I could make it work, sure I could change my bad boy into my Prince Charming."

There seemed nothing else to say. Jaime had heard the same story all too often. The movie climaxed, and then the TV clocked off. The boys, followed more sedately by Rebecca, tumbled into the kitchen.

"Looks like it might rain." She followed Molly and the boys to the door.

Ignoring that, Molly turned to her. "Thank you so much, Jaime. It was very—helpful to get some things out in the open. It was wonderful for the kids to come over, too."

"Thank you for letting me make the cookies." Rebecca stared shyly at the floor.

Impulsively, Jaime put her arms around Molly and hugged her. She could feel her bones through her thin clothing. "I hope we can do this again.

Elijah stuck his forefinger into his mouth. "Two girls hugging. Yuk."

Molly smiled at Jaime, finally a real smile that seemed free of shyness or embarrassment. "I'd like that. I feel like a real person with you. I haven't felt like that for a long time."

As she closed the door after them, Jaime turned to her boys, who were helping themselves to more cookies from the pile on the kitchen table.

"Did you like having Elijah over?"

Josh slapped the edge of the table. "I hate this table. Tables shouldn't be *pink*!"

"I liked him." Jack talked through the whole cookie he had stuffed into his mouth. "He sure knows a lot of good cuss words."

Eighteen

June 14, 1951

The Senior Prom was perfect, perfect!

I went with Jim Walsh, who asked me at the last minute, and Sylvia hadn't come through with one of her fancy college boys anyway (except for herself), so I said 'yes'. Jimmy could make The Nine into The Ten if he wanted in, but he's too much of a jock to care about his social standing, and, like Donnie, he never sticks to one girl anyway.

Sylvia made a big splash in her expensive gown, and she did look like a queen with the perfect, slim body and her hair piled up on top of her head like a crown. I didn't describe the dress, did I? It was a gorgeous thing, off-white, I guess that's 'ecru' in the fashion world, and pure silk, overlaid with chiffon that almost invisible, it was so light and floaty. The back dipped down very low, which looked great on Sylvia, and not so great on Willow, who's built shorter and squatter than Syl, and the trim was hand-made lace and pearls in the same ecru shade.

Balls' timing was perfect! While everyone was standing around, drinking that god-awful red punch and gaping at

Sylvia, he and Willow made their entrance. I have to admit that Willow's 'knock-off' looked pretty good, for Willow, that is, but it was obviously not the designer model that Sylvia wore, and even more obvious that it was a copy of Sylvia's.

Well, Willow was the hit of the evening! Everyone except The Nine and their dates clustered around her, complimented her, and all the non-Nine guys danced with her at least once. Balls and Forrest snuck in liquor in their rented tuxes and got pretty looped, so they and Willow were 'asked to leave' before the shindig was over, but they had made their point, and I think Willow had the best time of her life, while Sylvia probably had her worst. Good! 'Bout time she got a taste of how it feels to be the outsider.

The Nine included Jim and me, Syl and her date—Brad Something, Paul and Barb, Francie and Donnie, Suki and Marc, who are not romantically involved but get along well together, and obnoxious Janie, who looked just too sweet in pink and white, and her date, a guy from Sandville she picked up somewhere, I don't even remember his name. She couldn't keep her eyes off Donnie, as usual, but he was all over Francie, obviously hoping the evening would end in a way he hoped it would.

The Nine stuck to one end of the room and sulked for the whole night, as Willow had ruined Sylvia's queenship, and didn't even attempt to mingle with the rest of the class. Forrest asked me to dance a couple of times, and I did, passing it off as a joke, until Jim complained, "I don't even feel like touching you after you've danced with that greaser!" Balls asked 'Baby Blue' a few times, and she didn't even answer him. He didn't stop until Paul got up and almost punched him, and if Mr. Anderson, the gym teacher, hadn't intervened, I guess Paul might have done it, too. Well, enough of that. It was a great night, and one I'm sure The Nine will long remember. By the way, the band was just super!

Jaime put the diary down and stared off into space, brooding. Wasn't 'Baby Blue' what Alden used to call Molly, before he got depressed and mean? There just seemed to be so many coincidences, she and Janie, Francie and Francesca, Molly and Barbara, Donnie and Dane. Where did Evan fit in, she wondered. She reached for the phone and dialed Francesca's number.

Francesca's cheerful voice responded.

Jaime plunged in. "If your reincarnation theory is correct, and I'm Janie, and you're Francie, and Molly is Barbara—how about the rest of The Nine? And Forrest and Balls? Where are they, and *who* are they?"

Francesca was quiet for a moment. "I think Dane was Donnie, since you felt so strongly that you already knew him."

"I agree, but I didn't want to be the one who said that." She laughed. "Guess I never got him out of my system."

"And I got him this life, just the same as the last time we were here," Francesca said. Jaime visualized her grin. "I beat you out again!

"I'm happy with Evan." Jaime's feathers were slightly ruffled, even though she knew Francesca was kidding. "Do you think he was in this mix, too?"

"You know what I think?" Francesca suggested. "I think I should bring over a bunch of yearbooks from Mill Pond, and we'll try to figure out who the rest of them might be."

"They might not be from here, Molly and Alden aren't."

"I'll be right over. Put on the coffee."

~ * ~

The pictures of the graduates and the clever captions under their pictures had no effect on Jaime, but she listened intently as Francesca pointed out people she thought they might follow up on.

None of what Francesca said rang any bells with Jaime. Finally, she pushed the pile of yearbooks aside. "I'm interested in the writer of the diary. Kathy Kelly was killed that night, too. Is there anyone from here who became a published author, that you know of?"

Francesca closed the yearbook and rubbed a hand across her eyes. "You know who would know that—?"

"Willow," they both said at once.

"Yeah, but try to get her to tell us anything. She and Jane-Michelle clam up—like clams—around me. I can't get a word out of her."

"Who else?" Francesca asked. "You being the new kid in town, who has made an unusual impression on you?"

Jaime gazed out the window, which afforded her a partial view of Jane-Michelle's green Victorian. "I'd like to talk more to Sandy Gleason, the boys' kindergarten teacher—and how about that really out-there guy who teaches fifth grade? Could he be Marc?"

"Well, his name is Matt, and everyone thinks he's gay, although there's no proof of that." Francesca smiled wryly. "He's probably afraid of losing his job if he 'came out', as they say, especially in this town."

"Do you think he'd be open to talking with us?"

"I'd say anyone who wears orange socks, or lime green jackets, or those atrocious print ties he wears as a trademark would have a fairly open mind."

They grinned at each other.

"Evan and I think it's time we began to entertain. Maybe a cocktail party, with a buffet dinner, so we can get around and talk to everyone."

"Great idea! Are you going to level with Evan? About what we're doing, and what we think?"

Jaime hesitated. She downed the rest of her coffee, which was now cold. "Not about going into the Snyder's house, but maybe about what we think might be happening. And about Kathy's diary if he's still not convinced."

"And you know what else?" Francesca leaned toward Jaime with a conspiratorial look on her face. "You could wear that necklace you found at Molly's. We'll just see if anyone reacts to that."

Jaime nodded and returned her smile. "I've thought of that. The trouble is, is that if anyone reacts to that necklace, it will be Dane."

Nineteen

"You look great!" Evan exclaimed, as Jaime twisted and turned before her dressing table mirror. "And the cocktail party was such a good idea, too—you are definitely an asset, Jaime. I think I'll keep you."

Jaime swept him a curtsy. "Thank you, m'lord! I wonder who will show up."

"I would think just about everyone, my lady." Evan fumbled with his bow tie, trying to get it to sit just right.

She laid her necklace down on the glass-topped table and went over to help him. "There! Perfect!."

Jaime relished the way his eyes swept over her.

"You haven't worn that dress in a long time."

He looked so handsome, just turning forty, a hint of gray that hardly showed in his sandy hair. He was more upbeat than he had been in weeks, since she had proposed the cocktail party, and then, with Francesca's help, sent out all the invitations that she had made herself—a quick Impressionist painting of their wonderful old Victorian house, run off on watercolor paper on her printer—and gone about organizing and preparing for it.

"I haven't had much occasion to wear it, since I've been up here in the hills." Jaime wrinkled her nose at him, so he would know she was kidding. She adjusted the wide cummerbund, looking at herself critically again. The halter dress was gray silk, plain except for the slubbed texture of the fabric, and the last third of the full skirt, which was embroidered with vines and flowers in the same silvery hue and accented with a few pearls and crystal stones here and there. It was an elegant dress with which she had fallen in love at first sight in an Atlanta boutique. And the cleaned-up silver *J* with its tiny sparkling stones was the perfect thing to wear with it.

Evan leaned down to give her a quick kiss on the bridge of her nose. "I'll meet you downstairs. I want to make sure the bartender is all set up and has everything he needs."

"I'm sure he does. I saw that liquor bill."

"By the way, the bartender is Ryan Barrett. He moonlights doing this, as a way to meet and connect with people for his business. And I'll bet the liquor bill wasn't as much as that dress cost." He gave her a wave and headed toward the stairs.

He stopped outside the bedroom door, poked his head back in around the corner and mouthed, 'I love you!' before he disappeared, and she heard his footsteps going down the staircase.

Jaime picked up the necklace and held it up to her throat. It was not only the ideal choice to wear with that dress, but as she and Francesca had discussed, she needed to wear it, just to see if it got a reaction from anyone. She had cleaned it with jewelry cleaner, and it shone with a quiet elegance. It didn't look new, but it didn't look fifty years old, either. She slid it around her neck and fastened the clasp. It sat there, the lyrical *J* resting in the creamy hollow of her throat, and it looked very much as if it belonged right there, and nowhere else.

She wondered if Molly would come. Alden was still in jail, and she might very well not have the confidence to face a crowd of people who had been there when he fired his gun at the board meeting. On the other hand, she had called after receiving the invitation, thanked Jaime warmly, and had asked what kind of dress was expected. Jaime had bitten back the words she wanted to say, offering Molly a cocktail dress to borrow, and had just said, "Something very dressy, if you have it. Otherwise, just come. We'd love to have you." Molly had rung off without committing herself further, and Jaime had not seen her since. Would she come, or not? The Bauer brothers and their wives had not acknowledged the invitations, thus indicating their continued opposition to Evan and his new policies. But, as far as she knew, the rest of the board would be there, and a lot of the school faculty from all three towns.

Jane-Michelle and Willow had not given her any definite answers. Jane-Michelle repeated that she wasn't much of a party person, and Willow, as usual, evaded the question entirely.

She gave herself a final look, ran the brush through her hair one more time, and went downstairs.

The bartender was a still-handsome man, perhaps fifteen years or so older than she and Evan. "Ryan Barrett." He grinned, showing perfect, very white teeth, and extended his hand to her. 'Thanks for hiring me for this gig. It's sort of my moon-lighting job, and after all day at the lumber company, it's a welcome change."

She raised her eyebrows. "Oh, you're one of the P & B Lumber company sons? I'm so glad to meet you."

"I already know your husband." He ran a cloth over the surface of the already immaculate marble portable bar they had set up at the far end of the living room. "The house looks beautiful." He looked around appraisingly. "I've never been inside before, but people the age that my parents would have been, and Jane-Michelle Taylor, of course, have told me what a great house it used to be, when the Porters lived here, and then how it went down during the years they rented it. Looks like you're bringing it back to its former glory."

"Thank you." Jaime bit her lip and stared at Ryan. *There it is.* He's one of the Barretts, son of Donnie and Francie, who were killed in the Mill Pond Massacre, one of those, who, like Jane-Michelle and Willow, had never left the town in search of greener pastures and who were all interwoven in each other's lives. He might be willing to tell her something about the massacres. She took a chance.

"The age your parents would have been? I'm sorry, Ryan. How did you lose your parents?"

"Oh, I think you know." He didn't look at her. "They were killed in that Columbine type of event we had here, years before Columbine. They were at their tenth class reunion when they were murdered by those two deranged maniacs." He picked up a highball glass, squinted at it, and wiped the inside with a paper towel.

"Yes, I've heard." Her voice came out a whisper.

"I suppose you're wondering how I can even live in the same town as Jane-Michelle and Willow, when it was Willow's brother who killed my parents."

She spread her hands in protest. "Ryan, I would never ask you that!"

"Well, others have." He answered without a trace of bitterness. "And the answer is, Jane-Michelle wasn't even born yet, and Willow couldn't help who her brother was, and she's not cut from the same bolt of cloth. He was burlap, and she's linen. It wasn't their fault, and this whole town decided that if we were going to live together in peace, we couldn't have tribal warfare, so to speak, the Hatfields and the McCoys."

"Hmmm." Jaime was impressed in spite of herself. "I guess that's why no one will talk about what happened then."

Ryan nodded, as he judiciously arranged bottles of red and white wine on the counter. "You have to realize that outsiders are suspect here. We don't want to talk about that with people who are just curious, or nosy, or looking for info to write a book about it. That's why we clam up."

"Tell me one more thing. How is Lily of Lily's antiques tied into this? Rob Brass was her nephew?

"Balls was one of three brothers. Lily was an aunt or great-aunt, not sure which, and she fancied herself quite a lady. When *that* happened, she was absolutely apoplectic about it. She moved to Connecticut and never had anything to do with anyone from here anymore."

"And what about Rob's brothers?"

"Moved out of town, never heard from again."

"I appreciate your telling me that, but I would like to hear the whole story from someone who knows it firsthand, like Willow. But Francesca and I can't get a thing out of her."

Ryan began setting out wine glasses. "Why do you want to know?"

She hesitated, and when he shifted his gaze to meet her eyes, she read something strange in them. "Because..." She hesitated. "Some people think it might happen again, and there are some of us who would like to prevent that."

He nodded, not even appearing to be surprised at her remark.

From across the room, Evan came toward them, a drink in hand,

Ryan laid a hand on her arm. "I know who you are, Jaime Reid. I have dreams, several a year, in which something horrible is about to happen, but it doesn't, because a group of people show up to stop it. A group of people and one particular woman."

Jaime stood frozen to the spot.

He went on. "I know you because I have seen you in those dreams. I know you came here for a reason."

She couldn't answer. Was there a change in his eyes, in his tone? Was there something emanating from him that she hadn't sensed at first?

Evan came to claim her. "Hey, our guests are starting to arrive. Come and meet the Waltons and the Pattersons."

Ryan handed her a long-stemmed glass of white wine and gave her a little bow as she went off with Evan. Her head whirled, and her thoughts tumbled like clothes going round and round on top of each of each other in the dryer.

She met the Waltons, and the Pattersons, and the Bartons and the Drakes and the Blakes, and so many more that the names and faces became a blur. All she heard as she smiled and greeted couples and singles was Ryan's voice saying over and over, *I know you, Jaime Reid, and I know you came here for a reason.*

Molly Snyder came in, sliding timidly into the room, and headed straight toward Jaime. Jaime hugged her. "I'm so glad you came! And don't you look pretty!"

Molly did look pretty. Her hair, obviously having been cut and highlighted, framed her thin face with springy curls, held in place with a blue velvet band. Her silky blue dress was almost the same azure hue and ended above her knees in a flirty skirt, showing off a pair of surprisingly beautiful legs.

"This is almost ten years old," Molly confessed. "Senior prom. The skirt used to be long, but I cut it off." She twirled around. "I think it looks, okay! Don't you?"

"I think it's beautiful." Jaime turned her over to Francesca, who put her arm around the younger woman and guided her toward the bar. Jaime watched as Francesca steered Molly through the crowd. Jaime didn't notice any antagonism as Molly met some of the other guests. Either people were very well mannered, or they weren't holding Alden's actions against Molly. And, she hadn't said a word about the necklace.

The crowd swelled and overflowed from the living room and dining room, into the kitchen—much to the distress of the caterers—into the den, and even out onto the heated back porch, where some of the guests went to grab a cigarette, even though the February night was chilly. She and Francesca had spoken several times during the party, exchanging brief observations, and repeating bits of conversation to each other, but Jaime had not had the chance to confide to her privately what Ryan had said.

"Did you get a chance to talk with Matt Thompson?"

"Only to compliment his outfit." Matt had worn a white sports jacket with a bright red shirt and a pink tie. "He's oblivious, I think."

"Sandy brushed me off again," Jaime confessed, "and left soon after I asked her about the class of fifty-one. I guess I shouldn't have brought it up."

It was well into the evening when she finally came face to face with Dane Summers.

"What a great party! And what a beautiful dress! You look marvelous, Jaime, and I want to thank you for throwing this shindig. I have been able to talk to so many parents and board members, as well as just people around town. I think Evan and I have both made a lot of valuable connections tonight."

"Well, that was the point of it all." Jaime noticed with a little flutter that his eyes had dropped to the necklace at her throat.

A subtle change flicked over his face, but what the change meant, she couldn't tell. He reached out and took the little silver *J* in his hand. His touch against her throat felt familiar to her, weirdly familiar, not like Evan's hand, but like someone known well to her, nevertheless.

"Where did you get this?"

She caught her breath. "Oh, it's something I've had for a long time." She tried for a casual tone. "An old boyfriend gave it to me."

"I don't know why it looks so familiar to me. Maybe I've just seen one similar when I was picking out jewelry for Francesca."

"Probably." Jaime nodded, afraid to breathe.

Dane seemed to relax a little. "When you wear it," he teased, "does it make you think of the old boyfriend?"

"I—I was just kidding about the old boyfriend." Jaime, caught in her own choice of words, was thrown off-guard. Before she could continue, Francesca was at her side, linking her arm through Jaime's.

"Isn't that pretty, Dane? Can you believe she found that on one of our antiquing mornings?

Jaime held her breath. Would Dane believe the fib? He dropped his hand and let the necklace rest against her throat again. His face relaxed as he shook his head in bewilderment. "I must have seen something like it somewhere. It's pretty, so simple, but sometimes the simplest things are the most meaningful. It actually is something I would have bought for a girlfriend."

Yes. It is *something you would give to a girlfriend, and a long time ago you did. When your name was Donnie, you gave it to me.*

Twenty

"I think she was Barbara," Francesca agreed, getting up herself to refill her coffee cup.

She sat again, and poured cream into her coffee. "Did you see how she changed from mousy little Molly to someone really sure of herself as the evening went on? I could tell she used to be popular and self-confident, and the men all thought she was adorable."

"And Dane was obviously Donnie, given his reaction to the necklace." She put her hand to her throat. "And you were Francie, and I was Janie. I'm finally convinced. The Nine are coming back together again. It's really sort of spooky." She reached across the table and rescued the cream pitcher from Francesca.

"But necessary." Francesca sipped her coffee. "Now we just have to find Sylvia, and most of all, we need to locate and recognize Kathy Kelly. Any bright ideas on how we proceed from here?"

"Ryan Barrett? I told you what he said to me at the party. And he *is* Donnie and Francie's son."

"How old do you think he is?"

"I would guess early fifties," Jaime said, and then doubled over with laughter. "Don't you know how old your own son is? He's older than *you* are!"

Francesca joined in her laughter. "It's too bizarre. I didn't really feel any connection with him, but maybe if we can sit down and talk with him, something will hit me."

~ * ~

Ryan Barrett sounded as if he had been waiting for Jaime's call. Without preamble, he suggested meeting at a restaurant, ten miles or so from the edge of town. "Not likely to run into many of the locals there." He paused. "I wouldn't want anyone overhearing the kind of conversation we're likely to have. How about lunch, one' o'clock or so?"

"Brookfield's on Foster Road." Francesca nodded. "I know just where that is, and Ryan's right. It's a very secluded spot."

"What about the kids?" Jaime asked. "I guess I could call Evan and—"

Francesca shook her head. "No need. Dane is home, and when Jack and Josh get here, we'll just whisk them over there, and tell Dane we've decided to treat ourselves to a good lunch."

"I'm thinking more and more that we should be leveling with our husbands." Jaime rested her chin on her hand. "Except—" She bit her lip and looked at Francesca. "They're likely to have us committed, it sounds so crazy."

She pictured the wheels going around in Francesca's head, as she thought about what Jaime had said. After a pause, she drained the last of her coffee and set the mug down on the table. "Let's see what Ryan adds to the mix. Then I'd like to try to find Kathy Kelly and Sylvia. If we had the whole gang together, or most of The Nine, we could all sit down and present them with Kathy's diary, and lay it all out for them."

"Just what are we trying to achieve? We have to be very clear on this before we try to persuade those two brilliant, accomplished husbands of ours of anything like what we're thinking."

"We'll figure it out." Francesca turned as they heard the boys' voices shouting and laughing, and the sound of their footsteps pounded up the slate path to the kitchen door.

~ * ~

Jaime and Francesca managed to locate Brookfield's without getting lost in the winding maze of woods in the softly falling fairy-tale snow. The restaurant itself was a building of indiscriminate style, painted pale yellow, with lots of randomly designed additions. The January wind sprayed snow around their feet as they made their way to the door of the restaurant.

Ryan got up from his seat at the bar and walked toward them as they came in the door. "We already have a table, although as you can see, there wasn't any real need to reserve one."

Jaime shivered from their brief walk in the snow and agreed with that. The three of them made their way to a table near the back of the room. There were only a half dozen other tables occupied, and as she made a quick check of the diners, she saw no one she recognized. It was not a large room, and it presented an intimate atmosphere, with yellow walls, a warmer shade than the outside was painted, lacy curtains, and paintings of idyllic landscapes on the walls. A small bouquet of flowers in assorted colors sat on each of the tables, which were covered with starched white tablecloths.

"I asked for a table overlooking the lake." Ryan pulled out their chairs for them and then sat himself. The waiter approached with menus, but Ryan held up a hand. "Let's have some wine first. Is white all right with you?" They nodded. Ryan ordered without consulting the menu. He tossed off the name of something French-sounding as if it were his daily drink. The waiter nodded and set off toward the bar.

Jaime and Francesca raised their eyebrows at each other. "That's—*expensive!*" Francesca blurted.

Ryan laughed. "Lunch, and the wine, is on me, ladies. I know why you're here. As I mentioned to Jaime at her party, I've had dreams and premonitions for years. I know Jaime is the key to this, to preventing another Columbine in Mill Pond, and I need to honor, and avenge, my parents by helping to avoid another slaughter."

In spite of his noble words, something wasn't ringing true. Was it the tone of his voice, just a little too assured, too smooth? Was it his manner—too rehearsed, as if he had been waiting to play out this scene with them? Out of the corner of her eye, Jaime saw Francesca staring at Ryan. Was she trying to feel something, find something familiar, perhaps, in this man who would be her son, if she had indeed been Francie Barrett?

Jaime leaned toward him over the table. "Why do you think I am the key, Ryan? And what do you mean, 'the key'? I'm hardly the heroine type."

"I told you—I have dreamed about you for years. I knew your face the moment I first saw you. And by key, I just meant that events couldn't be put into place until you got here. That's how you're the key."

"Why didn't you approach me earlier, then?"

"I didn't know where you were, mentally, or what kind of psychic experiences you might have had, or not had. I had to wait until you were ready, so at the party I just dropped a hint. I thought you would either take me up on it, or think I was nuts and ignore it."

"Pretty big chance to take," Francesca suggested.

The waiter brought the bottle of wine, and with great ceremony uncorked it. He poured a little into an exquisite cut crystal goblet and handed it to Ryan. Jaime watched in amusement as Ryan swished the wine in the glass, inhaled its aroma, and then took a small sip, letting it swirl in his mouth before swallowing. The ritual completed, he nodded at the waiter, who filled all their glasses half full and placed the bottle on the table.

"Are you ready to order?" The waiter remained polite to a fault.

Ryan waved his hand. "Give us twenty minutes. We're in no hurry."

When the waiter left, Francesca raised her glass. "Here's to us, and to the success of whatever it is we need to do."

They touched their glasses together, their faces solemn.

"You certainly have great taste in wine." Francesca took an appreciative sip.

"For a lumber guy, you mean?" Ryan grinned. "I went to a pretty fancy business school, spent the junior year in France, where I learned about some of the finer things in life."

"Okay..." Jaime plunged into the subject that concerned them all. "What is your take on this situation, Ryan? What do you know, or suspect?"

"What I know, or suspect is that your husband, Evan Reid, is not very popular in some circles of town, with the likes of the Bauer brothers or Alden Snyder, for instance. They are trying to organize the opposition to his modernist, liberal education reforms."

Jaime gasped and felt her face grow pale. "You're not saying *Evan* is their target? That they would actually use violence against him?"

Ryan quirked an eyebrow and nodded, looking at her with concern. "Yes, I think they would resort to that, as well as violence against those of us who support him. Evan is the trigger, Jaime."

"Alden works for you," Francesca said. "He gets out of jail in a few days. You are going to fire him, aren't you?"

Ryan met her eyes. "No, I'm not. I want him right there where I can keep an eye on him. As a matter of fact, so I can learn what's really going on, I have pretended to agree with him. So if you hear me quoted, and it's not favorable to Evan, that's what's going on."

Again, Jaime experienced a gut feeling, little stab of doubt. Could Ryan actually be trusted in what he said? Her head was spinning, and she knew it wasn't because of the wine. She put her elbows on the table and dropped her head into her hands. "Oh, my God!" was all she could manage. "Oh, my God!"

Ryan reached over, took one of her hands, and forced her to look at him.

"Listen." Jaime heard a new urgency in his voice. "For some reason I don't understand, I feel as though you two will be open to this." He took a deep breath and looked at each of them in turn. "Do you believe in reincarnation?"

Jaime shot a glance at Francesca, who gave a gasp of surprise. "Do you?"

"Absolutely. It's the only theory that makes any sense to me. You learn and experience as much as you can in your life, but one life is hardly enough to become all you could be. And... I think some cosmic method is necessary to avenge the injustices from one life and reward the good deeds. Thus, we come back, again and again, if need be."

"Isn't that all sort of against religious thought?" Jaime asked.

Ryan smiled. "Many religions around the world believe in reincarnation and live their lives in expectation of being punished or rewarded in the next life. And..." He lifted his wine glass in another toast to them. "Some sources suggest that reincarnation was actually part of the Christian religion, until Constantine threw it out at the Council of Nicea in three-hundred and something."

Francesca blew out a long breath of air, speechless. Jaime stared at Ryan. She had never heard that before. Could it be true?

He drained the rest of his wine and leaned over the table toward her "I have heard rumors for years that Kathy Kelly kept a diary, and it might be hidden somewhere in the Porter house." His voice came out low and hard. "Why don't you look for it, Jaime? I'm sure that would give us a lot of clues about how this situation might develop."

Twenty-one

The sumptuous lunch they had enjoyed had hardly registered with Jaime. She sat staring out the window, and with Francesca at the wheel, they headed back over the snowy roads toward Mill Pond and home.

"He wants to see Kathy Kelly's diary. You're not going to give it to him, are you?"

"No way. There's just something about him that makes me uneasy. I don't know if I totally trust him."

"He gave us some terrific pointers. For instance, he thinks Kate Knight, the reporter on the *Springfield Register* staff, might have been Kathy."

"Same initials." Jaime watched the falling snow out the car window. "As if that proves anything."

"Cute name for her column, 'Knightly News'." Francesca gave a little chuckle. "I like puns. Very clever."

"Just like Francie." Jaime tossed her a glance. "She loved puns, too."

"And Sylvia..." Francesca tapped the steering wheel. "He says the Mason and Crenshaw families both moved out of town after the massacre. But the company who bought their law firm from them is still there. Of course, coming in from the outside, they wouldn't know anything.

"Right. Now, just suppose that Kate Knight is Kathy Kelly. How many of the original Nine do we have here?" She counted off on her fingers. "Me, Janie. you and Dane, Francie and Donnie. Molly, Barbara. We're still missing Suki, Paul, Sylvia, and Marc. Any ideas about any of them?"

Francesca was quiet as she concentrated on her driving on the snowy road. Jaime gazed out the window at the blur of icy tree limbs whizzing by, thinking. All of a sudden two yellow diamond-shaped road signs, each with a leaping deer symbol, rose up in her mind.

"Francesca, maybe you should slow down. There might be deer out here in, and it's hard to see around the curves."

Francesca applied her brakes hard and cut her speed, just as two deer burst out of the woods and raced across the road in front of the car. Francesca skidded to a stop and pulled the car over to the side of the road. Shaken, the two women looked at each other.

Francesca shivered. "Nice to see your ESP is still working, If you hadn't said anything, I would have hit them."

"Oh, deer!" Jaime giggled in relief.

~ * ~

Evan had left a note that he had taken the boys to watch an ice hockey match in Westlake. She put together a chicken casserole for dinner, mixed up a salad, and put it all in the refrigerator to await her family's return. She dug Kathy's diary out from behind the family Bible. Then, even though she had read the entire diary several times, she curled up in the easy chair to see if she could find some passages that would give her some clues about Suki, Marc, Sylvia and Paul. Tired from the emotional toll of the lunch meeting, she drifted off, the diary open in her lap.

~ * ~

She felt like Cinderella! The white satin gown had a halter back, and the hem, embroidered with delicate pink flowers and pearls, swirled around her ankles. One of the senior girls whispered 'Good luck!' in her ear, and Janie realized with a shivery little thrill that she was in the running for Prom Queen. She looked up at her date, but he had no face, as if someone had scrubbed all the features away. Balls Brass loomed up behind him and tapped him on the shoulder. 'May I cut in?' Janie turned her back on him, and her date, who suddenly morphed into Dane Summers, punched him in the face, and Balls, laughing maniacally, floated up through the ceiling and disappeared. Barbara, enveloped in misty blue, drifted by in Paul's embrace, and they all laughed, as their eyes followed Balls.

In the next scene, she was herself. The girls paraded with their dates so that the band could choose a queen for the Junior Prom. She felt ridiculous in her jeans and tee shirt as she walked behind Francie, regal in green velvet, with her hair up and held with a jeweled comb. Jaime glanced behind her, looking for Sylvia, who would probably be voted Prom Queen, just because she was Sylvia. Instead, there was a young man, looking like a young Matt Thompson, dressed in a sequined-covered pink tux, escorted by— another Matt Thompson, who wore an identical outfit.

They didn't seem at all out of place. Jaime flashed what she hoped was a radiant smile at the band as the contestants glided past. There was no sign of Sylvia, but sitting with the band, taking notes on a yellow legal pad, was Kathy Kelly, wearing a cat mask and a ragged green gown splotched with dark red stains. Blood? Green, the color of envy. Who was Kathy jealous of? And there was Evan, standing on the platform with the band. He held an oversized trumpet in one hand and the Prom Queen crown in the other. He raised the trumpet to his lips, but before he could blow it, the sound of gunfire filled the air. Jaime turned slowly, feeling the horror fill her from the toes upward as she recognized the shooters. Alden Snyder and the Bauer brothers, and a mysterious figure all in black wearing a mask, were everywhere, multiplied like twins and triplets, their faces contorted in a variety of menacing expressions, shooting, shooting, shooting...

Jaime awoke with a gasp. What a horrible dream! But it had told her several things. Dreams were full of symbols. Green for Kathy's envy of the other girls, probably, whose coattails she clung to for her own popularity, such as it was. A young man escorted by Mr. Thompson, who was certainly very odd, and might be gay, having a lover somewhere. What else? She grasped for the fading images of the dream.

She laughed out loud. Oh, yes, Evan with his trumpet. How symbolic of the new message he was attempting to sell the three-town community. Then the shooting at the end—the Bauer brothers and Alden Snyder, and many more of the same persuasion.

She stood up, trying to shake off the remnants of the dream, as she replaced the diary behind the Bible, but the feelings of the horror she had experienced in the dream lingered.

~ * ~

Later, Evan listened with a thoughtful expression as she told him about the dream.

"I believe that dreams can tell us what's on our minds," he told her after a brief silence in which he seemed to be mulling over what she said, "and I can see why you're worried about another massacre here, but pinning that on Alden Snyder and the Bauer brothers—

well, I think that's stretching it a bit." He grinned. "I like that bit with me and the trumpet, though. That's just what I'm doing."

She took a deep breath. Now was as good a time as ever to tell him about the reincarnation theories she and Francesca had come up with. "Do you think reincarnation is possible?"

He shrugged. "You know my theories on that. I don't think about it much."

She had made a raspberry pie, Evan's favorite, and he cut another piece for himself before he answered.

"Whipped cream or ice cream with it?" she asked.

"No, it's great just the way it is. You must be the only modern wife on earth who still makes her own pie crust."

"Probably. But it's really not that hard." She stared at him, pondering. "You know the diary I told you I found, Evan?"

"Uh huh." He seemed more interested in the pie.

"I'd like you to take a more serious look at it. Francesca and I think it's sort of a message from the past, warning us about the future. About the present, actually."

She handed it to him, and he leafed through it with casual interest. "Where did you say you found this?"

"In the cellar, along with some used condoms and cigarette butts. Apparently Kathy Kelly and the guys broke into the house that way and went up into the attic through the back stairway in the kitchen, had a few fun-fests up there when the house wasn't occupied."

Evan rolled his eyes. "Kids! But I wouldn't doubt it. It agrees with the time period when the Porters had left but hadn't yet rented the house." He handed her the diary. "But it doesn't prove *anything,* Jaime. Just because there are similarities between you and this Janie and Francesca and Francie doesn't mean you are reincarnations of these people. My God! That's a depressing theory! We have to live through all that again?"

"We're here again to stop it from happening again." Jaime's voice fell to a whisper. "If we can."

Evan shot her a lopsided grin. "And who am I supposed to be in this life? Your beloved Donnie whom you could never quite get over?"

"Evan, be serious!" She hoped he wouldn't push for an answer on that question.

"I am serious. I'm so serious that I'm going into the den and spend several hours writing a proposal for an integrated arts program: art, music, dance, and theatre, all conveniently located in one place, to include field trips and an after-school program, beginning in kindergarten."

"That's wonderful." She meant it sincerely. "But you'll never get it off the ground, unless we stop the opposition. It's growing, you know, even now. already building, and you've only been on the job a few months."

He had gotten up to put his empty pie dish in the sink. He turned and gave her a level look. "How do you know that?"

She swallowed. "Okay, here goes! Not everyone thinks our theory is nuts, Evan. Francesca and I had lunch with Ryan Barrett today."

He threw up his hands. "Ah! The intrigue! Well, what did the son of the guy who started P & B's Lumber have to contribute to your theory?"

"Don't be snide. He's a college grad, spent a year in France, and is nobody's fool. His parents were killed in the massacre, remember?"

"Yeah?" Jaime felt his restlessness growing. He wanted to end this discussion, go into the den and work on his proposal. His mind had already left the conversation. He headed out of the kitchen toward the den.

"Evan. Ryan recognized me the night of our cocktail party. He said he'd had dreams about me, and he knew I would come. He wanted to see Kathy's diary..."

He turned back at the kitchen door. "Jaime, your reincarnated Donnie is going into the den to work on his awesome arts idea, and he really doesn't want to be interrupted. Okay?" He smiled, but his tone was all business.

"Can we please talk about this some more, some other time?" He was already gone, the door closed firmly behind him. In the den, the phone rang, and she heard him answer it.

"You weren't Donnie," she whispered after him. "Dane was."

Twenty-two

"Have a good day, sir, and try not to come back."

Alden Snyder sneered at the guard who had unlocked the cell door for him and walked with as much dignity as he could muster, considering his slight limp, down the hall and into the main office of the police station. The officer at the desk nodded to him.

"Hope not to see you back here, Mr. Snyder."

Alden grunted, deigning not to answer, and limped to the front door. Several of those stupid cops sat at desks sipping coffee from that poison-brewing machine they had here, and a couple more stood around comparing notes on something, as if they were real detectives.

A young cop who looked about twelve years old opened the front door for him, and Alden walked out of the Mill Pond Police Station a free man.

Outside, a chill wind had risen, and the snow blew through the February air. It was a typical winter day in New England, although it certainly wasn't as severe as northern Vermont, where sometimes it seemed summer never came to call at all.

He pulled the collar of his worn leather jacket up around his neck and buttoned it up. He looked around for Molly, who was supposed to pick him up in the truck. His temper had not been cooled by his month's stay in the cell, and his ire began to rise as he waited. Just as he decided to set out for home on foot, the rusty red truck, its brakes squealing like a wounded animal, pulled up beside him. He opened the door and climbed in.

He glared at her. "'Bout time."

"Sorry. The kids had a field trip, and I went along with them. The bus was a little late getting back. The roads are slippery."

"Always some lame excuse." He looked more closely at her and suddenly noticed that she looked different somehow. Her hair, her makeup, her whole demeanor. She looked more like the cute, classy high school girl he had married than the dowdy, tired housewife she had turned into.

"What have you been doin' while I've been sittin' in an eight-by-eight-foot cell drinkin' rot-gut coffee for thirty days? You look like you spent the entire time in a beauty parlor. You better not have blown any of my hard-earned dough on that!"

"Not to worry." He couldn't believe that she actually turned and smiled at him. "A couple of new friends gave me a make-over. I feel like a different woman."

"New friends?" He studied her, curious. She looked like the Molly Hart he had pursued on a dare some ten, twelve years ago. He'd lost track of time. She'd been so pretty, so classy, so desirable, he'd thought there'd be no chance at all that she'd go out with him. But she had, and gradually he'd torn her away from her family and their put-on values, and she'd seemed happy to have a chance to start over without all their unrealistic expectations. They'd eloped when she turned eighteen, the college plans forgotten, her freakin' family left behind, bewildered and heartbroken. They moved to northern Vermont, bought the trailer, and he got a good job in construction. But then the children had been born, and somehow there had never been enough money, or time, or energy to buy that plot of land and start their own house. After he'd lost the job at the construction site—damned stupid to show up drunk on the job!—he'd found the job at P & B, located the house they could afford a down payment on, and started over in Mill Pond.

"Drive to P & B. Have to see if I still have a job." He stared out the window at the ice-frosted trees as the truck rattled along the country road. "Probably not, though." he added. "What do you think the chances are, babe?"

"Slim, but I have a surprise for you, Al. I got a job. I start on Monday."

He was not just surprised; he was astounded. "No kiddin'? Where and how? How did a little mouse like you find the courage to apply anywhere?"

She threw him a glance that was not at all what he expected. Somehow she had regained all that confidence she used to have, before he got her under his influence and managed to stomp all over her self-esteem. He wasn't sure at all that he liked this new Molly—especially if it turned out he could no longer control her.

"I didn't have to apply for it," She turned the truck into the P & B parking lot. She drove to the door marked 'Office' and parked the truck. "The Reids gave a cocktail party and invited me. I met the woman who runs the little craft shop near the beauty salon, and she just asked me if I'd like to work part time. I said I'd love to. I start Monday." She looked him straight in the eyes, as if she thought he'd oppose her decision.

The Reids! Shock ran all through him as he thought of those fancy people who had always been too good for him, including his wife in their social circle. Or maybe... they just wanted to pick her brains, what brains she had left, to find out what *he*, Alden, was up to. That was mostly likely it, as they couldn't possibly have any interest in Molly, either as an employee or as a person.

"Huh," he grunted and opened the door to the truck, which gave with a loud creak. "Well, it's probably a good thing, as I wouldn't lay any bets on my still havin' a job here." He headed toward the office door.

~ * ~

Ryan Barrett looked up from his computer. "Hello, Alden. I heard you were getting released today. I'm glad you came in. Have a seat." He pointed to a chair.

"I can stand while you fire me. Just get it over with."

"I'm not going to fire you. Please sit down, Alden."

Alden turned the chair so the back was toward Ryan's desk, and straddled it like a horse. Ryan didn't even blink at this symbol of defiance.

"Alden, you're a good worker. I want to keep you on."

"Yeah? In spite of what I did at the school meetin'?"

"In spite of that. A lot of us are upset at what the new super wants to do, and many of us are gun owners who don't want their rights taken away. I'm not saying what you did was right, but I am saying I understand how you feel."

Alden crossed his arms on the back of the chair and punctuated his nod with a grunt. "Yeah. What was good enough for me is good enough for my kids. They need to learn reading' and writin', and not be drawin' pictures and listenin' to fancy music they're never goin' to hear again."

Ryan nodded as if he agreed. "Well, there are two sides to every question, Alden, and we have to all respect the other person's viewpoint. This is a rural community, Things won't change overnight."

143

"That's why I moved my family here. I don't want my kids in one of them city schools, mixed up with all them... ethnic types." He noted the change of expression that flashed across Ryan's face. "Well, 'twas mostly the *job*. That and the house."

Ryan nodded. "Okay. Well, why don't you get back to work? Joe and Frank need some help with the new load of lumber that just came in."

Alden stood up and nodded. He turned, left the office and let the door close behind him of its own accord. He knew it wouldn't close completely, and Ryan would have to get up and shut it.

"Prick!" he muttered, as he strode toward the truck where Molly waited, expecting that he had been fired. She had even left the engine running while waiting for him and was listening to some talk program on the radio.

He motioned to her to roll down the window.

"Still got my job, babe. They can't get along without me. Pick me up at six." Alden turned on his heel and walked away, refusing to react to her expression of amazement. After a moment, he heard the truck pull away and roll down the frozen dirt track toward the road.

Twenty-three

Kate Knight was taller and thinner than her photo in the paper had led Jaime to expect. She had a full, round face and a short, shaggy haircut, which was all the style in the fashion magazines but not seen around Mill Pond. Kate wore black pants and a pale green cashmere sweater set and a chunky gold necklace and earring set. She looked both professional and stylish, and in spite of her Atlanta background, Jaime felt a little like a hayseed, even though both she and Francesca had dressed up more than they usually did.

Kate looked around the living room. "How pretty. These old houses are always so charming." She managed somehow to sound disparaging at the same time as she handed out the compliment.

Just like Kathy Kelly. Same initials, and same snotty attitude. Like Springfield is any kind of a metropolis. Jaime managed a half-felt thank-you smile.

Francesca leaned forward and spoke directly to Kate. "What we have to tell you, and show you, is strictly off the record. That is, we hope you're interested in what we have to say, but we don't want you to write a story on this, for obvious reasons."

Kate put down her flowered teacup and put away the notepad and pen from her Coach purse. "Why am I here then?" She nodded toward Francesca. "Your husband is principal at Mill Pond School," She switched her gaze to Jaime. "And your husband is the controversial new superintendent of the three towns." The tone of her voice indicated that that neither did not much impress her. "Is this what you want to talk about? You want me to give him some free publicity for his new programs?"

Jaime felt herself flush. "Well, he's controversial for all the right reasons. People who try to make changes for the better always run into opposition from those who want things to stay the same way forever."

Kate smiled. "That's what makes news. Now what's the scoop? Have you found a future Thomas Kinkaid or James Taylor lurking undiscovered in the senior class?"

Francesca erupted. "Look! If you're going to be condescending—"

Kate cut her off. "Oh, sorry." She didn't sound sorry at all. "Of course I was intrigued by your phone call. It's just hard to think of anything really that exciting happening out here in the hills. Please fill me in."

"Oh, please," Francesca let her disgust show. "You're from here, too, Kate. Stop pretending you're not. You may not remember me, but I remember you. You were only a few years ahead of me.

That seemed to deflate Kate a bit. "Okay, you're right. I'm from here, too, but I pretend I'm not. Let's hear your story."

Jaime regarded the reporter for a long moment, wondering if they'd made a huge mistake in inviting Kate to meet with them. Then, silently, she picked up Kathy's diary, which she had placed beside her on the sofa and handed it to Kate. "This is a diary written by Kathy Kelly, one of the victims of the sixty-one massacre. I found it in the cellar shortly after we moved in. Some of the people and conditions described in it sound eerily like what's going on around here today."

Kate's face lighted with interest as she took the diary from Jaime and began to leaf through it.

"We don't want you to do a story. We hoped we could find out what you know about this. Obviously, I'm not going to part with the diary itself."

"Some of the people mentioned are still around," Francesca offered, as Kate skimmed through Kathy's entries. "Willow Brown runs the beauty shop in town, and her daughter, Jane-Michelle Taylor, lives in the green house next door."

Jaime nodded. "And Ryan Barrett and Jason Peller, sons of two of the other victims, own the P & B Lumber Company at the edge of town."

"Really?" Kate asked

She was losing her 'attitude'. Jaime watched as Kate leafed through the diary. She stopped at some pages to read them more thoroughly and actually back-tracked several times to read certain sections. Her tea sat cooling on the coffee table. Jaime and Francesca exchanged glances and hopeful smiles. Kate was acting as if she were on the scent of something, a great story, perhaps. When at last she laid the diary down, her expression was thoughtful.

"Janie and Jaime," she said, staring out the tall window into the yard. "Francie and Francesca. Kathy and Kate. The names are so similar."

"Uh huh!" Jaime and Francesca echoed together, leaning forward.

"Please don't think I'm crazy." Kate shifted her glance back to Jaime and Francesca. "But have you read any books on reincarnation, like those by Shirley MacLaine?"

"Everything she's written and a lot of others." Francesca jumped in before Jaime had a chance to say anything at all, so she simply nodded agreement.

"And do you think that people are sometimes brought together for a *reason*?"

Again, Jaime and Francesca nodded in agreement.

"Well." Kate sat back and regarded them with new interest, her haughtiness all gone.

"This is so eerie. A cousin of mine is very psychic and tends to have visions and get messages..." She threw up her hands. "Don't look at me that way. "I'm telling you what she says. I know it sounds crazy."

Jaime let out a long breath. "We really want to hear about it. What does your cousin say?"

"She's been worried about Mill Pond for a long time, maybe years. She thinks there may be another massacre, like the one that happened in sixty-one. She says she has dreams about it, and sometimes 'sees' it in her mind, even when she's awake."

Jaime and Francesca were quiet, staring at Kate.

"My cousin also thinks 'The Nine' who were murdered on that night, as well as the two guys who killed everyone, have reincarnated, and are here, now. She thinks there's going to be a repeat of the whole thing. Unless someone stops it."

"Hmmm." Jaime shivered. "Would you return to the scene of your own murder, if you thought it might happen all over again?"

"Would you return to try to stop it?" Francesca countered.

Kate tapped the diary. "Do you think it's at all possible to think that maybe we're Janie, Francie, and Kathy, all brought back together for a reason? Like maybe Balls and Forrest are back here, too, planning more violence?"

Jaime exhaled a long sigh of relief. "That's exactly what we think." She and Francesca filled Kate in on their conversation with Ryan. "And of course, you've heard what Alden Snyder did at the school board meeting."

Kate nodded. "Yes, I heard about that. Is he Balls or Forrest, do you think?"

"We don't know," Francesca said, "but we're pretty sure his wife, Molly, is Barbara, and Balls always had a thing for her, way back when."

Kate looked thoughtful again. "This is so fascinating. You know, I always wanted to be a writer. It was as if I had no other choice when I was growing up."

"Just like art for me," Jaime said. "My mother said when I wasn't even three years old I drew a shape like a rock and colored in one end of it. I said to her, 'This side is darker because the light is coming through the window over there.' She was so impressed by that she never tried to change my mind about going to art school. She said she knew it was just 'in me'. And it was."

Kate turned to Francesca. "And how about you?"

"Well, I dressed up in my mother's high heels and old prom dresses a lot. I guess I always wanted to be prom queen, and I was, you know!"

"Yes, twice!" Jaime quipped, and they all laughed.

"Well, I have to get back to the paper," Kate said, "but I will thoroughly read the copy of the diary you made for me, and see what I can come up with. I have a feeling that I know someone you two will be very interested in meeting."

Before Kate could rise, the phone rang. Jaime went to answer it, feeling more lighthearted and hopeful than she had in weeks. Maybe it was Molly, and they could bring her into the discussion.

It was Evan, sounding tense and out of breath.

"Jaime! I want you to go to the school and pick up the boys. We've had an incident here."

"What!" Her high mood vanished in an instant. Kate and Francesca looked up, startled at the tone of her voice.

"Dane and I were heading out for lunch, and when we got outside the school, there was a group of about a dozen people with homemade signs. They were really hostile, and there was some pushing and shoving, before the cops got there."

"Oh my God. Are you all right? You're not hurt, are you?"

"Got punched in the jaw, but I'm okay. Dane got roughed up a little more. Come and get the kids, will you? Is Francesca there with you?"

"She is! I will! We both will!" Jaime made frantic motions at Francesca and Kate. "Just tell me, was Alden Snyder part of it?"

"No," Evan said, "but the Bauer brothers were. I have to talk to the police now, Jaime. They want you to pick up the boys, just in case." He hung up.

Jaime raced around getting her coat and purse, while breathlessly relating what had happened at the school.

"Let's both go in my van," Francesca said. "It'll fit everybody." She pulled on her jacket and flew out the door, Jaime struggling into her coat right behind. Kate raced out behind them, digging her cell phone out of her purse. "I'm going over there, too. I'll call you later, Jaime."

Both women jumped into the SUV, which skidded on the snowy driveway, as Francesca started up too fast. They sped down the street toward the school, which was only a couple of blocks away around the corner. The boys walked to school through a little trail the neighborhood kids had made through a patch of trees between the two houses across the street. Jaime supposed it had always been that way, and nobody objected, or built a fence, or put up a *No Trespassing* sign.

It wasn't a sound, but more of a feeling that made Jaime suddenly turn around in her seat. As Dane's face had hung in the air against the white background of the refrigerator, another face hung in the air against the tan leather of the car's interior. She gasped as its malevolent gaze fixed on her as if trying to send her a message.

Alden Snyder. His dark eyes burned through her and sent a wave of hatred washing over her.

"Oh, my God!" she whispered. "It's going to happen again, and it's beginning now."

Twenty-four

The phone rang just as Jaime and the boys, shaking the snow off their coats and boots, piled back into the house.

The first call was from a reporter from the Worchester newspaper, who had already heard about the scuffle at Mill Pond School. Jaime told him she had no facts and couldn't comment. As soon as she hung up, it rang again, and a man's voice, husky and threatening, came over the line.

"That's a warning. Next time he won't get off so easy. Why don't you and your jerk-offin' husband go back where you came from!"

Jaime slammed down the receiver, then took if off the stand and laid it on the counter. Shaking, she leaned against the kitchen counter. 'Jerk-off'. That was the same phrase used in Kathy Kelly's diary, when she wrote about what Balls and Forrest called the popular kids, The 'jerk-off Nine'. Could anything that specific be just coincidence? Did the voice belong to Alden Snyder? The only time she had heard his voice had been when she sat beside Molly at the school board meeting, and she hadn't heard him say enough to be able to identify his voice.

Francesca called on her cell phone and asked if she could drop Kevin and Kyle off there, as Dane had been roughed up more than Evan had, and she wanted him checked out at the local doctor's office. Jaime, thanking God that the children were all okay and virtually unaware of what had happened, settled all four boys in the den with snacks and a video game before Evan came home.

She heard the car stop in the driveway, and ran to the door as Evan got out. He gave her a reassuring wave, but, dismayed, she saw the dark bruise already swelling at the side of his face.

The boys were hyper with excitement. Jaime shooed them into the den and put one of their favorite movies into the DVD player. She supplied them with juice boxes and cookies, although heaven knew they didn't need any more sugar right now.

She pulled Evan into the kitchen and made him sit at the table. She ran upstairs to the bathroom and retrieved medical supplies form the cabinet.

"It's not too bad." He flinched a bit as she applied a soothing ointment, and she could tell it hurt

"Damn them!" She couldn't hide the heat in her voice. "You're just trying to help them, trying to drag the school system into the twenty-first century. What's the matter with them?"

"I probably moved too fast. This town, and this is one of the things I truly love about it, is still fifty years behind the times. It's just emerging from being a farming community. The majority of the high school graduates still don't go on to college—the attitude hasn't changed much since what you read in Kathy Kelly's diary. Boys go to work on the farm or in the mills, which are starting to close up now, and girls get married and have children. If they want to work, it's at the grocery store or the craft shop."

Jaime laid the folded washcloth and astringent on the table and sat, facing Evan. "What in the world do you *love* about it? I'm beginning to think we never should have come here. I'm scared—for you, and the boys, and yes, for me, too."

Evan met her eyes, and his voice held all the honestly and conviction that she admired about him. "I can make a *difference* here. They need me here. Dane has been frustrated beyond belief at not being able to move forward. Now he has someone he can work with, someone who wants to go in the same direction he wants to go. We can bring an explosion of knowledge in here."

"Except, they don't want it. What was it you said you truly love about this place?"

"The—quaintness of it... the possibilities here."

"That sounds a little down-putting," Jaime pointed out. "Like we think we're better than they are because we're from a big city."

"Just the opposite," Evan protested. "I would have *loved* to have grown up here. Freedom to run around in relative safety, woods to explore, sand-lot baseball, walking to school, instead of riding an hour on a bus, your best friend living next door, or at least on the same street—there's a lot to be said for a town like this."

She saw he meant it. "An honest-to-goodness swimming hole in the river, with rocks to sun on, and a little waterfall people come from all over to take pictures of. Real tomatoes and squash and cucumbers from gardens of people you know. Sam at the gas station he actually owns, knowing I won't get ripped off when I bring the car in to be checked over. It's America the way it used to be."

Jaime smiled. "You make it sound like a Norman Rockwell painting."

Evan nodded. "I love the charm, the innocence, the neighborliness, but educationally, it's not fair not to give the kids coming up a fighting chance. If they want to stay home and run the farm, that's fine, but they should have a chance to go to college, become an engineer or a nurse or an astronaut, if they want to."

"Kids went to college from here," Jaime said. "Ryan's dad went to UConn, and so did Ryan himself. He chose to come back and run the lumber company. And the ones from the diary, Janie and Sylvia and Suki. They all went on to school after high school."

Evan took her hand and held it. "You're forgetting those were the elite. Their parents were the very small minority who had the resources, but the school system hardly did them justice. I remember the story you told me from the diary—when Janie had her interview with the guidance counselor. Janie should have had the art background she needed right here in Mill Pond, not just an after-school program."

"You're right." Jaime nodded, pushing back her hair with her free hand. "Things have changed. I never would have gotten into the art school I went to if I hadn't had a good high school background. I couldn't have gone anywhere."

"My point exactly. I want to give every kid in Mill Pond, Sandville, and Westlake that kind of opportunity. I want the special-needs kids to have their own classes where they can have the specially trained teachers they need."

Jaime looked off toward the den. "It's too quiet in there, I'd better go check on the boys." She stood up, bent down and kissed Evan behind the ear. "I understand why you want to make a difference here, and I adore you for it, but I'm worried about your safety, and for Josh and Jack. What if your opponents target *them* next?"

Evan winced as he put a hand to his swollen cheek. "I wouldn't say I have all that many opponents. Maybe a few malcontents. We'll bring them around. It'll just take a little more time than I expected."

Josh was asleep, huddled in one corner of the overstuffed leather sofa, and Kyle knelt at the coffee table and colored a drawing he had made with magic markers, which now littered the floor. Jack and Kevin watched Animal Planet, fascinated as several snowy polar bear cubs frolicked around the ice floes.

"Did you know the ice is melting up there?" Kevin looked up at her from Francesca's brown eyes. "The polar bears might go extinct."

Jaime couldn't help but smile at him. "Yes, I've heard about that.

His face, so much like his mother's, wore a serious, worried expression. "I want to help them when I grow up. I want to go to college and learn how to save the polar bears."

It hit Jaime like a rock. This is what Evan meant! Of course, Kevin Summers would have the opportunity to go to college and study environmental science, or whatever else he might choose to do, but what about Elijah Snyder? If the school system did not provide him with the background and the incentive to go on to college, what would his future hold?

She sank down onto the sofa to watch the TV with the boys. She remembered almost to the word what Kathy Kelly had written about Janie's interview with the guidance teacher. The words ran through her head like an old song she couldn't forget.

September 14, 1950

Sweet little Janie (gag! gag!) is all upset over her guidance interview with Miss Kensington yesterday. Apparently the old bag asked her what she wanted to do with her life, which is the line she uses on all of us, and Janie said, "I want to go to art school."

Janie said Miss K. shook her head ever so sadly and said, "Janie, nobody goes to art school from here." She advised her to go to secretarial school in Springfield, or if she had to go to college, to take home ec at UMass. She said, "All you're going to do is get married and have babies, anyway. Why waste your parents' money?"

Suki had the same kind of story. She wants to go to this hoity-toity fashion school, Traphagen, in New York City. Miss K. doesn't think she's got a prayer of getting in, and neither do I.

September 28, 1950

Janie brought in her 'portfolio', which consisted of a manila folder with a couple dozen colored pencil drawings in it. Oh, yeah, she had a watercolor or two and a pastel portrait of someone, I think, from that six months that we did have an art teacher, before the board, in their infinite wisdom, decided we didn't need any frills like that.

Well, I had to take a note from Mrs. Mullins to guidance, and when I got there, nobody was there, but Janie's art stuff was sitting on Miss K.'s desk. Miss K. never saw it, because I took it and made sure no one will ever see it again. Let's see Janie go to art school now!

Jaime leaned back into the leather cushions. Yeah, sure. Janie did go to a two-year art school. Maybe her talent showed up on her entry exam, or something. Maybe she was just lucky to be accepted. But the tri-town kids deserved a better foundation than Janie'd had—or didn't have, as the case may be. Evan wanted to make sure the students at Mill Pond and the other schools had a fair chance, along with everyone else.

Twenty-five

Jaime left Evan snoring in bed and gave the boys their cereal and juice. Full of weekend energy, they raced outside to give each other rides on their sleds in the snow.

Jaime loaded the dishwasher and turned it on, relishing the quiet of the morning. The telephone interrupted her.

"Hello?" She wiped her hands on a dishtowel.

Kate Knight's smooth voice came over the wire. "How is Evan? I'm so sorry about all that trouble yesterday."

Jaime reassured her that Evan had suffered only a minor bruise and that his enthusiasm for the job was not at all dampened. "I suppose our little ruckus made all the papers? I haven't turned the TV on yet."

"It got a few small mentions." Kate snorted. "It wasn't enough of anything to push aside what's going on in Springfield, or the state, or the country as a whole. Most people still don't even know where Mill Pond is. What's the population there now—about two thousand?"

"Hmmm, Just about."

"Well, it's just a few malcontents. I wouldn't worry too much about it. The police were on the scene in seconds."

Jaime barely had time to wonder why Kate was calling, before she changed the subject, her voice moving from smoothly professional to excited. "I read and re-read the copies you gave me of Kathy's diary. I think I know who Sylvia and Suki might be!."

Jaime drew in her breath as she caught the excitement in the reporter's voice.. "You do? Who are they?

"Suki is still Suzanne, same name, and writes as the fashion editor here at the paper. Isn't that convenient for us?"

"Maybe a little too convenient. Why do you think she's Suki?"

Kate laughed. "Well, if you go back to Kathy's diary, Suki was rather aloof, a little superior, and that's just the way Suzanne White is, too. Fortunately, if *I'm* Kathy, I don't have to hang onto her coattails in this life."

Jaime was not convinced. "Hmmm... I don't know about that, Kate."

"*And,* if you remember Suki's passion for fashion—this Suzanne is the same way. Clothes, clothes, clothes, ad infinitum. It gets old fast for the rest of us, but she's great at her job."

Jaime, holding the receiver in the crook of her neck as she talked. wiped off the kitchen table. She opened the cupboard door and put the box of Lucky Charms back on the shelf. "So, Kathy's diary really did resonate with you?"

"Did it ever! As I read more and more of it, I was beginning to *feel* like I was Kathy Kelly, writing the diary myself. My God, Jaime, it was an eerie feeling."

Jaime caught her breath. "Maybe you were. And what about Sylvia? I haven't seen or heard about anyone around here who fits that bill. If she came back, in this day and age she would be following a really ambitious path, don't you think?"

"Yes, I do," Kate agreed, "and I think she has. I think Sylvia is Skye Weston."

For a moment, Jaime didn't react, the name not meaning anything to her at first. Then it hit her. "Skye Weston? *Senator* Skye Weston? But she's not in our age group at all—she must be almost fifty!"

Kate laughed. "Don't let her hear you say that. She's forty-six. Obviously she wanted a head start, being the impatient, ambitious person she was. There's no reincarnation law that says we all have to wait for each other, is there?"

Jaime shrugged, then realized that Kate couldn't see her. "I wouldn't know." When Kate didn't say anything else and seemed to be waiting for Jaime to speak, she ventured, "But do you think she really would come to a meeting with us about this?"

Kate sounded amused. "You still don't get it, do you, Jaime? Well, I guess there's no way you could know, thought I would have thought someone from Mill Pond would have bragged about it."

"About what?" Jaime shifted the receiver to her other ear.

"Skye Weston graduated from Mill Pond High in 1985. She was a cheerleader, prom queen, on Student Council, class president all four years, and valedictorian."

"Wow. She came right back and did it all."

"Yes, she did. And now she's on the political fast track and being talked about as a shoo-in for the US House of Representative for the next election."

Jaime was impressed. "She could end up being president. One of us—imagine." Of course she had heard of Skye Weston and her meteoric rise in politics, but being new to Massachusetts and busy settling her family, and having little interest yet in Massachusetts politics, she had paid little attention when Skye Weston had been mentioned.

"She'll still never meet with us," Jaime insisted. "We're small fry, and this isn't a topic everyone is eager to discuss."

"She will. Leave it to me." Kate sounded mysterious. "What day would be good for you? Lunch at Chez Cherie, Smithtown road, twelve-thirty. I'll make reservations."

Jaime glanced at her calendar "I'll have to call Francesca, and Molly, but Tuesday might be good. Yes, Tuesday. I'm almost sure Molly has it off, and Francesca and I were going to go antiquing anyway."

"Do you know how to get to the restaurant?"

"Francesca will know. Thanks a mil for setting this up, Kate. Gosh, I can't believe we're going to have lunch with Skye Weston. You must be a miracle worker."

"Not so much." Kate laughed. "Skye Weston is my cousin, and she's the one who got *me* interested in reincarnation."

~ * ~

Molly had needed some persuasion, but in the end, she agreed to go with Jaime and Francesca to Chez Cherie. Jaime glanced at her in the rear view mirror as they chatted and Francesca drove. Molly had blossomed; she was no longer a shrinking violet but was emerging into a full-blown rose. A look of serenity replaced her pinched, haunted expression Her timid demeanor had vanished, and in its place Molly's self-confidence was growing by the day. She was doing well at her job and expected to be promoted to assistant manager sometime soon.

She looks so pretty! Jaime felt a little flow of self-satisfaction, basking in how good it felt to know she'd had a lot to do with

Molly's new life. True, she was still married to a sour, angry man, but she was coping with him much better, asserting herself and refusing to be cowed by his controlling tactics.

"Blue is a great color for you," Jaime called back to Molly. She smiled to herself as she remembered that according to Kathy Kelly, Barbara had worn a lot of blue, too.

"It's my favorite color," Molly replied. "Always has been, all shades of it."

Francesca slowed the car as Chez Cherie came into view. Although positioned on a main highway between Mill Pond and Springfield, it looked like an English tea-house, a long, one-story building with a faded gray façade, managing to look old and elegant at the same time. Francesca pulled into the parking lot.

"There's Kate's car." Jaime pointed at the dark gray BMW parked in one of the end spaces. Francesca parked next to it.

The inside of Chez Cherie was as charming as the outside, but not particularly French, Jaime thought as she looked around. It consisted of a series of very small rooms, with only three or four tables per room. Antique-looking lace curtains framed the windows, and an assortment of old-fashioned objects such as picture hats, long gloves, and button-up shoes sat on shelves or were displayed on the walls themselves. She didn't have much time for examining the décor, however, as she spotted Kate gesturing to them from another room. Francesca sprinted toward them, and Jaime and Molly followed, weaving their way around the other diners' tables. Jaime noticed there were no other customers in the other room, and as soon as they went in, the waitress pulled a red braided cord across the door and hung a *'Private Party; do not enter'* sign on it.

Kate, sporting a big grin, waved them to the table. "Meet my esteemed cousin, Skye Weston."

They shook hands all around. Skye looked surprisingly normal, although she was tall, with a rather regal air about her. She wore her ash blonde hair pulled away from her long face into a braided coil at the back of her neck. Her complexion was flawless, and her dark blue eyes sparkled with intelligence.

The waitress came in from the kitchen via the back room, in order to keep from disturbing the rope and the sign. She took their orders for drinks and left the menus for them to peruse at their leisure.

Francesca leaned over the table toward Skye. "So you're a believer in reincarnation?"

Jaime smiled to herself. *Leave it to Francesca to jump right in.*

"I am." Skye's eyes twinkled. "But I don't tell my constituents that. I'd lose a lot of them for sure and be labeled one of the 'left wing loonies'."

"When did you start to believe in this theory?" Molly asked, her shyness returning a little in the senator's presence. "I'm not completely convinced yet, but these gals do make a good case for it."

Skye sat back as the waitress came with the drinks and set them down in front of the women. Trying not to stare, Jaime did notice that there was a faint resemblance between Kate and Skye; their faces were the same shape, with high cheekbones, and they both had sharp, elegant noses and slightly jutting chins.

When the waitress had gone, Skye lifted her wine glass in a toast, and they all followed suit. "Here's to us... together again."

"You really believe that?" Jaime took a sip of her Chardonnay. It was exceptionally good—icy cold and tart, clear as crystal.

"I was *born* knowing it," Skye answered simply. "The older I got, the more certain I was that we would all meet again eventually, and here we are. We were waiting for you to come along and get the pot boiling."

Kate grimaced. "Except Suzanne. She told me she had 'deadlines' and couldn't come. I did ask her. Not sure she buys into this, anyway."

"I can convince her." Skye smiled. "I know things about her that no one else knows, and I've never even met her."

Jaime observed that everyone regarded her with interest and something like awe.

"Look." Skye lowered her voice. "I've known since I was two or three years old that my name was once Sylvia. I used to tell my mother things about "when I was here before", and the older I got, the more I remembered. I *was* Sylvia Mason Crenshaw. I *was* a lawyer, married to John Crenshaw, and I did have a baby the summer between my junior and senior years, just as Kathy Kelly suspected. And—" She broke off, looking around at the other women, who sat like statues listening with entranced expressions. "Please don't think I'm nuts. I think I've proved by my academic credentials and my career that I'm completely sane, and of a clear and practical bent of mind."

Kate grinned and looked at her cousin with admiration. "I had a very weird experience once that can't really be explained except by meeting someone from a previous life."

"What?" Jaime and Francesca chimed together.

Skye nodded. "Yes, that's a powerful story. Tell them about that."

"Well," Kate began, "I was vacationing with Audrey, an old friend from college who has a place at the Cape—great house, by the way, cedar with a wraparound porch, on stilts—and she wanted me to meet some writer friends of hers. She was working on something she hoped to publish at that time, and these friends were part of group she met with. Well, two of them came, Diane and Dawn, and Diane's husband, Bill, was supposed to join us a little later."

"And you had never met these people before, right?" Skye prompted.

"Never!" Kate continued her narrative. "Well, we're all chatting and comparing notes on writing, drinking tea, and having a good time, when Diane looked around toward the driveway and said, "Oh, Bill's here.""

"And—" said Francesca, "—what? You felt an instant attraction to him? I've heard that story before, I think.

Jaime laughed. "Oh, shut up."

"No, just the opposite." Kate ignored their banter. "I heard him coming up the steps, and when he opened the sliders I looked around—and every bone in my body turned to ice, and a voice in my head screamed, 'Oh! God—*no!*' It was *visceral—I was filled* with absolute terror from head to toe, and I could hardly move."

Jaime, trying to gauge their reactions, glanced at Molly and Francesca. Both sat motionless, hanging on Skye's every word. "What happened then? Did he feel it too?"

"I tried to act and sound as normal as possible when Audrey introduced us, "but I could hardly look at him. I was so uncomfortable, and I'm sure I was pale as a ghost. After a while he started saying things that forced me to relate to him, such as 'Everyone who's really important is already here, like Kate.' Eventually my insides stopped churning, and I could talk with him. And I still have no idea what *that* was all about."

"Is that it?" Jaime asked. "Didn't you mention it to him?"

"No, I felt like an idiot. What was I going to say—why am I terrified of you? He was a mild-mannered college professor, nothing scary about him."

"So that was it?"

"Not quite. When they all left, I stood in the doorway and watched them pick their way down the cedar stairway. He was the last in line, and on the third step down, he turned around a looked at me, a look of complete of mystification on his face. I shrugged one shoulder and smiled a little, as if to say, 'I don't know,' and that was it. But it was very, very strange."

"Very strange indeed," Skye agreed, "but it had to be someone from a past life, with whom you had a terrible experience. It's the only thing that explains it."

Kate nodded "I think everyone has had at least one weird experience in his or her life, if one is just open-minded enough to remember it and think about what it might mean."

Everyone joined in a chorus of "Oh yeah!" and "Sure" and "Of course."

Skye went on. "I not only remember my past life—which included all of you—but I'm also psychic. I've always known we would come together again, because there is something we have to do."

Little cat claws climbed up Jaime's spine, and she felt as though she had frozen into a chunk of ice. How could it be that she knew, *she knew!* exactly what Skye Weston would say next?

"Because if we don't do something very soon..." Skye stared down into the dregs of her glass. "Columbine is going to happen in Mill Pond again."

Twenty-six

"For God's sake, Molly! You didn't work today. Didn't you have time to cook a decent meal for your husband?"

Molly ignored Alden's complaints about the hurried macaroni and cheese dinner she'd thrown together after returning from Chez Cherie. She was far too upset about what Skye Weston had said about the certainty of a Columbine-style disaster happening in Mill Pond again to care what he thought about dinner.

"The kids like it." Elijah and Rebecca shoveled the creamy yellow mixture into their mouths with great gusto.

"What *did* you do today?" Alden demanded. He shoved his plate aside, the mac and cheese untouched. He lifted his can of Bud, the third or fourth since he had come home, and drained it. He tossed the can into the trash and glared at her. "Well?"

She put down her fork and looked at him. "I had lunch with friends, Jaime and Francesca, and some others."

"Others?" He screwed up his mouth at the corner. "Who else? You know I don't like you palling around with those fancy people. We're not like them, Molly—rich bastards, noses in the air, looking down on the likes of us."

"I don't find them that way." She tried for a calm tone. "They accept me, seem to like me, and are helping me find myself again."

His face turned bright red. *"Find yourself again?* What the hell do you mean by that? We're not enough for you?"

She weighed her answer before she spoke. "I didn't say that, Alden, but I want to be able to do something—I want to find the self-confidence and hope for the future that I once had."

"Before you married the loser known as me," he sneered.

"I didn't say that either," she repeated. *But that's what I meant, yes!* She was afraid to meet his eyes now. His anger swept over her like a swarm of angry bees. The almost-physical force of it nearly knocked her off her feet.

She flinched as the sudden motion of his arm sent his plate across the room. It crashed into a cabinet and sent golden smears of macaroni across the linoleum floor and splattering against the wall. He stood up and glared down at her, his eyes narrowed, his mouth tight.

"Make me a decent sandwich and bring it into the den, your highness, when you get around to it, which had better be pronto." He yanked the refrigerator open and snapped the tab on another can of beer. "And I'll have chips, pretzels, and a couple of pickles if you ain't been too lazy to buy them." He stomped off as she watched him in astonishment. The kids cowered in their seats, and Rebecca began to cry. He was crude, rude, and always angry, but he had never shown this propensity for violence with her, never.

Except when he pulled a gun at the town meeting and fired several shots into the ceiling. She stared after him as he showed her his back. It hit her with sudden force; she didn't love him, and if she ever had, which she doubted, she certainly didn't any more.

She put her arms around Rebecca. "Don't cry, honey. He isn't going to hurt you."

Elijah muttered something into his plate.

"What was that, Elijah?"

"I don't like Daddy anymore. He's always mad."

"I know it seems that way. He does love us all, though." She ruffled his hair. "Specially you and Becca."

She found leftover ham and turkey, and she added several slices of American cheese, which was the only kind he would eat. Swiss, provolone—they were for the "Frenchies", the people who thought just being plain American wasn't good enough. White bread, of course, nothing healthily whole-grain, which she was trying with some success to introduce to the kids.

Molly put the sandwich on a paper plate, then thought better of it and got another china plate out of the cupboard. It wasn't good china; actually it was plain white stock she had bought at the Dollar Store, where she bought everything she could—soap, shampoo, toothpaste, trash bags, lunch bags for the kids, and much more. But she wasn't buying her makeup there anymore. Since she had a job and was earning some money of her own, she was spending a little more on herself and enjoying watching her forgotten prettiness slowly return. She'd even stopped hacking off her own hair and had gone twice to Willow's beauty shop in town, once for a cut and once for highlights.

I could have a life again, a better life, if I took the kids and got out. Leave him here with his never-ending anger for company. But where could I go?

She put the plate on a tray and added two large piles of chips and pretzels. There were two lonely dill pickles in the jar in the fridge, and she placed them on either side of the sandwich. She added half a dozen Oreo cookies to the repast and took the tray into their tiny den, hardly bigger than a closet, that had been outfitted with one of the new, flat-screen TVs, flanked by two brown and orange plaid armchairs that Alden had picked out. Molly hated them, but he had said this was *his* den, his place to relax. After all, women just watched soaps and Oprah anyway, so she could watch TV all day when he was working at the damned, stupid lumber company run by those Frog-loving libs, Ryan Barrett and Jason Peller.

Alden had his feet up on the small walnut coffee table Molly had so painstakingly refinished, but he took them off with a great show of reluctance, as she set the tray down in front of him. She turned to leave, but stopped just outside the door as Elijah rushed past her and went into the den.

Alden yelled out a string of cuss words. "Don't stand in front of the TV!"

Molly turned in time to see the crestfallen look on her son's face. Gamely, however, he stood his ground. "Dad, the red wolf is now extinct. There are no more left alive. Did you know that?"

Alden grinned and held up his sandwich. "This was the last red wolf. I'm eating it, and it's delicious." He took a huge bite and smacked his lips.

"Daddy!" Elijah began to cry.

"How can you be so cruel?" Molly demanded, her anger surfacing at last. She knelt down and put her arms around her son. "That's sandwich meat, honey, not wolf. Daddy's teasing you. He thinks he's being funny."

"Don't you care?" the boy asked, his thin face wearing an anxious look.

"Nope." Alden took another bite of the sandwich and chewed nosily, staring at the TV and ignoring the boy.

"Well," Elijah continued, stammering a little, "K—Kevin Summers wants to save the b—bears, and I want to save animals, too. I want to go to some college where they teach me how to help the animals. Do you know of any colleges like that?"

Now Alden was interested. Molly watched from the doorway as his expression flashed from indifference to rage.

He exploded, his anger sending Elijah reeling backwards. "So! Working at the lumber company ain't good enough for you, huh? Elijah Snyder's gotta be better than his old man, is that what you're saying?"

"I—I don't want to do that. I—I want to do s—something good for the world. The TV shows say the w—world is in trouble. Miss Gleason says so, too. An' she says you have to take special courses in j—junior high and high school, and I want to be ready."

Alden gave his son an incredulous look. "And where do you think the money for a fancy education is going to come from? You can just forget about college. You'll work in the lumber company with me, or at the paper mill—"

Elijah twisted away from Molly, who tried to sweep him up in a hug as he brushed past her. "No! I don't want to do that!" Elijah ran from the room. She heard him sobbing as he clattered up the stairs.

Alden glared at her. "What are you looking at? Why don't you go do the dishes and mind your own business? Be a wife, if you haven't forgotten how."

She tried for a conciliatory tone. "We could send him to college, Alden. "You're making decent money now, and I'm working part time. Even if he just goes to one of the state schools—"

"He don't need to go." He didn't look at her, his attention back on the TV screen.

"Don't you believe in education, Alden? We didn't get a chance to go, to do what we might have done with our lives, but the kids *can* go. That's what the Reids and the Summerses are trying too hard to get across to this community." The minute the words were out of her mouth, she knew it had been the wrong thing to say.

He turned his eyes on her then, looking her up and down. "That's what's *wrong* with this town, the Reids and the Summerses, and their 'progressive' ideas. Elijah can work, take mech-tech courses at the high school, and work at Sam's Repair—or at the paper factory—and maybe make foreman someday if he works his lazy ass off." He turned away and picked up his sandwich again. "And Rebecca can meet some guy and get knocked up, just like her mother did."

At her gasp, he chuckled. "You know, Molly, they had a really bad sort of thing happen here fifty years ago, and if they don't watch out, it could happen again." He paused and grinned at her as she stared at him, aghast. "Yep. It just might happen here again."

~ * ~

Jaime sat at the pink kitchen table with her steaming mug of hazelnut coffee. Evan had left for work, and the kids had scooted off for school by way of the well-worn neighborhood trail. She flipped through the phone directory, looking for Ryan Barrett's number at the lumber company.

She found it, but before she could punch the numbers in, the phone rang. Looking at the screen, she saw with both pleasure and concern that it was Molly.

Jaime listened with growing concern as Molly told her of the events of the previous evening: Alden's rage at dinner, his response to his son's desire to go to college and save the animals, and his final words before Molly fled back to the kitchen to pick up the pieces of broken plate and wipe off the macaroni and cheese from the floor and wall.

"I just can't stay here with him. I need to get the kids away from his influence, before they start believing what he says."

Jaime clenched her fist so hard her nails bit into the flesh of her hand. "I agree with you completely. Let's keep our eyes out for an apartment for you. Can you afford to move out soon?"

Molly hesitated. "Well, I've been putting aside some of what I earn, but I don't think I can afford first and last month's rent, plus security deposit, like most of them ask for. I looked in the newspaper this morning. And there's not too much available here anyway."

Jaime didn't hesitate. "I'll lend you whatever you need to get started. We have to get you out of there."

"Oh—thank you so much!" Molly sounded close to tears. "Once I had too much pride to accept help like this, but not anymore."

"I bet you could get a handsome price for your quilts. They're gorgeous." Jaime spoke without thinking.

A sudden silence made her realize what she had said. She bit her lip. *Uh oh.*

"How do you know about my quilts?"

"We-uh, we were talking about our hobbies, or whatever one day, and I said I paint and would like to find a place to sell my paintings, and you said that you quilt—"

"I don't think I told you that." Molly's voice was soft. "And how would you have seen them?"

"Well," Jaime blundered on, "maybe I got you mixed up with someone else. Anyway would you ask Grace if I can bring in a couple of paintings for her to see?"

"Yes, I'll do that. She does take small paintings sometimes."

"And," Jaime continued, her voice turning hard, "if he *ever, ever* hits you or abuses the kids, I want you to come here, pronto. We'll figure something out from here."

After she hung up with Molly, Jaime sat and thought about the assignment she had been handed. She punched in Ryan's number and tapped her fingers on the tabletop until he picked up on the fourth ring.

"Ryan Barrett, P & B Lumber." His tone was cool and professional.

"Hi, Ryan. It's Jaime Reid."

"Hi, Jaime." His voice warmed. "I wondered when I'd be hearing from you."

She had to smile, in spite of herself. "Well, Ryan, how did I know you would say that?"

He laughed. "I always know, don't I? Are we going to set up a meeting?"

She couldn't contain her curiosity. "How can you possibly know that?"

He hesitated for a few breaths. "I guess you already know I'm weird, so no use pretending I'm not. I was sending out new orders on the computer yesterday before going to lunch—just before one p.m. I'd guess, and then all the words and numbers on the screen vanished, and I saw you at lunch with some other women. Was that accurate?"

Startled, she hesitated a few seconds. "Yes—I was at lunch with Molly, Francesca, Kate Knight—and Skye Weston, can you believe that?"

"I can." Jaime heard the amusement in his voice. "Because I saw it. Chez Cherie's, right?"

Doubt suddenly grabbed her, working her stomach into a tight knot. "Ryan—you didn't just happen to be there, too, did you? You didn't see us in person, did you?" *He must have been, or had a spy there. He must have been spying on us.*

Ryan laughed. "No way! I told you I have psychic experiences. I can't explain it, but it sure comes in handy sometimes."

"I'll bet." Jaime relaxed a bit, although her misgivings regarding him prickled at her. After all, Ryan was a successful businessman, well-respected in town. He had no reason to be messing with her mind, did he?"

Ryan took the wind out of her sails again. "I bet this is about Alden Snyder, isn't it?"

She backed off a little. "Why would you think that, Ryan?"

"Oh, he's been stomping about and muttering things when he thinks no one will hear him, about your husband and Dr. Summers, about how his kid is getting grand ideas, about how Molly thinks she's too good for him now—"

"Oh Golly!" Jaime clapped her hand over her mouth. "Molly called me, all upset this morning, and that's exactly what she said."

"We'd better get going on this, then. You call everyone together, including your hubby and Dr. Summers, who, even if they don't buy the reincarnation thing, they will still be mightily concerned about Alden's behavior."

"I will." She rang off, feeling hopeful that when the group met all together to discuss the situation, something could actually be done to avoid another mass murder in Mill Pond.

Ryan Barrett replaced the receiver and grinned at Alden Snyder, sprawled on the black leather sofa lining one wall of Ryan's small, tidy office.

"It's all coming together just like we planned. I've got that Reid bitch right in the palm of my hand."

Twenty-seven

Jaime admired how regal and elegant Skye looked, in a simple, short black dress, a red blazer, high-heeled boots, and a chunky, Aztec-looking necklace. Her shoulder-length streaked-blonde hair, so much like Kate's, hung straight and shiny, adding to her infinitely polished look. However, as the women all greeted each other and made themselves comfortable in Francesca's cozy but terminally beige den, her first words raised the hair on Jaime's arms and sent shivers creeping along her spine.

"You can't trust Ryan Barrett, Jaime. Kate told me you called her about setting up a meeting with him for all of us. That's why I called this sort-of emergency meeting of just the three of us, so we can figure out our strategy against him."

"*Against him!* But he's the one who introduced himself to me at our cocktail party, told me he was psychic and we needed to work against a massacre again."

"He also told you he knew you were coming to town, and that he had been waiting for you, right?"

"Yes." Skye's question took her by surprise.

Skye smiled at her. "I told you that I'm psychic, too, and I also knew you were coming. I knew we'd all come together again, and although I don't know Ryan Barrett personally, I know enough about him to know he's not on our side."

Francesca flashed Skye a curious look. "What do you know?"

"I'm just a bit older than the rest of you—couldn't wait to get back, I guess, and I've heard a lot about Ryan over the years. He was a wild kid, and everyone thinks he's settled down into a respectable businessman, but I think he may have some very bad genes. He's probably Forrest Brown's kid, not Paul and Francie's, and that makes him related to Willow and Jane-Michelle."

"Ah, the joys of living in a small town." Without asking, Francesca refilled all the teacups, and the scent of herbs and lemon filled the room. "Yeah, I've heard that about Ryan all my life. From the yearbook, though, I think he resembles Francie, so there's no telling that way. It might just be small-town gossip."

"I have a bigger bombshell to drop on you." Skye sat back and regarded with other women. "I think Alden Snyder is Rob Brass. Remember how, according to Kathy's diary, those guys were always plaguing the pretty, popular girls, because they couldn't get one of them? Well, Rob finally got Barb."

"Oh, Heavens!" Jaime gasped. "All the more reason she's got to get away from him."

Francesca made a face. "So, essentially, I'm Ryan Barrett's mother. I sure don't like that idea."

Skye smiled. "It doesn't work that way, Francesca. You *were* Francie, but you're not now. You have the same soul, and you may have some or many of the same qualities that she did, but you're your own person. You're *you*."

Jaime leaned forward, staring at Skye. "I guess I just don't get how that can be. How could I have been Jane, but now I'm Jaime, and we're both *me?*"

Francesca nodded in agreement as she took a sip of her tea.

"I explain it like this." Skye's long index finger traced a line on the surface of the coffee table, then reversed it. "You can drive to Boston in a Volkswagen and drive back in a BMW. Are you still the same person?"

"Oh! I get it." Francesca nodded. "It's just the outer shell, but inside we're the same person, just living a different life."

"That's a genius way to put it." Jaime grooved into Skye's explanation. "So we come back, building on the experiences of a previous life—"

"*Lives.* We've all been here many times."

"Sometimes with a purpose, sometimes not?" Jaime beckoned to Francesca to fill her cup again, which she did, spilling a little of it on the coffee table in her excitement. Jaime swiped at the spot with her napkin and smiled at her friend.

"I'd guess it's more for experience." Skye put a finger to her lips in an 'I'm thinking' gesture. "Every life is a grade in school. Except when there's a job to be done, like this time around. We never got to finish our life experiences last time. We have to set things right and not let it happen again."

"What about Forrest?" Jaime asked. "*Who* and where is he?"

Skye threw up her hands in mock dismay. "I don't know *everything*. But I'd be willing to bet that he's around, maybe working at the lumber company—"

Jaime pondered. "He could be one of the Bauer brothers. They give Evan and Dane and the school board no end of trouble."

Skye shook her head. "They're too old. Maybe since Forrest's evil genes are lurking around in Ryan, he went somewhere else to do some damage. All I know is that the core of who we used to be is back here—most of the Nine who were murdered that night, plus

Rob Brass and Forrest's son, Ryan. I have seen us..." She hesitated. "...in visions and in dreams. I have seen us the way we were, and as who we are now. And I know we're back for a reason—to stop it from happening again."

"Let's make a list of names and see just who we have." Francesca jumped up and grabbed a memo pad and a ballpoint pen from the desk in the corner of the den.

Jaime caught Francesca's eye. "Haven't we gone through this several times already? What good is it going to do to go over it again?"

"For Skye's benefit. We have more connections now than we did when just you and I were involved reading Kathy's diary." She marked off two columns on the pad. "Me, Francesca. I was Francie, the accidental Prom Queen."

"And me, I was Janie, the condescending snob. And I'm still painting, and not doing much else, just like Janie."

"I wouldn't say you're doing *nothing*," Francesca protested. "The paintings you put in Grace's shop are lovely, and the one you painted of the Adams farm in the snow was beautiful—and it sold."

Jaime smiled her appreciation.

Skye leaned toward the other two. "And I was Sylvia. And I'm in a tearing hurry to succeed, just like the old Sylvia."

Jaime gestured at Skye. "And you're convinced Alden is Rob Brass, and we think Molly is Barbara."

"And Kate Knight is Kathy—well, she made a better life for herself this time," Skye said, "and it's pretty sure Suzanne White is the previous Suzanne, or Suki. Kate snoops and writes, and she's a whiz at it, and Suzanne is all clothes, clothes, clothes, just like before."

"And Dane is Donnie, and probably Evan is Craig," Jaime added. "Or—he might be Paul. Why do we have almost the same names? That's a little weird, don't you think? Do we pick them for ourselves before we get back here?"

Francesca looked up from her pad. "That's a good point. I think I told you, Jaime, my mother said when I was born she had 'Jessica or 'Stephanie' picked out for a girl—she'd never even *thought* of Francesca, but when she first looked at me, it just popped into her head. She said that's what I *looked* like."

Skye shrugged. "That's probably how it works most of the time. Not in Molly's case, obviously, but Barbara's not a name that's currently in vogue. Kathy got changed to Kate, almost the same thing, but more of a *today*-name. Same with me. Nobody's named Sylvia now, but Skye is very trendy."

"Who else?" Jaime glanced at her watch. "The boys will be home from school soon, and I have to be there. But—what about Paul Peller and Marc Foster? If we could locate them, we'd have all the original Nine."

"Maybe we won't get everybody". Skye sighed, and rubbed her knuckle across her cheek. "I don't see much connection between Paul Peller and Jaime's Evan, but maybe we can't account for everyone. It's much more likely that Evan is Craig, since Craig was a teacher. Evan feels he has an educational mission here. That makes a lot of sense."

"And what about Forrest himself?" Francesca made some meaningless scribbles on the side of the pad. "He and Rob Brass are the ones we have to pinpoint, so that we don't have a repeat of the deadly performance."

Jaime shook her head. I don't think we can hope to find everyone. Marc Foster? I don't have a clue, but I'll reread Kathy's diary and see if I can pick out any identifying characteristics that might have come through. I wish we could find Forrest, though, before he does any more damage."

Skye stood up and shrugged into the red blazer. "I have to go, too. If they were younger, I'd make a guess. I'd say Forrest is one of the Bauer brothers, but that just can't be."

"No way of just jumping into a life at six years old, eh?" asked Francesca dryly.

Amid the laughter, Jaime went to the closet and retrieved her coat. "Almost March. We can put these heavy coats away for the season soon, and I for one, can't wait for the warm weather."

"I'll bet, Southern girl," Francesca teased. She laid her pad on the table. "Jaime and I will get in touch with Ryan and see if we can set up another meeting. You're sure we can't trust him, Skye, that he's on the other side?"

"Absolutely." Skye turned toward the door. "I've locked psychic-horns with him before, and he's definitely not on our wavelength." She hesitated. "And I'm not sure we all want to get together at a meeting. Maybe we can do this some other way, like on the computer by e-mail."

Jaime knew the answer before Francesca turned to Skye. "Why shouldn't we have a meeting of everyone concerned?

"Remember what happened last time," Skye reminded her, "the last time we were here?"

Twenty-eight

Alden sweated in the hot sun. Even though it was only March, it was an unseasonably hot day for early spring in Massachusetts. Lifting heavy boards and stacking them in piles hadn't improved his temperament all day, either, already bad after the quarrel he'd had with Molly last night. He had raised his fist to her, almost swung at her, but stopped himself at the last moment when he saw the fear and loathing in her eyes. What had he ever done to make her hate him? He'd married her when she got knocked up, had provided for her and those two spoiled, whiney kids, and even bought them a nice house in a great town where they could at last settle down and be a family, without the constant criticism and looking-down-their-noses at him from her family.

The loudspeaker came on, and he paused, wiping the sweat from his face, as he heard Ryan's voice. "Will the following people come to Mr. Barrett's office at once: Pete Finch, Jackson Roach, Ed Finley, Rick Botticelli and Alden Snyder. Right now, please for an important meeting."

Alden knew his name would be included as soon as he heard the first two, Pete and Jackson. They were all blue-collar rednecks and proud of it. He started for Ryan's office at a trot, wiping his sweating hands on his jeans as he jogged toward the door. He met Ed and Rick at the door, saw Jackson coming toward them from a distance. Pete was already there, sitting on the leather sofa. Alden sat beside him and left the three hard wood chairs for the others.

Ryan sat behind his desk, its glass surface occupied by a sleek computer, a wire 'in' basket, which was empty, his telephone, and a pad and pencil. The man was organized to the hilt, and Alden admired him for it, as well as for other things, as they had gotten to know each other. Frankly, he'd thought it strange that Ryan had sought him out for conversation after he came back to work from his brief stint in jail. Ryan kept his eyes on him but rarely spoke to him at all. But—he'd grown to understand Ryan's interest. They were all on the same wavelength, all of them, and Alden thought there might well be more at P & B Lumber, from some of the snippets of conversation he'd overheard.

Ryan greeted everyone with a nod, motioned them to sit, but didn't speak. He wore a thoughtful look, lips pursed, as he rocked back in his executive chair, arms crossed, waiting for their undivided attention.

Jackson was the last to arrive; he swung the middle chair around and straddled it, like a horse. Ryan acknowledged him the same way he had the others.

"Houston," he said, "We have a problem."

Alden felt a shock of apprehension, but that only inflamed him further. What in Sam Hill was the matter now? Five pairs of eyes regarded Ryan with curiosity.

"I just got a call from Jaime Reid, the new super's wife. Remember how I was talking about getting all those liberal sickos with all their fancy new educational ideas together—"

"Just to scare 'em." Jackson grinned. "Do a lot of yellin' and throw some chairs around and stuff. I'm ticked off the way they want to change everything."

"Yeah," Pete grunted. "We gotta make 'em understand we like our town just the way it is. The wife and I hate the way they wanna change it into some fancy suburb and attract a lotta people into it that we don't want here."

Ryan nodded. "It seems that several of *them* got together, and well, they're just all too busy with their children and their social obligations to find a convenient time to meet—so they want me to talk this out with them by email."

Alden snorted in disgust. "That ain't going to work. I'm lookin' forward to scaring some of those fancy bitches right out of their fancy underpants. Can't do that over the computer."

"No." Ryan nodded. "We need an actual get-together."

"Which you won't even be at, right?" Rick grinned and leered at Ryan.

Ryan affected an air of innocence. "I'll be right here, going over accounts with Alden, and a couple of you will vouch for that, right?"

"Right!" they all repeated.

Rick looked doubtful. "We're just gonna scare 'em, right? Wear black bags with eyeholes cut out over our heads, or ski masks, and make a lot of noise—but no real violence, is that the plan?"

Alden regarded him with a smirk. *Maybe you just wanna scare 'em, buddy, but I intend to cause some damage and give them treatment they won't soon forget.*

"Right." Ryan rocked back in his chair. "Just give them some actual second and third thoughts about changing everything around here." Alden caught the glint in Ryan's eyes. "Say, Al, your wife is friends with some of those people, isn't she?"

Alden grimaced. "'Fraid so."

"So, can she get them all together for some sort of soiree at your place?"

Alden retreated. "Oh, I don't think so. Our place isn't set up for fancy entertaining."

"On second thought..." Ryan tapped his finger on his desk and looked out the window, as if he hadn't even heard Alden's answer. Ryan turned his gaze back on the group. "My partner, Jason Peller, and I could invite them all to a party, maybe at his place. That way, I could say Alden and I had to do some work here, but would be along later, and when we got there, the damage would already be done, and the police would be there. We would be completely vindicated, since we weren't even there."

Pete leaned forward. "Jason? But from what I've heard him sayin', he's all for these new programs and reforms. Does he know you're not on that bandwagon?"

"No, he doesn't. And that's what makes it a perfect plan. I'll get into a conversation with him about what a great job Reid is doing and how we ought to give a nice party for him and his wife. That should work. We're doing some rehab on my place, and he has a bigger house anyway, so his hosting it would be logical. If the five of you are with me, that is." He rubbed his hands together and grinned. "This could work, guys."

Alden nodded, along with a chorus of grunts and 'yups'. *But I will be there. I wouldn't miss that chance for anything in the world. I hate those bitches so much, with their high-flyin' ideas and how they're givin' them all to Molly, too. She's my wife, and they got no right to interfere with how I run my family affairs.*

Ryan dusted off his hands. "Well, that's it. You guys knock off for the day, and I'll meander over to Jason's office and get a little conversation going."

They filed out, grinning and slapping each other on the back. Alden noticed that of all of them, only Rick seemed less than enthusiastic. His long, thin face wore a worried expression.

"Hey, Rick." Alden accosted him in the lumberyard after the office door closed behind them. "You don't look so sure. Are you with us or against us?"

"Does it have to be one or the other? I just don't want any violence, Al, and after what you did at the School Board meeting, I'm not sure you just want to scare 'em..." His voice trailed off.

"Oh, sure, that's all." Alden tried to sound sincere. "You like what they're doing to our school system, bringing in all these fancy new ideas? Jeez! If everyone goes to college, who'll run the gas stations and work at the paper mill? Who'll fix cars and do electrical work and build houses? Who'll deliver groceries and drive the beer trucks—plus they'll hike our taxes to the sky to pay for all this new stuff."

"Yeah, yeah, I get the idea." Rick still looked unhappy. "But if I had a kid, which I don't, since I'm not married, I might hope he'd do better than I did. Yeah, on second thought, Al, I'm gonna go back and tell Ryan to count me out."

He turned and headed back toward the office. Alden narrowed his eyes as he watched him, and he felt his anger rise. He strode toward his battered truck, jumped in, and headed home, taking the curves too fast and not caring that the wheels squealed and the brakes screeched. No cops flashed him down; he would almost have been glad for the confrontation. He swerved into the parking lot of a package store and bought a twelve-pack. Well, so he would be home a little early, but this wasn't one of Molly's working days, so she had just better have some decent kind of supper going— meatloaf and mashed potatoes, maybe. TV and beer, then dinner, then get those two spoiled kids to bed, and then—well, Molly was his wife, and she'd do what he told her to. And she wasn't going to be seeing Jaime and Francesca and those other fancy women any more, either, if he had anything to say about it, and he certainly was going to have a lot to say.

He pulled into his driveway, grabbed the beer, got out, and slammed the door. Let that little bitch know he was home. His fury rose as he noticed that their old blue Ford that Molly drove to her pitiful little job wasn't in the driveway. He stalked toward the door and threw it open. It only took him a few seconds to look around and realize that Molly was just not home.

She and the kids were gone.

Half the twelve-pack later, Alden, muttering to himself, staggered down the cellar steps into the small, cramped basement, where all the debris from their former abodes lay in disorderly piles. Tossing piles of clothing aside, pushing aside objects in his way, he searched for a certain old black trunk that he knew was there somewhere. He finally found it, and with an oath, he wrenched the lid open. The light was dim, and he could hardly tell one object from another—all his old tools, out-of-date license plates, broken toys... you name it, it was in that trunk. But there was something else, too, something he remembered packing in there, just in case he ever needed it. He felt for it, and there it was. He dug it out and rubbed it on his jeans. It looked to be in good shape. He went upstairs and finished off his twelve-pack, yelled at the danged stupid wrestlers on TV, and stroked the old shotgun as he might have a favorite dog as he balanced it on his knee.

Alden aimed the gun at the window. "Bang! Bang!" he whispered. He threw the empty beer can at the TV and stood up, tucking the gun under his arm. He had a mission.

Twenty-nine

"Holy cow." Francesca's breathless voice came over the phone. "Have you heard what happened last night?"

"I just turned on the TV." Jaime set her own plate on the table. "Evan and I are watching it now."

Evan laid down the newspaper, his eyes glued to the television, as he worked on his pair of poached eggs. It was a rainy Saturday morning. Out of sight, in the den the boys ate Cocoa Crispies out of the box and played an easy card game Kevin had taught them.

"Who in the world would want to kill that guy?" Jaime heard the bewilderment in Francesca's voice. "These things just don't happen in this town, a random murder like this."

"Robbery?"

Francesca snorted. "He lived down near the river, near Willow's old place. He couldn't have had much worth robbing him for."

"A vagrant, then. Somebody just passing through."

Jaime pictured Francesca's shrug. "That's more likely. Things do happen down by the river, as we know."

Jaime let out a long "Uhm." She remembered Kathy Kelly's detailing her meetings with Rob, Forrest, and Willow. "Speaking of Willow..."

"Which we weren't." The frustration in her voice came over the line, loud and clear. "But, what?"

"I wonder if we should fill her in on what we've been thinking and doing. Maybe she should be in on this."

Too late! She heard the newspaper crunch on the table behind her and cringed as she wished she could recall her last words.

"Exactly what does that mean, Jaime? What *have* you and Francesca been up to?" Evan did not sound amused.

She glanced around at him. He didn't *look* amused, either. "I'll have to call you back, Francesca." She wished she could stall for time. She reached for the coffee pot. "Do you need a refill, Evan?"

"You know damn well I don't! And neither do you, so sit down right now and tell me what's going on. First of all, why does this guy's murder have any interest for you two?"

"He—he worked at the lumber company, with Alden Snyder."

"So?"

"And Jason Peller and Ryan Barrett."

"And this concerns you, how?"

Jaime reclaimed her chair at the table and let out a long sigh. "I don't think you're going to like this."

~ * ~

"He read me the riot act." Jaime was disheartened, as she and Francesca strolled down Main Street, peeked into the windows of the quaint little shops, and looked for a place to have lunch. "I've never heard him so angry. The boys even came unglued from their card game and came out into the kitchen to watch him yell."

"Wow. The mild-mannered Evan Reid... hard to believe." She pointed to a pair of shoes in Bossidy's. "I got it, too, but not as badly. Dane is a little more open about—and I must say, much more amused by—the reincarnation thing than Evan is. But, after he hung up with Evan he did reinforce Evan's point that the superintendent and the school principal shouldn't be famous for having wacko wives."

Jaime stopped to look at the shoes Francesca had indicated. She wasn't really interested in shoes right now, but it was something to do. "And he's right, of course, but we can't just ignore what Skye told us—and what Ryan himself said, before we knew he bats for the other team." She paused and gestured to a tiny deli with half a dozen red and white table-clothed-tables inside. "Want to get a bite here?"

Francesca didn't answer her, and when Jaime glanced around at her, she saw that Francesca's eyes were fixed on Willow's Beauty Shop across the street. She turned back to Jaime. "Don't you need a trim?"

They hardly bothered to check for traffic as they walked across the street. The street, and the town itself, seemed deserted. It was almost eerie, Jaime reflected. As was frequent in New England, the weather had changed, bringing forth a crisp spring day, as if repenting for the rain that had fallen that morning. The sky gleamed a picture-book blue, the mountains in the distance showing off new pale greens among the perennial dark evergreens. And yet the town was quiet, seemingly deserted, like the calm before a storm.

Willow's shop didn't seem to be busy either, as they stood in front of the window displaying bottles of shampoo and conditioners of all makes and sizes and boxes of hair coloring products— all the beautiful women on the containers grinning inanely. At least, at the moment, that was how it struck Jaime.

Francesca grabbed her arm. "Wait! Didn't Willow have a sign in the window about an apartment for rent on the second floor of the building?"

"Yes, I think so." Jaime remembered that the sign had been red and white, hand-lettered, but neat. "I wonder who rented it?"

Francesca tossed her a grin. "You wait a sec. I'll run in and say I have a friend who was interested, and is it still available?"

Jaime waited, tapping her toe on the sidewalk in time to a snappy tune that sang inside her head. Suddenly she felt a heavy grip on her arm, and she was jerked around, nearly knocking her off balance, to face a red-faced, snarling Alden Snyder.

"Where are my wife and kids, you bitch?"

"I don't know!" Jaime tried to pull her arm away. "Let go of me!"

He pushed his face up close to her and crowded her with his body, until she was pressed up flat against the window of Willow's shop. "I know you damn women got something to do with them being gone. Now, where are they?"

She pushed hard against him, but he thrust her against the wall and snarled into her face, "If you know what's good for you and that high-falutin' husband of yours—" He paused and sneered. "And *your kids,* you'll see that Molly and my kids go back where they belong. And soon." He gave her arm a hard squeeze, sending bolts of pain up to her shoulder, and stalked away, a man who radiated rage in every step.

Grinning widely Francesca bounced out of the shop. She stopped short. Her face lost its grin as she saw Jaime, flattened against the window, gasping and gripping the window ledge with her hands.

"Jaime—what is it? What happened?" She dropped her handbag on the ground and threw her arms around her friend. She drew back as Jaime winced in pain.

"Alden Snyder. Molly and the kids are gone, and he thinks we know where they are." Jaime rubbed her arm. "He grabbed me so hard, I'll have a bruise for sure."

Francesca picked up her handbag and searched for the cell phone. "We'll call the police, have him arrested for assault. This time they won't let him out so fast."

"No, wait!" Jaime closed her hand over the phone.

"Wait? Are you crazy, Jaime? The man is dangerous. He can't go around assaulting people. We have to call the cops on him."

Jaime shook her head. "I don't want to get Evan upset with me anymore than he already is." She rubbed her arm. "Alden's upset about Molly and the kids leaving. It doesn't have anything to do with us, or me specifically."

"He thinks we know where they are—and we do."

Jaime looked at her blankly. "We do? Where are they?"

Francesca grinned at her and pointed upwards. "In Willow's second floor apartment. Remember that we noticed the sign was gone?"

Jaime looked up at the second-story windows facing the street. "Well, good for her. But how is she going to afford that?"

"You ought to give me more credit for being a first-class detective." Francesca poked her with mock severity. "Willow also had an opening for a receptionist part-time, and she hired Molly for that as well, when she's not working at the craft shop. Molly confided in her, and anytime Alden shows up and makes any kind of scene when Molly's there, Willow or one of the staff will call 911 immediately for help."

"Wow." Jaime breathed. "Give the girl credit! But he'll get to her sooner or later. She can't avoid him forever."

"Let's not sell Molly short. She's come a long way in a short time. I think she can take care of herself." Francesca paused and glanced at her watch. "Now, I'm hungry. How about having lunch with Willow, ala our original plan?"

"Fine." Jaime rubbed her arm again. "We can ask her, although she has never been very open with me. Do you think she will come?"

"I already asked her." Francesca flashed her mischievous grin. "When I told her how involved with Molly we are, she agreed right away. Seems she's taken quite a shine to her. She'll be out in a minute. Now, Jaime..." She turned serious again. "Are you sure you don't want to report Alden for what he did? Before we go on with this and get in even deeper?"

Jaime took a moment to reflect, then shook her head. "I really believe what Skye told us, and even what Ryan Peller said. A mass murder is going to happen again here unless we act to prevent it, and getting Alden arrested will only add to the fire and get Evan even more upset."

Francesca nodded as the door to the beauty opened and Willow breezed out to join them. "It's been a long morning and I'm starving. Where are we going to eat?"

Thirty

Top Dog was the kind of bar in which Alden Snyder felt comfortable: small, dingy, the wooden booths scarred, with the one-time paint worn down to the wood, half a dozen stools at a ragged bar with a tired, bleary-eyed bartender futilely scrubbing down its grubby surface. And none of those fancy Mill Pond people were likely to be in there to raise his ire higher.

He was already seething. Before he passed Main Street Manes and had that little showdown with Jaime Reid, he had passed by the craft shop where Molly worked part time. He'd lingered around outside for a few minutes, hoping for a glimpse of her. She never showed, but his eyes lit on several small paintings in the window of the shop and a hand-printed sign that announced '*Original watercolors by Jaime Reid*'.

He was still thanking his lucky stars that the Reid bitch hadn't called the police on him. He hadn't meant to grab her so hard, but his anger got the best of him. He *knew* that she and her friend, the principal's wife, knew where Molly and the kids were. They had no right to be interfering in their lives, but they'd get their comeuppance—just let them wait and see. Even his boss, Ryan Barrett, had no idea how far Alden was prepared to go.

The small TV over the bar had continuing local news coverage of the murder of Rick Botticelli. Alden smirked into his beer. He'd been so clever. He felt good about himself for a change.

"We have no leads," announced the chief of police, who was a *woman*, and whose name appropriately and amusingly was Connie Ketchem, This struck Alden as very funny, and he found it difficult to keep from laughing. She and the mayor of Mill Pond, John Roach, stood side by side in front of the small, picturesque town hall and wore expressions of deep concern on their oh-so-important faces.

Alden ordered a second and a third bottle of beer as he watched the town officials try to reassure the citizens. He noticed that nosy bitch, Kate Knight, in the crowd of reporters. Molly had mentioned that she'd met her at some luncheon. Not mentioned, *bragged!* Well, he, Alden, was her husband, and his wife was not going to be palling around with those people much longer, if he had to take care of them all, one by one, all by himself.

He had been so very careful. He'd called Ryan from his car, said he'd be late for the meeting, but he'd be there, made a swift detour to Rick's shabby little house by the river, pulled on his rubber gloves, tiptoed up to the front porch, opened the door, and killed Rick as he snoozed in front of the TV. The revolver was old and had belonged to someone else, God knew who, and could not be traced back to him. Even Molly hadn't known he had it, as he had never told her when he found it in the rushes near a stream in Vermont where he was fishing. He'd just thought it might come in handy someday, and *someday* had arrived. Alden messed up Rick's small, shabby house by overturning smaller pieces of furniture, sweeping dishes and knickknacks onto the floor. Several pictures of families—Rick's brothers and sisters?—sat on a makeshift desk with a computer on it. Alden threw them on the floor as well and took great pleasure in stamping on the frames and breaking the glass. He left as efficiently as he had come in, leaving no evidence that he was ever there, and went on to the meeting with Ryan and the rest of the boys.

Alden beckoned to the bartender and ordered another beer. Just one more—one for the road. Connie Ketchem was still holding forth on the courthouse steps.

"Do you think it might be someone who worked with Rick Botticelli at P & B Lumber?" The camera zoomed in on Kate Knight's face.

Alden stared at her. He had never seen her up-close, and there was something familiar about her face, her manner. Something tugged at him deep inside, like a memory long buried. He realized, even through the wooly haze of alcohol, that something else had stirred in him, too, in recent weeks. He had seemed to have been born with an angry streak and a frightening inability to control his temper, but lately his anger had developed into something more like a smoldering rage. He wasn't even sure what it was all about; he just knew he felt compelled to act on it. It was the only thing that relieved the pain.

Chief Ketchem gestured to Jason Peller, standing to one side in the front of the small group of people. Jason joined the chief and Mayor Roach and took the mike as it was passed to him. His handsome face had sprouted new worry lines overnight.

Alden sneered. The other half of P & B Lumber, unlike Ryan Barrett, had no idea in hell about what was going on right under his nose.

Jason adjusted his tie and stared into the camera. "We at P & B Lumber are a very close-knit group, almost a family, you might say."

Alden snorted. "Self-important idiot."

The red-eyed bartender glanced his way as he wiped down the bar.

Jason continued. "It just doesn't compute with me that anyone from the company would have murdered Rick Botticelli. As far as the police and I can tell, all my employees have an alibi for last night. All were either home with their families, who can vouch for them, or in a planning meeting with my associate, Ryan Barrett."

Chief Ketchem nodded, her face sober. Mayor Roach looked off into the distance over the assembled group. Jason handed the mike back to the police chief. She cleared her throat, and when she could speak, said, "It's most likely that Mr. Botticelli was murdered by some vagrant just passing through."

Alden snickered.

"Something funny?" The bartender continued polishing a wine glass on a none-too-clean looking dishtowel.

Alden nodded and grinned. "Didja ever hear the saying 'the left hand doesn't know what the right hand is doin'?'"

The bartended nodded, and as Alden gestured at the television, he turned to look at it. "Yeah. So?"

"You might say that about P & B Lumber. They ain't got a clue what goes on there."

"You don't say. You work there or something?"

"Yeah, something like that," Alden got up and plunked a twenty dollar bill on the counter. "That cover it, buddy?"

"And then some." The bartender pocketed the bill. "Come back soon."

Alden cast a last look at the screen, picking out Kate's pretty face from the group around her. "Bitch!" He muttered. "Effin, nosy bitch." Wobbling slightly, he left the bar, enjoying the warm, fuzzy feeling that filled his head like a wad of cotton wool. He sensed the bartender's eyes on his back as he opened the door and staggered out onto the street. He'd spent longer than he intended in there; he'd drunk his lunch, and now it was nearly time for dinner.

He looked up and down the nearly empty street and wondered where he'd left his car.

Thirty-one

Jaime sensed as soon as she walked into the house that Evan's mood had not improved a heck of a lot since their conversation that morning. Peeking into the dining room, she saw that the table was set as if for company, and an aroma announced that something savory and herbal was cooking in the oven.

"What's up?" Her tone was tentative, as he had not turned to greet her in his usual welcoming manner. He offered no 'hi', no hug, no kiss. He busied himself stirring the pot of whatever he was cooking on the stovetop.

Evan turned, tight-lipped. "Dane and Francesca are coming for dinner, and we're going to have it all out about what you and she have been doing."

She wanted to wilt, but she steeled herself in the face of his opposition. If she had to tell him what Alden Snyder had done and said, she would. She didn't want to escalate this whole situation, and she certainly didn't want to bother Evan with it or cause him difficulty, but...

"You're really making things difficult for me, Jaime. I'm hearing things I really don't appreciate hearing about my wife. I'm working hard to overcome the opposition to change here, and then someone tells me my *wife* is running around saying Columbine is going to happen again, and all the people who were killed in '61 are back, *reincarnated as other people!"*

At a loss for words, Jaime looked at the two plates with leftovers of chicken tenders and French fries sitting on the pink enameled kitchen table. "Where are Jack and Josh?"

"Jane-Michelle took them to the movies and is keeping them overnight."

Jane-Michelle?" She stared at him open-mouthed. "How? Why?"

Evan picked up the two dishes from the table, scraped the leavings into the trash, and set the plates in the sink. He put a lid on the pan he'd been stirring, set it on the back burner, and turned the heat on low. "Willow called Jane-Michelle, all upset over what you and Francesca had to say at lunch. She called me. I asked her to take the boys, and I called Dane, who was also, shall we say, *perturbed,* with his wife."

"Do I have time to shower and change?" she managed to ask, feeling as though her legs might collapse under her.

"Just." Evan nodded at the kitchen clock. "They're due in half an hour."

His voice had not warmed toward her one degree. She dashed for the shower. She adjusted the water to hot, hot, and hotter, trying to wash away the trepidation she felt about the meeting that was going to happen. Then, steaming and feeling cleansed, her resolve returned. She and Francesca would convince them; they *had* to! If they failed to do so, their lives would again be cut short. For the sake of the children, if nothing else, she and Francesca had to succeed at this.

She pulled on silky black slacks, appreciating the fact that in her late thirties and two children later, her waist was still slim. But... evidently she wasn't as slim as she used to be. The slacks were a little tight. She tossed on a soft pink, short-sleeved sweater, then noticed in alarm that her arm, where Alden had squeezed it, was bruised and turning blue.

"Jaime!" Dane and Francesca are here," Evan called from the bottom of the stairs.

"Coming." She tore off the pink sweater. She fished in her drawer for something with longer sleeves and took out a cream-colored V-neck top with three-quarter sleeves that just covered the developing bruise. On the spur of the moment, she opened her jewelry drawer and fished out the necklace Donnie Barrett had given Janie fifty years ago. She fastened it around her neck, gazing at it in the mirror.

Maybe that would awaken something in Dane Summers' psyche, something buried, that he didn't remember on the conscious level at all.

Dane, casually dressed in a gray cashmere sweater and charcoal pants, didn't look nearly as—well, *pissed off*—as Evan seemed to be. He shook hands with her, a grave look on his face, but his eyes twinkled at her. "Well, it seems that you and my wife have been up to some serious mischief around here." His eyes fell on the necklace, and as he had the first time she'd worn it, he reached out and touched it. "This—reminds me of something, Jaime. Where did you say you got this?

"I—I found it." *You gave it to me, Donnie.*

"Where?"

Her search for an answer was interrupted as Francesca came in from the kitchen carrying a large steaming platter of chicken, vegetables and potatoes.

Jaime raised her eyebrows.

"I was pressed into service," Francesca explained. "And glad to do it, too."

I bet. Anything to forestall what we're in for tonight.

Evan brought a salad and a basket of hot rolls as he followed Francesca into the dining room. He had already poured white wine into the wine glasses at each place setting. "Sit," he invited with a sweep of his hand, but no smile.

They circled the table and sat down in their accustomed places. Of all of them, only Dane seemed relaxed and vaguely amused as he looked around the table. "Well, Evan, when we hired you, we didn't know you could cook like this. We might have to begin a yearly tradition of an all-school barbeque, with you as chef."

Jaime had to admit; it looked impressive, and it smelled wonderful. The roasted chicken, golden with an herbed glaze, sat in the center of the platter, surrounded by onions, carrots, green beans, and small red potatoes. The salad, mixed greens with tomato and cucumbers, glistened with an oil and vinegar dressing.

"All stuff we already had in the freezer and fridge," Evan said.

Jaime met his eyes and nodded. "You did a superb job, Evan. It looks and smells delicious. What are we having for dessert?"

"Vanilla recrimination and repentance with caramel sauce." He showed a trace of his usual good humor. "We'll have coffee and a very serious discussion. But for now, let's enjoy." He picked up the platter and passed it to Francesca, who helped herself to a hefty serving of everything. Dane, also, did not seem to have lost his appetite. As for Jaime, she took small servings of everything and picked, having little appetite. She had to admit it was really good. Evan had cooked dinner from time to time, but had never put his culinary talents to work like this. Evan himself ate in an efficient and business-like manner, saying very little between bites. Jaime couldn't wait for this uncomfortable dinner to be over. At the same time she wished desperately to prolong it so that the inevitable discussion to follow would also be delayed. Evan wasn't having any small talk, however. Everything she said was either met by silence or a minimal reply. He wasn't much better when Dane or Francesca tried to make conversation.

Too soon she and Francesca carried the plates and leftovers back into the kitchen.

"We'll wait for you in the den." Evan set his jaw even firmer, and he and Dane headed off for the small room with the refinished bookshelves and Kathy Kelly's hidden diary and shut the door behind them.

Francesca breathed a sigh of relief. "Whew! That was fun, wasn't it?

Jaime grimaced. "Not really, but the food was good. Too bad we couldn't enjoy it."

Francesca began to rinse the dishes off and handed them to Jaime, who placed them in the dishwasher. She shot Jaime a mischievous look. "It's every woman's dream to come home and discover her husband has made dinner."

"Not in these circumstances." Jaime wiped her hands on a dishtowel. "We're in for it, you know." She threw the towel on the counter. "We might as well go face the lions." She turned and walked toward the closed door of the den.

"Wait!" Francesca grabbed her arm, just in the place where the bruise was under her sleeve. "How much are we going to tell them?"

Jaime pulled away, wincing. "Ow! Everything, Francesca. We're going to come clean. All of it, like we did with Willow."

"Yeah, that was sure a good idea, wasn't it? Here, Jaime, let me see your arm."

Francesca pushed up Jaime's sleeve to reveal the darkening skin. "This is what Alden did?" Concerned, she straightened, anger flashing across her face. "Yes. It's time we laid it all out. We have to convince them that the threat is real."

"Or else..."

"Or else, yes. If I have to, I'll read them excerpts from Kathy's diary."

~ * ~

Dane flicked a brief smile at them as Jaime and Francesca entered the den. Francesca sat on the leather sofa, opposite the two men seated in comfortable chairs. Evan tapped his fingers on the arm of the chair. Jaime hesitated a second, then went to the bookcase lining the back of the room and removed several books on the third shelf. Fishing around for what she knew was there, she pulled out Kathy Kelly's diary. As she seated herself beside Francesca, she stole a glance at Evan, who seemed a little more relaxed, but whose face still refused to entertain a smile.

Evan leaned forward, his elbows on his knees and met Jaime's eyes. He looked at the book Jaime held on her lap. "Okay, ladies, it's time to come clean. What is this all about?"

Jaime swallowed and held up the diary. "This is Kathy Kelly's diary. I found it the day we moved in, hidden in the rafters in the cellar."

Dane sat up straighter in his chair, his interest obviously piqued by this revelation, but Evan still regarded her steely-eyed. "Yes. You've shown me that before. So?"

"Just listen, Evan," Francesca cut in. "Kathy wrote about all the Mill Pond grads who were murdered in the reunion of '61, and she had a lot to say about everyone. Try to keep an open mind."

"Pretty hard to do," Evan snapped, "when my wife is running around town sabotaging the job I worked so hard to get."

Jaime felt as though he had slapped her. Never had he spoken to her or about her in such a manner. She took a deep breath. "Evan, Dane, do you think reincarnation is a possibility, even a very, very small one? Can you accept that theory at all?"

"No," said Evan

Dane shrugged. "I believe everything's possible but I don't spend much time wondering about it. I know Francesca believes that, but I would need some concrete proof."

Jaime hesitated, then raised her hand to her throat and cupped the delicate *J* on its tarnished chain in her palm. "You said this reminded you of something," she said to Dane.

"Well..." He squinted at it. "It does, but I don't know what."

"You gave it to me fifty years ago—when you were Donnie Barrett and I was Janie Carlson."

Dane put a hand over his face, as if he could not process what she had just said, and Evan broke out laughing. "And how did you come to that remarkable conclusion?"

"Listen," she said, and opened the diary.

September 10th, 1954

Donnie came home from his three-year stint in the Marines a couple of months ago, and those of us who are still around went out to dinner to welcome him home. Janie finally got her chance with him, and she's deliriously happy, as they have been going out, and this is what she's wanted since third grade, I think. She was showing off a necklace he gave her—a silver J with rhinestones in it. Well, good luck to him; we all know Janie isn't going to give it up, and he'll get tired of waiting and move on sooner or later.

"That doesn't prove anything,"—Evan leaned forward, his hands flat on his knees—"except that you have a necklace something like the one Donnie gave Janie. It's not necessarily the same necklace."

"It *is* the same necklace."

"What makes you think it is?"

"Uhm." Jaime cast a sideways glance at Francesca. "You aren't going to like this at all, Evan."

"I already don't like any of this. You can't make it any worse."

"Oh, I can," she assured him. Bolstered by Francesca's nod, she told him about the painting of the Snyders' house she had seen in Willow's shop and how somehow deep inside she had known that she, when she was Janie, had painted it. As the men sat with disbelief etched on their faces, she told them how they had driven there, and how she had gone in and retrieved the necklace beneath the radiator floorboards, knowing exactly where to find it.

Evan sprang to his feet, shouting at her, "You broke into the Snyders' house? What were you thinking, Jaime? Good God!" He paced around the small room, pulling at his hair and muttering "Good God! Good God!" over and over.

Dane regarded her with a thoughtful look on his face but didn't say anything. Francesca threw him a pleading look and held out her hands to him. He got up and took Evan's arm, guiding him back to his chair. "Let's hear the rest of it, girls. Try to calm down, Evan."

They plunged in and told them the story of what was first an interesting discovery, but how, as the coincidences grew and the personalities and traits of the slain Mill Pond graduates emerged to fit themselves and others, they became convinced that it was more than mere coincidence. They were the reincarnated Nine, and there was a reason for them to all come together again.

Evan sat very still, his head buried in his hands, but Dane listened with what seemed to Jaime to be intense interest. When she described seeing his face floating in the air, he nodded without an expression of surprise. She told them what Ryan Barrett had told her when he bartended at their cocktail party, and she and Francesca related how they had met Skye Weston, Kate Knight's cousin and state senator, at Chez Cherie, and what Skye had said.

Evan looked up, his face drained of color. "For the love of Pete, Jaime! How far off the deep end can you go? Don't you care at all if you ruin my career?"

"Is that all *you* care about?" Jaime shot back. "Aren't you at all concerned that we just all might be murdered if we don't stop it?"

Dane held up a hand. "Evan, I think we should take this seriously. Although I don't totally buy into reincarnation, I admit it is a possibility, and look at the similarity in names and personalities: Janie, Jaime, Francie, Francesca, Kathy and Kate, Skye and Sylvia."

"Donnie and Dane," Francesca added.

Evan snorted. "That's all coincidence. It means nothing."

"Too much coincidence always means something," Dane retorted.

"Donnie got a scholarship to UConn for basketball, and so did Dane," Jaime put in. "Donnie dated Janie for that summer, but then went on to Francie, who was little more lenient with her favors, and married her."

"Hey, watch what you say about me and my favors," Francesca joked.

Evan got up again and began to pace about the small room. "There's nothing funny about this, and the similarities mean nothing," he tossed over his shoulder.

Jaime tried again. "Francesca was already pregnant by Forrest Brown, Willow's brother when she and Donnie married. That makes Ryan Barrett Forrest's son."

"So he could be carrying some very bad genes," Francesca added. "He could be as evil as his father was."

Evan threw up his hands. "Are you both *crazy?* Ryan Barrett is a respected businessman and outstanding citizen of Mill Pond. He has a wife and two little girls. If you try to ruin his reputation, we'll all be laughed out of town."

"Well, try this on for size." Dane spoke to Evan, but leaned forward to look Jaime in the eyes. "When I first met Jaime, I *knew* I already knew her, and when she wore that necklace at the cocktail party, Evan, I knew I had given it to someone. In my mind I could see myself fastening the clasp around a girl's neck. It was a very weird experience, I have to say."

"Jaime," Francesca said. "Read that last entry to them."

Jaime flipped to the last page, and her voice shook as she read it.

June 18th, 1961

It's all set. I can't believe it. Saturday night at the Lakeview Inn. All The jerk-off Nine will be there: Barb and Paul of course, and Francie and Donnie. No prob because they're local. Janie and her schoolteacher husband Craig are coming from Pittsfield, and Marc and his new boyfriend from Hartford. It was a little harder to get Suki—excuse me, Suzanne—to take a break from her round the clock fashion job, but she'll be here, staying with me. Snotty Sylvia and her aristocratic husband, who deigned to come back to Mill Pond and do us a favor by opening Crenshaw and Crenshaw law firm, had to be coaxed a bit, but they're coming, too.

And they are finally going to reap their just rewards. Forrest has a hunting rifle—he actually kills things out there in the woods and eats them—and Balls has an old revolver he found in a bedroom closet in the old Porter house. We tried it out. It works just fine, for what we have in mind.

I have already taken everything I've saved out of the bank, and Balls got seven thousand from the jewelry store he robbed in Springfield last month. After we kill them all, we'll just disappear, start a new life someplace warm and beautiful, and never set foot in Mill Pond, Massachusetts, again.

Evan took a seat again, shaking his head, dismay written across his face. After a long silence, he turned to Dane. "Okay. This all ends here, all of it. Technically, Dane, even though we're good friends, I'm your boss in this situation, and I say we will not discuss this again."

"Technically, you serve at our pleasure," Dane retorted mildly.

Evan looked at Jaime and Francesca. "And you two will go back to being wives and mothers and supportive spouses, and find something else to occupy your free time. Get a part time job, join a book group or a bridge club. Whatever. But no more of this. Give me the diary, Jaime."

"No!" she exclaimed, but as he held out his hand and as she read the expression on his face, she reluctantly held it out to him. He took it, and with a look of disgust, shoved it into the pocket of his tweed jacket. "I'll put this where it won't cause any more trouble," he said. "And this nonsense is over *now.*"

"What if it's not nonsense?" Francesca asked. "What if the murder of that guy who worked for Ryan is tied into this?"

Evan shook his head as the phone sitting on the computer desk rang into the heavy silence.

"I'll get it." Jaime was glad to have an excuse to escape Evan's ire, even for a moment. "Maybe it's Jane-Michelle about the kids." She lifted the receiver. "Hello?" she said into the receiver.

As the voice on the other end of the wire related its news, Jaime swayed and nearly fell, keeping her balance only by grabbing the edge of the desk. "Oh, please—no!" she sobbed, holding fast to the desk, the phone clattering to the floor.

Evan was beside her, holding her up, his strong arms around her. "What is it? Are the kids okay?"

She heard his voice and felt his strength supporting her, but reality had vanished and a gray haze enveloped her, as if she were in a dream, one of those lucid dreams in which one is aware that he is dreaming but can't break out of it.

"It was Willow," she managed to gasp through the fog. "Kate Knight was found dead, at the corner of Elm and Spencer, around the corner from the Town Hall. Her throat was slit..."

The gray haze advanced, smothering her like a blanket, and she slumped unconscious into Evan's arms.

Thirty-two

The media had dutifully reported the death of Rick Botticelli, but it hadn't dominated the airways. However, the murder of Kate Knight was a different ball of wax. Jaime and Evan sat, frozen to the TV screen, as reporters from Boston and Hartford blanketed the town. Kate had been a well-known reporter for the *Springfield Register*. This was no loner, living in a shack down by the river, apparently murdered by a wandering vagrant.

"Kate Knight was a highly esteemed reporter for the *Springfield Register* who had won numerous awards for her reporting," the seasoned, middle-aged reporter from the Hartford Courant intoned. As Jaime swiped at her tears, she wondered if the woman, meticulously garbed in a charcoal pants suit, would be so dispassionate if she had known Kate personally.

"Why are you crying, Mom?" Josh came in from the den. He held out his bowl for a second helping of Cheerios.

Evan jumped up and refilled Josh's bowl. "A friend of Mommy's got hurt. Go back into the den. You're getting a day off from school today."

Jack, coming in behind his brother, brightened. "We're not going to school today? Are you going to work, Dad?"

"'No' to both questions." Evan shoed the boys out of the kitchen. "We'll do something special today, though, like maybe go to the zoo in Westfield. We didn't see it all last time we went."

"Is Mommy going, too?"

"All of us. We'll pack a picnic lunch and have a family day out."

He returned to the table, to the echoes of the boys' whoops of joy.

Jaime tore her gaze away from the screen. "Do you think that's a good idea, Evan, to leave the house today?" She picked up the remote, and the screen went dark.

"I think it's the *best* idea to leave the house today." Evan's face was grim. "I didn't see any connection with you and your so-called reincarnated group with the lumber company guy, but I do with Kate Knight's murder. I don't believe she was a random victim."

Jaime gasped. "You think *I'm* in danger?"

He nodded. "You're not only one of that group, you're my wife, and this person, or persons, is probably one of those malcontents who's against all our educational reforms."

"Alden Snyder?"

Evan covered her discolored arm with his hand, careful not to put any pressure on it. "He's certainly my number-one suspect, after what he did to you. Are you sure you don't want to charge him with assault?"

"No. I don't want to make anything worse. It's not really assault. It's just a bruise." She covered his hand with hers. "Oh, Evan, I'm so sorry! I just got so caught up in Kathy Kelly's diary and thinking we might have all been here before—I never dreamed it would cause so much trouble for you." She didn't attempt to choke back the tears.

"If it's Alden who's at the root of all this, he probably would have gone down this path anyway." Evan rubbed his chin. He scooted his chair over close to hers and put his arms around her. She leaned her head against his shoulder. How grateful she was to have him, and how devastated she would feel to lose him.

"Speaking of the diary..." Evan pulled away a little. "I read the whole blasted thing last night after tucking you in bed, and although I still don't buy the reincarnation theory, but I do admit there *are* a lot of similarities." He handed the book to her. "If certain people were familiar with the contents of this, they might brainwash themselves into thinking they were the 'bad guys' in that scenario, and that would give them sufficient reason to try to do it again."

"I don't know how anyone else could be familiar with this—"

"Kathy might have typed it up from this and made copies in that primitive way they used to do things, you know, carbon paper."

Jaime tried to smile, although she felt as though the ache in her heart might never go away. "Well, Evan, I promise to give this all up and stay out of trouble from now on." She got up, book in hand. "I'll throw this out right now."

"Good. Now, how about I get the guys dressed, and you pack us a picnic lunch, and we'll all get out of here?"

He bent down and kissed her, a real kiss with all his love in it, took the diary from her and tossed it into the trash basket. "There! Good riddance to bad rubbish."

She giggled. "My grandmother used to say that."

At the door he turned back, a hint of a twinkle back in his eyes. "By the way, Jaime, who was I last time? I don't sound like Craig, whom Janie was married to. And I sure wasn't Marc! You've got Paul and Donnie accounted for, but I don't find me in there."

"I don't know. I suppose you could be a new super-hero type who swoops into our lives this time around to save us all."

"Dream on!" He chuckled as he went into the den to round up the boys.

She listened as all three pairs of footsteps sounded on the stairs. When she was sure they were out of sight, she fished the diary out from among the papers and other leftover debris. She looked around. Where to hide it? At last she decided that the original hiding place in the bookcase in the den was still the best place, and she replaced the diary behind the tomes nobody ever read.

Back in the kitchen, she emptied the trash into a black plastic bag, tied the ends tightly together, and took it out to the garage, where she deposited it along with other identical black bags in the silver metal cans.

She went back into the house and dug out sliced ham, peanut butter, and jelly and began to put together the picnic lunch.

"I'm sorry, Evan," she whispered as she cut the sandwiches into neat halves, "but I just can't throw it out."

Thirty-three

Ryan Barrett turned his truck onto Oak Street and headed for Jane-Michelle's house to drop off the tiles she had ordered for her kitchen. They were a special soft green shade that they didn't have in stock but was able to order for her. Jane-Michelle was one handy lady who could do some very clever things with her hands, and she was going to set the tiles above her kitchen counters herself.

As he rounded the corner, he saw Evan Reid, his wife, Jaime, and their two little boys getting into their dark blue SUV. The back was open, and folding chairs and blankets filled the back. Jaime hoisted a large picnic basket into the car and closed the trunk. *Odd.* He wondered where they were going; it looked like an all-day outing to him—and on a day when Evan should be working at the Board of Education and the boys should be in school. *What gives here? Why are they taking the day off?* Slowing down, he passed the Reids' car, tooted his horn at them, waved, and went on to pull into Jane-Michelle's driveway. He couldn't shake off the feeling that something had happened, something was very wrong.

~ * ~

"Oh, they're perfect," Jane-Michelle exclaimed as Ryan toted the boxes in and set them down on the kitchen floor. She picked up one of the tiles and examined it. "They'll really brighten this place up. I can't wait to get started."

"Glad you like 'em." Off-handedly, Ryan remarked, "Just passed the Reids' place. Looks like they're taking the day off."

"Oh, right." Willow held a tile up to the wall where she intended to put them. "One of the kids told me when I went out to get the paper that their dad was taking them to the zoo in Westfield. He was all excited about it." She looked at him, then averted her eyes. Ryan read the signals; there was something she *wasn't* saying.

"I bet. What kid wouldn't like a day off from school to go to the zoo?" Jane-Michelle was some four or five years older than he, but he had known her all his life. Maybe he could pry some information out of her. "How's your husband over there in Iraq?"

"It's tough. He won't get a furlough for another six months or so." She glanced at him, then as if making up her mind suddenly, she added, gesturing to a chair, "Do you have time for a cup of coffee, Ryan? There's something I'd like to talk to you about."

Aha! I thought so. "Sure thing." He smiled at her, inviting her confidence. "I'm the boss, remember? I can take all the time I want to." He sat in the chair she had indicated. He watched her movements as she set out coffee mugs, sugar, and half-and-half. She was pretty and graceful for a woman in her late forties, her soft brown hair not streaked with a trace of gray, her skin still fresh and wrinkle-free. She didn't resemble her mother as Willow was definitely *not* willowy and never had been. In fact, Willow, judging by her looks now, had probably been a much plainer girl than Jane-Michelle had been. Willow didn't even have the dark, almond-shaped eyes that gave Jane-Michelle's face a slightly foreign look.

Ryan had heard the stories; nobody knew for sure who Jane-Michelle's father was, and Willow would never say. He didn't even know if Jane-Michelle herself knew. However, having one of his perceptive hunches, he had pored over the senior class pictures in the Mill Pond fifty-one yearbook, and he knew had those almond-shaped eyes. Rob Brass, that's who.

She put two mugs of coffee on the table and pulled up a chair opposite him. "I got a really disturbing phone call from my mother yesterday."

Careful not to react, he added creamer from the pitcher on the table and raised the mug to his lips. He sipped the hot liquid. Why did he have this odd feeling that what she was going to say had something to do with him?

"Mom had lunch with Jaime Reid and Francesca Summers," Jane-Michelle said, pursing her lips. "I just feel I should tell someone about this. It's really got me upset."

He lifted an eyebrow, encouraging her to go on. There was something about her that really attracted him. However, she had a husband, even though he was not in evidence, and she didn't seem like the kind of chick who would fool around on her husband. And, if what he had heard in whispers almost all his life was true, she might be sort of a cousin to him.

Her next words went through him as if she had slapped him. "My mom said that Jaime found an old diary in her cellar when she cleaned it out. It was written by Kathy Kelly, who was killed in that class reunion in 1961."

"Jeez! Kathy Kelly? Are they sure?

"Oh, yeah. And Kathy had plenty to say about everybody, including my mother and your parents."

"Has anyone else seen this?" Ryan asked. "They should turn it over to the Historical Society or someone. They don't have a right to keep something like that to themselves. We all have a right to see it."

Jane-Michelle let out a long breath. "Apparently other people have seen it, Including Kate Knight, who was murdered last night."

"That reporter? What does she have to do with it?"

"This is so far out, I hesitate to tell you," Jane-Michelle said. "But, apparently, Jaime and Francesca think they're reincarnated classmates from that '61 reunion, and they've got a bunch of people agreeing with them, including Molly Snyder, Kate Knight, and the fashion gal at the Springfield paper, Suzanne something, and even Skye Weston is in on it, believe it or not!" Her coffee sat cooling, untasted.

Oh, I believe that all right. The psychic tangles I've had with Skye Weston over the years would fill a book. He said nothing, hoping she'd go on, and she did.

"Well, that's not the weirdest part. Or maybe it is. They are all convinced that they've been brought together in the life because a Columbine-type incident is going to happen in Mill Pond again— and they're supposed to stop it from happening."

So that's it! All those premonitions I've had—what I told Jaime at her cocktail party. It's all coming together.

"Do you think that has anything to do with those two murders?" She hadn't touched her coffee, but now she added cream and sugar and stirred it with a spoon. "This is such a quiet little town, and all at once we have two murders. One of them was a prominent person who was involved in all this reincarnation nonsense, and the other—"

"Worked for me." He drained his coffee and glanced over at the coffeemaker. He wanted to ask for a second cup, but he didn't want to interrupt her train of thought.

"So, do you see any connection? My mom also said Molly Snyder left her husband and moved into the vacant apartment over her shop with the kids. Doesn't Molly's husband work for you, too, and wasn't he the one who shot off the gun at the school board meeting?" Molly got up and refilled his mug.

So that's where Molly went! I bet Alden would like to know that. Ryan swigged the rest of his coffee and set the mug down as he stood up. He reached over and patted Jane-Michelle's hand. "I think you're making too much of this, honey. Alden's loud and obnoxious, but he's harmless. Just an angry guy because life hasn't gone his way."

"I hope you're right." She sighed. "I don't buy the reincarnation thing, but tempers have been short around here in the last few months, and now these horrible murders..."

"Since the new super, Evan Reid, got to town and started changing things."

"Yes." She got up and walked with him to the door. "I believe in education and keeping up with the times, but I hate to see this little town change and become a suburb of Springfield. And our taxes will soar to pay for it all. I have enough trouble keeping up, as it is."

"Don't we all." Ryan smiled back at her as he took hold of the doorknob. "If you need help with those tiles, Jane-Michelle, just give a call. I'll send someone out pronto."

"I will." She stood in the doorway of her pretty house as he climbed into his truck. He waved at her as he put the key in the ignition and backed out of the driveway. He wasn't going back to work though. If Jaime Reid had Kathy Kelly's diary, and if the Reids were away for the day, well, that gave him ample opportunity to look for it, didn't it?

~ * ~

Ryan left his truck in an unused lot several streets over with the rear and the license plate backed up against a large maple tree. Ryan walked back to the Reids' house. Jane-Michelle's house was on the

219

other side from which he approached, so even if she happened to be looking out a window, or out in the yard, she wouldn't see him. And the Smith house on the other side had been vacant for several months.

It didn't take long to jimmy the lock on the back door. They would never be able to tell, even if they examined it. He crossed the enclosed back porch, opened the kitchen door, which wasn't even locked, and went in. He squinted at the hot pink enameled table and chair set. Whew! Jaime Reid sure didn't have the decorating sense that Jane-Michelle had—although, as he looked around at the quaint wallpaper she had chosen, and her other improvements, he had to admit that effect was charming overall.

Now, where would Jaime hide a diary?

The cookbook shelf didn't yield the book he was searching for, and as he left the kitchen, *Easy Dinners in No Time At All* fell from the shelf and landed on the counter near the sink. Oh well, leave it. A book could fall off a shelf without his help. He went upstairs into the master bedroom. The Reids had added a large bathroom for themselves, and again, Jaime had made the place welcome and comfortable-looking. Well, he didn't have time to ruminate about her decorating. He searched through the two bureaus, being careful not to mess up her clothing. Nothing. A fancy old Victorian desk also hid no diary.

He went back downstairs and into the den. There was potential there. A floor-to-ceiling bookcase lined one wall, and a desk with drawers held a computer, a printer. A tall, green metal file cabinet stood in the corner. The room was small, just large enough for the leather sofa and two matching chairs, a coffee table, which was bare except for an empty Cheerios box, the desk, and a small table next to one of the chairs. A green and gold vase, which looked expensive or old, or both, sat on a side table and held a bouquet of flowers.

He went through the desk, drawer by drawer. Everything was neat and organized, and there was nothing that looked like an old diary. He looked around the room again.

"Aha!" He saw the perfect hiding place, just where he himself would hide a diary he didn't want anyone else looking at. He crossed the room to the bookcase and pried out one of the ponderous reference tomes he was sure nobody ever consulted—and there it was, a faded brown leather book. It had to be Kathy Kelly's diary, and as he leafed through it, he saw that it was. He shoved it into his jacket pocket and turned around to leave.

Damn! He had forgotten about that little table, and he bumped into it—gently, to be sure, but enough to topple that vase, which, naturally, fell on the floor, not the carpet, and smashed into a zillion pieces. Well, he couldn't take the time to clean that mess up; he kicked the pieces into the corner behind the table, grabbed a pillow from the sofa and wiped it over the water spill from the vase. Then, the liquid absorbed by the cushion, he placed the pillow over the broken vase and flowers as if one of the kids had carelessly tossed it there. With luck, Jaime wouldn't notice it for a while, and he would have been long gone from the house.

Thirty-four

Although her heart was broken into a thousand pieces and ached in a way she had never thought possible at the violent death of her friend and cousin, Kate, Skye had to go on with the work of the Commonwealth. She needed to drive to Boston to help put the finishing touches on a health-care bill, which would bear her name. Tomorrow she would get together with Kate's parents, her two sisters, and other relatives and assist with the funeral arrangements, which would be private, family only. In a few weeks there would be a more public memorial mass. And before all that, she wanted another glimpse at something Kathy had written in her diary, something about the malignant relationship between Sylvia and Forrest Brown.

Skye Weston always perused several newspapers while she drank her morning coffee. *The New York Times*, *The Washington Post*, and *The Wall Street Journal* gave her a fairly accurate overview of what was happening in the country and what people thought about it. Of course, she had the papers from Boston, Hartford, and Springfield, too. You had to be up on the local issues if you were in the state legislature and hoping to run for U.S. Congress in the next election. It was difficult, if not impossible, for her to concentrate, so distressed was she about Kate's murder. But she had to be up on events, national and local, no matter what else went on, and she had to make this trip to Boston to fill the legislature in on the goings-on in her district.

Flipping through an editorial about educational standards in America, at first she ignored the telltale prickling in her neck and shoulders that almost always preceded a psychic experience. But then—suddenly, there it was: Ryan Barrett's face, so like the yearbook pictures of his mother, Francie Nacca, fifty years ago. He resembled her in her facial features and coloring—except for his dark, flashing eyes. Francie's had been blue, but a bit turned up at the corners, as if she had an Asian ancestor hidden away in her lineage somewhere. And where had Skye seen those piercing, dark eyes before? She knew she had, but couldn't quite place them. One thing was for sure; they hadn't been inherited from Donnie Barrett.

His eyes met hers and held them, and reluctantly she laid the papers on the table. "What do you want?" She didn't pause to wonder at the strangeness of the moment. Ryan Barrett was no stranger to her, although she had never met him in person. Skye was five or six years older than the thirty-five- to forty-two-year-olds who made up those who had possibly reincarnated and returned to Mill Pond. She had left Mill Pond after high school, gone to college, settled in Springfield, and commuted to Boston as she needed to. She never met Ryan in any of her social circles, and she had never needed to buy lumber or fixtures for her home. She knew who he was, but their paths had never crossed, in person, that is.

"It's going to happen again, and you can't stop it." His lips formed the words, but nothing audible moved through the air.

Nevertheless, she heard them in her mind. "Then why are you telling me? Why don't you leave me alone?"

He raised his hand and showed her a book, a small, well-worn leather diary. "Because they hate you the most of all of them. " An ugly sneer crossed his face. "So above it all, so perfect. My father hated you the last time around, and he passed it on to me. We'll kill you again, and this time it will be much more painful, a very difficult death for you. It's coming, Skye. We're coming for you."

His face began to fade, as if washed from a dirty window, but his laugh lingered, sending chills up both arms and down her spine.

The vision gone, Skye got up and refilled her coffee mug. She sipped it, leaning against the kitchen counter and thinking. Had Kathy Kelly said anything in her diary about the relationship between Sylvia and Forrest Brown that might be helpful to her at this point? There was that bit about Forrest's invitation to ask Sylvia to the prom, and Sylvia's laughing him off as a joke. Was that what all the hatred was about, and if so, how could it have transferred itself into this incarnation? It didn't make sense, that Ryan, even if he were Forrest's son, should hate her for what went on fifty years ago. But then, she hadn't been the one ridiculed and insulted.

Skye wondered if Jaime had been sitting around waiting for the phone to ring, as she picked it up on the first ring. "Is it possible for me to come over and look at Kathy Kelly's diary again? There's something I need to check out."

"Oh, Skye, I am so sorry, so devastated about—"

"Please, Jaime, I know. I just need a quick peek at the diary, okay?"

"Oh, sure," Jaime replied. "I just got the kids off, and Evan's gone, so just give me a few minutes to shower and dress."

"It'll take me more than a few minutes to get there, so don't hurry. But I'll be driving to Boston from there, so it'll be a quick visit."

"Sure, I'll have it out and ready for you.

~ * ~

Jaime dashed upstairs and jumped into the shower. She appreciated how busy Skye's schedule must be, but hoped she would have time for a cup of coffee before her long drive on the Mass pike to Boston. She liked Skye personally and admired her professionally. Here was a woman who was making a name for herself in the world, and there were no limits on how far she might go.

Unless someone kills her, like last time, a voice said in her head. Jaime froze, her hairbrush in the air. What was that? *Who* was that? She glanced at the clock and flicked a dusting of powder across her face and dabbed on a hint of lip color. Content that she looked respectable, even for a Mill Pond housewife—she really had to see if there were any career opportunities in the area—she hurried downstairs and into the den. She pulled out the heavy historical tomes that hid the diary. The book was gone.

She stared at the empty space, unwilling to believe her eyes. Maybe it had fallen down behind the bookcase—? But, no, there was no space for it to fall through. Had Evan found it and disposed of it once and for all? Had the kids been fooling around and taken it?

She put her hand over her eyes, willing Skye not to come until she found the diary. She raked the small room with her eyes and found the pillow thrown in the corner. It wasn't that unusual; the boys often threw the pillows around and didn't put them back. She reached down for it. A few shards of glass covered a small section of the rug. She gave a gasp of dismay. Here was Grandma's antique vase in pieces and dead flowers in a soggy mess on the floor. She bit her lip. It had to have been Josh and Jack—just wait until she got hold of them when they got home from school

The doorbell rang. Jaime left the soggy mess where it was and went to meet Skye, dreading the news she had to tell her.

Skye looked ravishing in a black suit and a pink blouse that reminded Jaime of the magnolias that had graced the Reids' back yard in Atlanta. Her neat hair was twisted up behind her head in a sophisticated knot, and she looked every inch the career woman on the way up. When she removed her dark glasses, however, her eyes were red and swollen. The surge of envy Jaime had felt turned to sympathy. She had cried her own tears for Kate, so bright, so funny, so interesting.

"Skye, I'm so sorry—"

Skye waved her off. "We're all devastated. She was my best friend as well as my cousin. I'm on my way to Boston to try and explain some of the things that are going on around here."

"Time for coffee?" Jaime asked.

Skye indicated that she did have time and sat down at the kitchen table, while Jaime got down hand-made ceramic mugs from the cupboard and poured coffee for both of them.

"The diary's missing." Jaime sat opposite Skye and spread her hands in an apologetic gesture. "I don't know where it's gone, or who might have taken it, but I suspect my darling boys took it. I found a broken vase and dead flowers hidden under a pillow in the corner of the den."

Skye nodded, as if not at all surprised. "I think I know who has it."

Jaime felt her eyebrows shoot up. "You do? *Who?*"

"Ryan Barrett. I saw him in a vision. He showed me the book, after threatening to kill me, that is."

With a chill, Jaime remembered what the voice in her head had said. Hardly able to breathe, Jaime set her cup on the table. "Ryan has it? But that's impossible, Skye! He's never even been in this house except for bartending at the cocktail party we had, and we've looked at the diary many times since then."

"He showed it to me, and unfortunately, my visions have always been right on."

Jaime shook her head. "I'm sure it was my boys. They knocked the vase off the side table, shoved the whole mess into a corner, and threw a pillow over it."

Skye shook her head. "You can ask them about it when they come home, but I'm convinced Ryan has it. Has the whole family been out of the house recently?"

"Oh!" Jaime gasped. "Yesterday, as a matter of fact. We took the kids to the zoo for most of the day. And—" She clapped her hand over her mouth as she remembered. "A P & B lumber truck pulled in at Jane-Michelle's house next door. Somebody waved to us, but I was busy getting things in and out of the car, and I didn't pay much attention."

"Ryan, I just bet. Can you find that out for sure from Jane-Michelle?"

"I can try. She hasn't been the friendliest of neighbors."

"But the much bigger thing is,"—Skye reached for Jaime's hand—"is that we have to figure out who's behind all this. I feel that time is getting short. If they are banding together and plotting another massacre, we have to stop it. We *have* to!" She stood, her face etched with sadness. "Losing Kate was the worst thing that's ever happened in my life, by far. We need to stop this."

Jaime watched her slide into her black BMW, and she waved as the car glided away. She ached for Kate, too, and she was afraid for the rest of them, herself, Evan and the boys included. Who knew what these maniacs had in mind? The diary was the key to it all, she was sure of that, but now the diary was gone.

Thirty-five

The rock sailed through the window and sprayed glass everywhere. It hit Evan's desk, skittered across the surface, and banged against Evan's knee before it fell to the floor. Evan's yell of pain, along with the noise of the shattering glass, brought his secretary on the run.

"Oh my soul, Evan! What's happening here?" Courtney Gill's face looked almost as pale as the computer screen as she stood in the doorway, shaking, staring at Evan's torn pants and bleeding leg. "Do you need a doctor? Should I call 911?"

Evan got up from his chair with difficulty, groaning a little. "Call the cops. I'm not that hurt." He limped as fast as he could manage to the window. Courtney fled back to the front office as Evan peered through the unbroken panes and took care to avoid the jagged edges left in place. He saw no one in sight who might have thrown the rock. He hobbled back to his desk, bent and picked up the missile. It was a good-sized rock, about the size of a grapefruit with sharp sides. A good choice to shatter a window, and possibly do worse damage. There was a scrawled message written on it in black magic marker: *Get out of town while you can.*

His desk phone rang, and he picked it up.

"What the hell was that?"

"Oh, Dane." Evan took several deep breaths, trying to calm himself down. "You heard that from your end of the building? Someone threw a rock through my window. Courtney's calling the police." As he said that, he heard the sirens begin to whine in the distance. "There's a love note on it. It says 'get out of town while you can.'"

"Jeez! I'll be right there."

Several blue and silver police cars roared into the school yard at the same time the breathless school principal arrived at Evan's office. Teachers who were on break or hall duty crowded the outer office door and demanded to know what was going on. Evan heard the word 'bomb' mentioned, and one of the women screamed. The group of five or six teachers broke, running down the hall, opening classroom doors and yelling, "Get out! Get out! There's a bomb in the school!"

Evan raced after them as fast as his wounded leg would allow, yelling, "It's not a bomb—just a rock! Everyone stay calm. Follow the emergency procedures, everyone." But it was too late. Students poured from the classrooms, running every which way, trying to be first to get out of the school, the bigger ones trampling the smaller ones. It was a full-fledged riot, and it was all Evan could do to back his way into Courtney's office. Dane pleaded for order over the intercom, but he couldn't be heard over the screaming and shouting in the halls. Helpless to stop them, he and Dane watched the police try to corral the students, but there were too few of them and too many terrified students. They scattered in all directions toward their homes, even those who lived several miles out of town down toward the river.

"Call the radio and TV stations," Evan yelled. "Let them know the students left school on their own and are headed home." Dane nodded and signaled to Courtney to get them on the phone. Evan watched her trembling fingers raking through the phone book. She dialed and handed the phone to Dane, just as several red-faced policeman burst into the office.

"What the hell happened here? Did you find a bomb?" Seth Foster was the same tough cop who had interviewed them after Jack's accidental shooting. He stared at the shattered window. "Holy Sheeeet!"

Evan handed him the rock. "This is the weapon."

Seth's pockmarked face was hard as slate. The cop looked him in the eyes. "You know, Super, personally I think you're an okay guy, but this town hasn't been the same since you got here. Ever think of taking this advice?"

Evan rocked back on his feet as if he'd been struck. "Are you saying this is my fault?" He clenched his fists by his side and hoped his Irish street-fighting days would not overcome his good judgment at this time.

"Let's go down to my office," Dane urged. He took Evan by the arm and motioned the three cops to follow him. He turned to Courtney, who was still shaking. "Court, I need you to stay here and field the phone calls. Just tell them, if they ask, that there was no bomb, and the students are all on their way home." She nodded as he called back, "and let my wife and Mrs. Reid know what's happened."

"Al—all right," she said, but it was clear from her expression that she also wanted to flee the school. The phone began to ring even as she returned to her desk and threw Dane a terrified look as she reluctantly reached to answer it.

Seth settled himself on the worn denim sofa in Dane's office as if he had a right to the best seat in the house. The other two men brought in wooden chairs from the outer office, and seated themselves on them.

"Where's Mary?" Seth's question referred to Dane's matronly secretary, who had been there longer than anyone could remember.

Dane forced a non-amused grin. "She was on a break when all this happened. I assume she ran out with everyone else." His cell phone, and Evan's, began to trill at the same time.

Seth made a cutting gesture with his hand. "Don't answer them. Courtney's calling your wives, and everyone else can wait."

Evan had been about to suggest that they turn off their cell phones, but he wasn't about to take orders from this robo-cop. He fished his out of his pocket and pressed the 'talk' button as Seth glared at him.

Jaime sounded rattled and upset. She wanted him home, *now*. Was he okay, did the rock hit him, was he hurt, couldn't he come home? She was insistent; she wanted him to come home. If not now, how soon?

Evan took several minutes to placate her, relishing Seth's steely stare. When he was sure she would be all right, he promised to be home as soon as possible and asked her to call and reassure Francesca. He clicked the phone off and replaced it in his pocket.

Seth pretended a great show of courtesy. "If you're ready, maybe you'd like to tell us what happened. All of it, from the beginning." He clicked on a small tape recorder.

Chin in hand, Dane sat rigidly with his elbows on his desk. He cast an occasional worried glance at the windows and, after a few moments, got up and drew the heavy tan drapes across the panes.

"It's pretty cut and dried." Evan reiterated what had happened as he sat in his office working on the computer.

"And this is the rock." Seth gestured to the stone Evan had placed on Dane's desk.

"Obviously."

"Just getting it down for the record." Seth flicked a stony glance at the other two policemen who sat like rigid statues in the folding chairs along the wall. "Why don't you two go look for clues outside, footprints, anything the perp might have dropped and so forth." He made an impatient gesture, and the two stood up stiffly and left the office.

"By the way,"—the policeman took off his cap and scratched the side of his head—"don't you people have a lock-down system and an orderly system to evacuate the school in cases like this?"

"Of course we do!" Dane spoke up. "The problem is in those situations, the drills and all, are always done with people in place, someone to man the doors, a warning that a drill will be held sometime in the next few days—so everyone always knows it's a drill. This time, someone heard the word 'bomb', and everyone freaked out. Would you stay in a building if you thought a bomb was going off any second?"

"Not on your life. Now..." He looked from Evan to Dane and back to Evan. "Why would anybody do this, Dr. Reid? Who wants you gone?"

"Well, there has been some opposition to some of the programs I've instituted, and some of the ideas I've proposed for the future," Evan began.

"The usual malcontents." Dane rode his chair forward so that it landed on all fours with a thump. "There's always opposition to change. Evan's doing what's needed doing here for a long, long time."

"But some people don't like it." Seth persisted. "People like Alden Snyder, who fire off guns at a school board meeting."

"He's a frustrated man who's mad at the world, not me in particular," Evan replied. "He did his thing at the school board meeting, but we haven't heard anything from him since." He paused. "Actually... there has been an incident."

Seth looked up from his pad. "What kind of incident, Dr. Reid?"

"My wife, Jaime, was waiting for Francesca Summers outside Willow's shop, and Alden approached her—rather roughly, demanding to know where his wife and kids were, and left a bruise on her arm."

"Did you report this?"

"I wanted to, but Jaime asked me not to. She and Snyder's wife, Molly, are friends, and she didn't want to make things any more difficult for Molly."

The cop's dour face took an even more downward turn. "We'll pick him up and ask him some questions, but we can't do anything if your wife doesn't want to press charges."

Evan shook his head.

"We haven't had any threats specifically from Alden," Seth continued, "but I've heard the Bauer brothers aren't any too happy, and Ryan Barrett down at P & B Lumber has been heard to make some remarks. And we've had two murders within two weeks."

"Do you think they're connected to the discontent with the school situation?" Dane raised his eyebrows, as if the thought had never occurred to him before. "The guy who worked for the lumber company was a harmless loner, and Kate Knight—well, I don't see how she could be tied into this at all."

"She was tight with your wives, right?" Seth looked from one to the other.

"Jaime just met her a month or so ago," Evan protested. He turned to Dane. "How long has Francesca known her?"

Dane shrugged. "They went to school together, right here in Mill Pond, so actually, they've known each other all their lives."

"But were they tight?" Seth tapped the top of the tape recorder, as if willing an answer

Dane tapped his fingers on his desk. "If you mean, were they good friends, I'd have to say no, not until recently, when Francesca and Jaime and Kate seemed to be getting together more often. And Snyder's wife, Molly, too."

Seth's face flashed with sudden interest. "Snyder's wife, too? And she walked out on him, right, got a place over Willow's salon? Is there anyone else in their little group?"

"Skye Weston," Evan said after a moment. "I believe she is— was Kate Knight's cousin. She was with them a couple of times."

Seth sat back, a thoughtful look on his face. "She's from Mill Pond, too, originally. It's beginning to look to me as if there's a tie-in here."

Dane looked at his watch. "I have to get home, but I hope, Foster, that you're not blaming this on Evan and what he's trying to do for the three-town school system."

"I just said there seems to be a connection." The cop got to his feet and clapped his cap on his head. "It gives me a place to start. I'm going to pay a visit to Alden Snyder, and his boss, Ryan Barrett, down at P & B. Meanwhile," he said, "you might want to soft-pedal things a bit, Dr. Reid. Just 'til things settle down." Seth's cell phone began an instant trilling.

"Yep." He answered in his no-nonsense police voice. "Uh huh. When? What kind of damage is there? Okay, tell her I'll be right there." He shoved the phone into its place on his belt and turned back to Evan, his face like steel. "That was Grace Gray. Her shop was vandalized last night, rock through the front window, and some paintings smashed."

Evan stared at the cop, his heart sinking. He had a feeling he knew what Foster was going to say.

"The paintings were the ones your wife had in the shop for sale."

Evan watched him leave and turned to Dane, still sitting behind the desk. "What are we supposed to do? We've started all these new programs, which will be immensely beneficial to the kids and the community at large, and now we're being sabotaged by some kind of maniac who has a vendetta of some sort. How do we fight this?"

Dane picked up a pen and scribbled on his desk calendar, not meeting Evan's eyes. Finally he looked up, and Evan read the pain in his eyes.

"Evan, this is the last thing I ever thought I would ever say to you, but I think you that you have to give some thought to resigning your position. As long as you're here, things are bound to get worse."

Thirty-six

"You are *not* going to resign." Jaime faced her husband, her hands on her hips. "You wanted this job—you felt *called* here—how many times did you tell me that, and now you're going to let them run you out?"

"Right now, yes, I feel as though I should go. Dane thinks there will be more violence if I stay." He put his arms around her. "I'm so sorry about your paintings. You had some really good work in Grace's shop, some of your best watercolors."

"Well." She choked back a little laugh. "It's not as if I were famous and they were worth a lot. I can always re-do them, although I'd guess Grace won't be too eager to display them."

"We'll see. She knows it wasn't your fault."

"Any more than the other things that have happened are *your* fault. Evan, we have to stay. We—"

"Turn on the TV," he said, interrupting. "Have you heard what they're saying? It's all over the news, how angry the parents are about the non-bomb thing, the school board meetings that keep getting interrupted by the noisy minority, even how the two recent murders in town might be tied in. Evidently, it is all my fault."

She picked up the remote and pushed the 'on' button. The screen flared into life, and the face of local anchor, Ted Ferris, glared out at them. He looked more like a used-car salesman than a professional newsman, with his greasy hair and shifty eyes, wearing a shiny blue suit and a red, white, and blue striped tie, but there he was, and he was spouting off with a vengeance.

"And, furthermore, the people of the tri-school district cannot afford to put up with this arrogant out-of-towner superintendent of schools any longer. And *afford* is the crucial word here, folks. Our taxes will go through the roof to pay for Evan Reid's outrageous 'improvements'. Why the combined school boards ever decided to bring in such a liberal person who has no respect whatsoever for our local traditions and values, I will never know. As an added thought, I would suggest that Dane Summers, principal of Mill Pond Central School, who was most instrumental in bringing Evan Reid here, be asked to resign also. Let's take our town and our school system back. This is my commentary for today."

Jaime caught her breath. "Wow! They're not wasting any time, are they?"

"No, they're not." Evan broke off as a loud commotion began over their heads. "What's that?" He glared at the ceiling in irritation as the bumping, pounding, and yelling increased.

"Just our lovely children. You should spend all day with them sometime. I'll go up and see what they're up to now."

"And I'll write my letter of resignation." She heard Evan close the door to the den, as she left the room at a run.

~ * ~

"Stop that! Boys—stop that immediately." Jaime waded into the fracas and physically separated her sons. Josh had pulled out a clump of Jack's hair, and Jack had paid him back with a long, bloody scratch across Josh's cheek. Toys and games lay scattered all over the floor, and a smashed lamp lay on the floor in pieces.

She hauled them to their feet and held them at arms' length. "What is this all about? How could you do this to each other?"

Both boys continued sobbing, unable to control their rage long enough to answer her. Anger gave way to love, and she gathered them both in her arms together, hugging them tight. "Okay, let's go get you cleaned up in the bathroom, put some medicine on those war wounds, then we'll go downstairs. Daddy's upset, too, and I think we need to have a family meeting."

As she tended to the boys, Jaime was vaguely aware that the phone had begun to ring. The abrupt breaking-off of the ringing when Evan answered it was replaced by more ringing almost immediately when he hung up.

"Is that what I think it is?" she asked, as she led the subdued boys into the den.

"Oh yeah," Evan replied. "The Bauer brothers, some parents irate about the school thing, the newspaper. Evan Reid is the villain of the hour." He continued typing on the computer and did not look up at them.

"What's a villain?" Josh sank into the leather sofa.

"Somebody who does bad things, but that's not your dad, no matter what he or anyone else says."

"A bad guy, like the giant in *Jack and the Beanstalk* who ruins things for everyone else?"

Jaime tried not to laugh. "That would be a good example, but that's not your dad."

"'Lijah Snyder says he's a bad guy," Jack contributed. "His dad says we're all evil, and we're going to hell."

"If someone doesn't shoot Daddy first," Josh added.

Jaime gasped and felt as if she'd been struck. Pulling the boys with her, one by each hand, she sank down on the sofa. She noticed the phone resting off its hook and guessed that Evan had removed it.

The printer began to grumble, and a piece of paper slowly emerged from its jaws. Evan picked up his pen and scribbled something on it, then held it up for her to see. "My letter of resignation. I'll take it over to the chairman of the school board in the morning in person."

"Evan, I just can't let you do this."

He glanced at the boys. "Did you hear what Josh said?"

"Oh, you can't possibly think—"

"Yes, I can." Evan folded his arms and looked at her. "That's just not a risk I'm willing to take. The family comes first." He paused and looked harder at the boys. "What happened to them?"

"Fighting. They caused a little damage to each other, but I haven't found out what it's all about yet. I thought I'd bring them down and all four of us could discuss it."

"Good idea." Evan laid a stern look on his sons. "I haven't really liked the behavior I've been seeing lately, guys. We need to have a talk."

"And I need to ask you about the broken vase in the corner with the sofa pillow hiding everything." Jaime pointed to the mess that she had left as she found it.

The twins' heads swiveled in the direction she indicated, like identical weather vanes.

"We didn't do that," they said in unison.

Evan made an impatient gesture toward the boys. "Who did, then? For sure your mom or I didn't do it, and nobody else has been in this house."

Jaime sighed in resignation. "I'm not so sure about that."

Evan swiveled around and gazed at her in amazement. "What are you talking about, Jaime?"

Before she could formulate an answer, the doorbell rang. Jaime got up. "I'll go. Why don't you talk to the boys about their behavior, or lack of it?" She got up and closed the den door behind her as she left.

Jane-Michelle stood on the front porch, shivering a little in her thin sweater. May could be chilly in New England, as well as unseasonably warm. 'Wait five minutes and it'll change,' the natives said.

"Oh, do come in," Jaime urged. "Would you like something hot, coffee or tea?"

"No, thanks," Jane-Michelle said. "I just need to tell you something, then I'll go."

Something in her expression warned Jaime not to interrupt her further. She waited for Jane-Michelle to continue.

"I'm at war with my conscience. On one hand, I'm about to betray an old friend. On the other, I can't just ignore what I saw."

"Okay." Jaime tried for a non-judgmental tone of voice.

"Yesterday, Ryan Barrett delivered some tiles to me, and we sat and talked for a while. I've known him forever. His folks were in the same high school class with—uh, my uncle Forrest."

"Yes, we saw his truck in your driveway, just as we pulled out to take the kids to the zoo." Jaime wondered where this was going.

"I'm afraid I let it slip to Ryan that you had Kathy Kelly's diary, and that you and Francesca and some others have this reincarnation thing going on..." She stopped and bit her lip. "I'm so sorry, Jaime. I should never have told him, but I didn't think he'd do anything about it."

Jaime didn't understand. "That's no big deal, Jane-Michelle. He told me he had some of the same reincarnation thoughts when he bartended at my cocktail party, months ago."

"He showed a lot of interest in the diary," Jane-Michelle said, "and I sort of regretted telling him about it, but he got in his truck and drove off, and I thought that was the end of it."

"But—it wasn't?" Suddenly she knew what Jane-Michelle was trying to tell her, knew who had broken the vase and hidden it with the pillow, and where the diary had gone. "Did you see him break in here?"

"There's only one spot in my house where I can see your back door and a bit of the back yard," Jane-Michelle said. She gestured toward the porch and the back door. "There's a small bedroom on the third floor that has a window facing that direction. It must have been fate; I went up there to look for a jacket I had stored in that closet, and I saw some movement over here. I looked out and it was Ryan. I watched him jimmy the lock, go in, and in less than ten minutes he was out again."

"Oh, damn it all!" Jaime breathed, covering her mouth. "Ryan has the diary."

"That's it." Jane-Michelle turned toward the door. "I had to let you know, and I did. I just don't want to get mixed up in this whole thing."

Before Jaime could thank her, she was gone, running across the lawn to her own house next door.

Watching her go, Jaime didn't hear Evan come up behind her. She jumped when he put his hands on her shoulders. "What was that all about?"

She turned slowly to face him and let out a deep breath. "Evan, we need to sit down and talk. There's something I have to tell you, and you're not going to like it."

He sighed. "It seems like there's a lot of that going around lately, Jaime."

Thirty-seven

There was no opportunity to talk until the twins were tucked into bed. Her husband had done a good job of laying down the law to the twins, and, chastened, they watched TV for a while after dinner, which was an unusually quiet affair and went to bed when it was suggested, without any fuss at all.

Evan poured a glass of wine for her and himself, and they went into the den and sat down. Jaime wished this were going to be just an ordinary pleasant evening, the kind they used to enjoy in Atlanta, but those days were gone for good. When she didn't say anything, Evan took the initiative. "Something to do with Jane-Michelle?"

"Yes. How did you know?"

"Well, she didn't stay long, didn't bring a casserole, so I thought she just came over to tell you something, which she did, and left. Am I right?"

"You are, Sherlock," She tried to portray a lightness she did not feel.

"So tell me what it is, Watson. It can't be that important."

She told him how she had dug Kathy Kelly's diary out of the trash after he had assumed she threw it away, how she had hidden it back in the bookcase.

He looked puzzled. "No big deal. We'll light a fire in the fireplace and burn it this time. But—what does Jane-Michelle have to do with that?"

"After we left with the kids yesterday, Ryan Barrett broke in here through our back door. Jane-Michelle saw him from third floor window and felt she had to tell me. She knew I had the diary, and she told Ryan that I did." She pointed to where the pillow had been in the corner. "*He* was the one who did that, probably backed up into the table while searching the bookcase."

Evan downed his wine in one gulp, set the glass down on the coffee table, and swore, something he rarely did. "That damned diary is causing more trouble around here—" He got up without looking at her. Evan went to the buffet in the dining room that held their hard liquor supply, then into the kitchen and got ice from the dispenser on the refrigerator. He came back with a tall glass of amber liquid, mostly rye or scotch, she guessed, and not too much soda.

He sat down opposite her, and his face wore a hard expression, one Jaime rarely saw on her husband's face.

"This reincarnation nonsense has got to stop. Meeting with these other women, one of whom has just been murdered by someone else who undoubtedly believes in this handed-down curse from the class of '51, has got to stop."

She couldn't believe her ears. "You can't tell me—"

He held up a hand. "Listen to me, Jaime. It's all over town what you and Francesca have been saying. I don't know if it's Willow who's spreading it around, or Jane-Michelle, or who, but the ridicule isn't helping matters here. It's making everything worse."

"How? How can it make it worse? We're just trying to alert people to the fact that the antagonistic conditions, as they are now, might very well lead to the same thing, or something like it, happening again."

"Yes, that's just it. The good people who think that will work to make sure it doesn't, but it also encourages those nut-cases out there who are so against what I'm trying to do to act in their own interests, also. In their minds, it justifies what they want to happen."

"Evan, that's the *last* thing we want to happen! If Kate Knight was the reincarnation of Kathy Kelly, and I was Janie Carlson, and Francesca was Francie—"

"Oh, for God's sake!" He exploded. "That is such a load of hogwash. How can a woman as talented and intelligent as you are believe that?"

"Evidently Kathy's diary didn't convince you. But it convinced me, and Francesca, and Kate, even Molly is on board now. Skye Weston has psychic encounters of her own. Ryan has actually *threatened* her..."

He snorted and shook his head. "I'm going to bed. Maybe in the morning I can talk some sense into you. I'm too exhausted to continue right now."

"Just listen for a second," she pleaded as he got up and started for the door. He turned and looked at her, his impatience obvious.

She forged ahead. "The first time I saw Dane across the school cafeteria, I *knew* that I had known him before. *He* admitted to the same feelings, and he got really strange vibes from that old necklace I found and wore at our cocktail party."

"Doesn't mean anything." Evan responded curtly. "We've been through all this before."

"And Ryan Barrett. He bartended for our party, and he told me that night that he had dreamed about our coming here. He and Skye have a sort of psychic connection that—"

"Jaime." His tone was flat and remained flat. "Sometimes I think you are actually trying to sabotage me so we have to move somewhere else—back to Atlanta, maybe? Either that, or you badly need to get a job again and get your over-active imagination working on something real." He turned and walked away, not giving her a chance to reply.

Jaime stared after him in disbelief. Never had he walked out on a discussion with her—never. She drained her wine, picked up the bottle, and poured herself another glass, this one full to the brim. After a few sips she got up and began to wander about the house, touching the pink enamel table, the backs of the chairs, the fireplace mantel, the smooth brocade of the living room sofa. She found herself at the window, pushing aside the sheer beige curtains that replaced the original heavy green draperies. She gazed out across the lawn, across the street at the other turn-of-the-century houses. Jane-Michelle's pretty house gleamed in the light from the faint half-moon. The old-fashioned streetlights highlighted the trees branches, which were only partially garbed with fresh new leaves

She lost track of time as she stood there, looking out at a setting so picturesque it might have been part of a Hollywood set. Her wine glass was empty, but as she stood there, staring at the scene outside, lost in her thoughts, new feelings rose to the surface. *I love it here, I belong here, I'm home.*

How could Evan possibly think she wanted to go back to Atlanta? She was home at last. She sighed. Evan was right. She had to cool it with the reincarnation stuff. It was beginning to affect their marriage, and she wouldn't let anything do that, if she could help it. She'd call Francesca tomorrow, and tell her... tell her what?

Just that she couldn't do this anymore. It was time to back off and give one hundred percent of her support to her embattled husband.

She glanced at her watch as the phone suddenly jarred her back to full consciousness. Ten forty-five. Who would be calling this late?

"Is this little Janie Carlson, back to the scene of the crime?" the muffled voice asked.

Jaime couldn't answer.

"The same fate is coming back for you, little Janie. And you're going to lose this husband, too, and you're going to lose Donnie, the guy you couldn't have and never got over... all over again."

The line went dead.

Thirty-eight

"Mom, Dad! There are trucks and people with cameras 'n everything outside!"

Jaime startled awake and sat up as the boys bounced on the bed like puppies.

"What is it?" Evan woke to consciousness more slowly than she had. He sat up and rubbed his eyes.

Jaime jumped out of bed and ran to the window. Sure enough, a large white van bearing the letters WWLP of the local Springfield channel was parked in front of the house. While she gaped at the sight of reporters and cameramen trampling the lawn, a van from a Hartford station, WDSB, drove up, parked behind the other van, and the crew began to pile out, hauling their equipment with them.

Evan joined her at the window, his sleepiness gone. "What the— ? What are they doing down there?"

Jack and Josh had already vanished, and Jaime flew down the stairs after them, catching them just before they managed to wrench the front door open. "Wait! We don't know what's happened out there. Let's let Daddy go check."

She glanced around as Evan, wearing jeans and a sweatshirt, ran past them toward the kitchen. "I'll go around the side." He unlocked the back door and slipped out onto the porch. She heard him run down the step; then his footsteps were muted by the grass. After a moment a commotion broke out on the lawn, and she heard voices shouting.

"Mr. Reid!"

"Evan Reid! Who would do this to you?"

"Do you know who did this?"

"Who's behind this, Dr. Reid?"

"Will you resign now, Mr. Reid?"

Jaime opened the door a crack and looked out. Evan stood, staring at their house, an expression of disgust and disbelief on his face. Several reporters stuck their mikes in his face, and several cameramen aimed their bland black boxes at him.

"Who did what?" Josh tried to force the door open wider so that he could see outside.

One of the cameras swung around toward her, and she pulled Josh back against her and shut the door.

"We'll wait and find out when Daddy comes back inside." She put her hands on their shoulders and turned both boys toward the staircase. "Go upstairs and get dressed, and I'll start breakfast."

They went, inching like snails toward the stairs, and she cracked the door open again, hoping she could get an idea of what was going on in their yard. Cars began to turn the corner and drive down their street. Slowing to a crawl, they drove past the house. Eyes stared, fingers pointed. A few horns beeped. The noise drowned out whatever Evan was telling the reporters. She watched the activity through the crack for a few more minutes. Evan waved a gesture of dismissal, turned his back and headed for the door, the front one this time.

:What is it?" She opened it wide enough to admit him and shut it behind him.

"They spray-painted our house." Jaime caught his tired-to-the-bone tone as he dropped into one of the. chairs. *Screw Reid,* and some assorted profanities that I wouldn't want the boys to see."

"Oh, God!" She gasped, covering her mouth. "Just when we thought it couldn't get worse—"

"I'll call Ryan Barrett and have him send a couple of guys to paint over everything. Try to keep the boys inside, at least until the reporters leave."

"Yeah, good luck with that." Jaime pulled the kitchen curtain aside and peeked out. "Looks like they got what they came for. They seem to be pulling up stakes."

"Good. I'll call Ryan, then Dane and Mack Blake to call an emergency meeting of the school boards. I'll tender my resignation, effective immediately." He looked around, a puzzled look on his face. "Why isn't the phone ringing off the hook?"

"I disconnected it," Jaime said. She blew out a long breath. "Obviously everyone in the universe would be calling. I didn't feel we needed that, added to everything else going on."

"Of course not. By the way, it's awfully quiet upstairs." Evan gestured with his chin. "Where are the boys?"

Jaime, alarmed, went to the foot of the staircase and called up, "Jack! Josh! What are you two up to?" When there was no answer, she went back into the kitchen, to find the kitchen door wide open and Evan not there. She looked around, puzzled, but the next instant Evan reappeared, leading a grinning boy by each hand.

"They're still wearing their pajamas. What were they doing out there?"

"Reading all the words I didn't want them to see," Evan replied, releasing their hands. "How they got out there without our seeing them, I still haven't found out."

"Well, I wouldn't worry about the words." Jaime smiled down at the boys. "They're only in kindergarten. They can't read yet."

"We can read *those* words," Josh piped up. "Elijah Snyder showed us what they looked like."

"Swell," Evan muttered. "By the way, guys, how did you get outside?"

The boys looked at each other. Josh shrugged, followed by a shrug by Jack.

"Tell us," Jaime insisted, "or there'll be no TV all day, and that includes your video games."

Jack squinted at her. "What will we do, then?" He looked at Jaime as if he were deciding what to say.

Evan folded his arms and regarded his sons. "I'm sure you can learn to use a paint brush and paint out some of those words Elijah taught you."

The boys exchanged glances. Jaime could tell they were weighing their options. After a moment, Jack, with an impish look on this face, told them, "We went out the window, onto the porch roof."

Getting in on the excitement, Josh got into the act now that they were sharing their secret. "And the big tree has a really big branch that you can crawl over, and then climb down the tree." His grin spread as wide as his outspread arms. "It's easy!"

"And you've done this before?" Jaime could tell that Evan was not amused.

They nodded enthusiastically.

"Guess I'll have to nail that window shut," Jaime told them. She tried to sound severe. She *was* amused at their daring and creativity, but there was no way she was going to let them know it. "That's not a safe thing to be doing, boys."

Over their protests, Evan said, "I'll call a tree surgeon and have that branch cut off. That'll solve that problem."

Jaime nodded and pointed the boys toward the stairs. "You two go up there, get dressed and come back down for breakfast. They headed upstairs toward their bedroom. "And use the stairs!"

Left alone, Jaime and Evan exchanged glances, and Jaime allowed herself a soft laugh. "Boys will be boys, but that's a dangerous trick."

"I did worse things and survived." He put his arms around her and nuzzled her neck. "But don't you wish all our problems could be so easily solved by just cutting a branch off a tree?"

Thirty-nine

A team of painters from P & B Lumber arrived within the hour and set to work painting over the offending messages on the front of the house. The boys, dressed and breakfasted, ran outside to watch and cheer the painters on.

Jaime reactivated the phone, and it began to ring immediately. Most of the messages, including the one from Jane-Michelle next door, were outraged at what had been done to their house and supportive of Evan.

Francesca, however, was more than just outraged—she was livid. "I cannot believe they would stoop to that." Her voice echoed the anger she felt. "Dane is just apoplectic about it. He said this has changed his mind about Evan's resigning, that now he's ready to fight for him to stay, that he's not giving into any neighborhood terrorists."

Jaime sighed. "He's made up his mind to resign. He wrote the letter and took it with him over to the Board of Education."

"Listen, Jaime," Francesca went on, "we all need to get together again. I know it's not the best time, but Skye called me from Boston. She's on her way back here and wanted us to meet for lunch, as many of us can make it."

Jaime thought about the decision she had made the previous evening. However, that had been before the spray-painting and the new rising support for Evan. It couldn't possibly hurt to hear what Skye had to say. After that, she'd ease off, she really would. Pulled in two directions, Jaime bit her lip. Should she, or shouldn't she?

Francesca pushed into her silence. "I know it's short notice, Jaime, but I think it's important to talk about what to do now that Ryan has Kathy's diary, and Skye said she had another one of those psychic episodes with him."

"Oh, Jeez! What about the kids—"

"I'll get a couple of high school girls to watch them all. I'll call Molly and see if she's available, too. Come over as soon as you can, Jaime, please."

Jaime didn't know whether Francesca sounded more upset about the possibility of Evan's being fired, or what Skye had told her. She took a final swig of her coffee, and then—overcome by a nausea that was suddenly very familiar to her—she dashed for the downstairs bathroom. Brushing her teeth afterwards, she counted back to when her last period had been. She put her hands on her stomach and smiled to herself. It might not be the optimum time, but babies came when they came. They didn't make appointments.

She shrugged into a dark red coarse-knit sweater, perfect for a cool spring day. She rounded up her sons and handed them light poplin jackets. They reluctantly put them on, making exaggerated faces of protest all the while.

Those poor high school girls. They have no idea what they're in for, with these two, and Elijah, and Francesca's boys. I'll have to get them in line before the next one comes along.

~ * ~

Skye's BMW already graced the Summers' driveway. Jaime pulled in behind it, and before she could unfasten her seat belt and get out of the car, her boys had already bolted and raced for the house.

Francesca and Skye sat at the kitchen table, Skye looking as pale and unsettled as it was probably possible for her to appear. The boys disappeared into the nether regions of the boys' bedrooms upstairs.

"You're going to want to hear what Skye has to say, but let's wait for Molly. She's on her way." Francesca poured coffee for all of them, in her easy hostess way.

Molly didn't waste any time and soon joined the others at the table. Her little girl, Rebecca, refused to play with the group of noisy boys, clung to her mother, and with wide gray eyes, stared at the grown-ups. She looked a little healthier since Molly had left Alden and the abusive home atmosphere they had all endured, but she was still a shy, scared child.

Francesca got a coloring book and crayons and persuaded Rebecca to sit at a small table in the corner of the kitchen. After a few moments she seemed content there and began humming to herself as she colored a picture. The four women relaxed.

Skye leaned over toward Molly. "I wouldn't want her to hear what I'm going to tell you. She's a precious little thing, and even though she probably wouldn't understand what I was talking about, I wouldn't want to scare her."

Molly nodded. "Thank you. She's in her own little world now. She won't hear a word."

Skye interlaced her fingers, separated them, and rubbed her hands together. "I had another—communication—with Ryan."

"He has Kathy's diary," Jaime told Molly, unsure if she had heard that or not. "He broke into our house while we were away and stole it. Jane-Michelle saw him from a third-floor window that overlooks our back yard."

Molly looked shocked, but then she shrugged. "Well, what good will that do him? He grew up in this town; he must have heard everything there is to hear."

"He could find out he's Francie and Forrest's son, not Francie and Donnie's," Francesca answered. "I think Kathy makes that pretty clear, although I'm sure he's heard the gossip over the years."

"And nobody may have said that to him in so many words." Jaime looked around, checking the other women's reactions.

Skye nodded. "Which makes him Jane-Michelle's half-brother." She sighed. "So many secrets in this one little town. I know we all feel we had to come back here to clean things up once and for all, but this may be a bigger job than we can handle."

Francesca's face took on the determined look that Jaime knew so well. "We have to try. Tell us about your vision."

"I woke up about three in the morning," Skye began.

"In a hotel?" Molly asked.

Skye looked at Molly for a long moment before answering. "No, I have a small apartment I rent there. It's very tiny. Sometimes it's almost claustrophobic. Anyway, I woke up a little before three, and—oh, it's so hard to explain this to people."

"Just say it," Francesca urged.

"It looked as if Ryan were hanging in the air over my bed—just part of him, hovering in a gray mist of sorts."

Molly gasped. "I would have screamed."

"I did, but then he laughed, the bastard. He said—well, not in so many words, but I heard it as if it *had* been words—he said 'this is the last time we will see each other this way. In another week you and your busybody friends will all be dead—*again*. And you can thank Kathy Kelly for it—once again. What goes around comes around'."

"That's an odd thing for him to say." Francesca wrinkled her forehead. "Whatever could he mean by that?"

Skye shook her head. "That's what we have to figure out, and that's why I'm worried that he has the diary. It must have something to do with Kathy or something she wrote in it."

"What could that possibly be?" Jaime spread her hands and glanced at Francesca, who shook her head.

Skye lowered her head pressed her palms against her eyes. "You two have read it cover to cover and are most familiar with it, I was hoping something would remember something that would jump out at you."

"Mommy, look at my picture," Rebecca demanded, appearing at Molly's side. She put the book on the table for her mother to see, then hid her face in her mother's lap as everyone praised her coloring.

"How about taking a doughnut and a glass of milk back and coloring another one?" Francesca got up to pour the milk, then carried it and the pastry over to the small table. Rebecca skipped behind her and settled down happily in her corner again.

"Well?" Skye prodded, looking at Jaime.

"Nothing specific. Just the whole thing about how much Forrest and Balls hated The Nine, that the hatred has an evil life of its own. It still has power, and the obsession to do it again."

"One thing is for sure," Francesca said. "We have to get our men on our side on this. We can't do whatever it is we have to do alone."

"Well, we won't get Alden..." Molly began, then turned bright red and began to tremble. "Oh, my God! Alden! You don't think he's involved in this in any way, do you?"

"We don't know, Molly." Jaime reached over to take her hand. She was glad she had never told Molly that he had roughed her up outside Willow's shop that day. And that *was* the same day that Kate Knight had been murdered.

Francesca hastened to reassure Molly. "Let's not jump to conclusions, Molly. We don't know who's responsible for the two murders in town, and we don't know who, if anyone, is involved in making plans to bring on another massacre. We just don't know." She looked stricken and glanced at Skye apologetically. "I'm sorry, Skye—that was insensitive."

"Kate was my cousin and my best friend. If she was Kathy and I was Sylvia—well, there's a bond there we made in this life that death will never shatter."

Jaime nodded. "I believe that. I believe we all have a bond that we knew before and will probably know again."

"And there's Ryan," Skye added. "Everyone in town thinks he's the upright young businessman, but I have had these visions and threats from him for years—and if he finds out that he's Forrest's son and has all that bad blood in him—"

"He's probably already read the diary." Jaime pursed her lips and shook her head. "Getting it back is not only *not* an option, but the damage, if any, has already been done. What we need to do now is figure out when and where the next massacre could take place, and how it would tie in with Kathy."

"Things are coming to a head." Everyone turned to Francesca when she spoke. "There'll be a big, open-to-the-public Board of Education meeting, probably next week, to hear what the townspeople have to say, and then take a vote on whether Evan goes or stays. I'm so sorry, Jaime."

Jaime felt tears burn her eyes but willed them back. "This is even affecting the relationship between Evan and me, but I feel so strongly that we have to do everything we can. Let's try again to get Dane and Evan to listen to us and to make sure any public meeting is well-protected."

"And meanwhile, keep our eyes and ears open." Skye stood up and smoothed down her skirt with a weary gesture. "I don't think I'll be hearing from Ryan again."

"You *could* try contacting him." Molly sounded hesitant, as if she thought no one would take her suggestion seriously. "Try to goad him into telling you what the connection is with Kathy Kelly."

Skye nodded. "If I have any emotional energy left after the next thing I have to do, which I am dreading with all my heart, I'll try. It takes a lot of out me to do that, and I already feel so drained."

Jaime sensed that nobody wanted to ask outright what the next thing was, but Skye told them anyway. "I have to meet with the newspaper staff and the priests of St. Mark's and help plan a memorial mass for Kate in early June. Let's meet again—tomorrow, maybe, when we know what happened at the Board of Ed meeting. In the meantime, I'll—"

Jaime reached out to steady her, as Skye suddenly seemed to lose her balance and wilted into the chair she had just vacated. "Oh, heaven help us! That's it—isn't it! The place and the tie-in with Kathy—or Kate. It's Kate's memorial service."

Forty

Ryan Barrett spied Alden Snyder coming up the walk toward his office and shoved the diary into his top desk drawer. Alden opened the door without knocking and walked in. He pulled a chair up to Ryan's desk and tossed his baseball cap onto another chair. His hair, Ryan noticed with disgust, looked even dirtier and more disheveled than usual. He swallowed his annoyance at being interrupted. This guy was annoying to the extreme and had no qualities that Ryan liked—but he might be useful to him in the end. Alden was just the kind of amoral malcontent he needed for the final showdown.

"Hi there, Al. What's up?"

"Just taking a break, Boss, if that's okay with you. I got that latest load of oak into the warehouse, and Jake and Bill are setting up a display in the shop."

"That's great. Everyone deserves a break when they need it. How're things with you? Any word on the wife and kids?"

"Oh, I know where they are, all right. They're holed up in a flat over Willow's hair place." He sniffed and wiped his nose with a finger. "I ain't seen them, though. That bitch Willow, and that bigger bitch, Jaime Reid, won't let anybody near her."

Feed on his discontent. "That's a rotten thing for them to do, Al. Can't you get a lawyer and go to court about it? I'll be glad to set you up with an attorney."

Alden spat on the floor. "No use doing that, Boss. These people all have the powers on their side. You know that. They think they're so much better than everyone else, like that Evan Reid and his fancy new ideas, and everyone else just goes along without thinking a twit—"

Ryan softened his tone. "What would you like to do about it?" The man disgusted him, but he was ready to be molded into his plans.

Alden rocked back in his chair and lifted the front legs off the floor. He nearly lost his balance, but caught himself at the last moment. "Whoa! Nearly lost it there." His face took on a crafty expression. "I thought that maybe a the next Board of Education meeting, I'd do a little more than fire a gun into the ceiling."

Ryan caught his questioning glance and nodded. "What might you do?"

"I just might shoot *somebody* for real this time."

"Like who, for instance?"

"Like that effin Evan Reid, for example. Or his interfering wife. Or both of them." He was shaking with fury, Ryan noted with glee. *Just egg him on. Get him worked up. He's almost there.*

The hatred on Alden's face was like a perverted portrait of a man. "Do you hate them all so much?" Ryan prodded.

"You better believe I do. Well, look—that whore Kate Knight got what was coming to her, didn't she, poking her nose into everyone else's beeswax."

"Ah, yes," Ryan agreed. "So you'd like to off the Reids, and who else?"

"Wouldn't mind getting rid of that faggy principle, Summers, and his too-fancy-for-words wife of his, either. I didn't like some of what my boy was learning, even in kindergarten, and I for sure didn't want him hanging out with the Reid kids."

Ryan thought quickly. Instead of asking him what Elijah was learning that Alden objected to, he decided to feed the fire with an example of his own. He tossed Alden a conspiratorial wink as he opened his desk drawer and pulled out a couple of joints. "Yeah, I know what you mean. Ashley and Kayla come home talking about the *contributions* black people have made to this country." He twisted his face into a sneer. "And the teacher is trying to get everyone involved in all this save-the-planet crap." He held one of the cigarettes out to Alden and took his own time to light his own first.

Alden's eyes widened, and he grinned with pleasure as he accepted one and held it out to Ryan's lighter. "Hey, Boss! I'll have to take a break with you more often!"

"Anytime." Ryan took a puff and inhaled deeply. He leaned across his desk toward Alden. "Al, if you really hate those people so much and are committed to doing something about it, I can provide you with a lot more than pot."

For the first time Alden looked doubtful, and a guarded look crossed his face.

"What do you mean? I don't wanna go to jail or nothing." He laughed. "Been there, done that."

Ryan chuckled. "Well, how did you expect to shoot a bunch of people at the board meeting and not get arrested? I have a much better plan." He examined the cigarette between his fingers as if he had never seen it before.

"What?"

Ryan kept silent and stared out the small office window, as if in thought.

"What?" Alden asked again, in a harsher tone. He puffed on the joint. "What have you got in mind?"

"Kate Knight's memorial service will be at two o'clock Saturday afternoon," Ryan made himself sound as if he were musing over possibilities. "Everyone we hate will be there."

"We?" Alden's jaw dropped. "You-you mean, you hate them, too?"

"Hell, yes. I just gave you two examples why. I don't want my girls going off to one of those fancy colleges—Smith or someplace where they learn to look down on all the rest of us. I want things back the way they were, before Evan Reid." He crossed his fingers under his desk, although he didn't believe lies would bring him bad luck. "I want Ashley and Kayla to stay right here in Mill Pond, marry a farmer or a drug store owner, maybe, have kids, and just live ordinary lives. Hey! Joe Palmer's boy is good enough for my girls, and me, too. What's out there is too dangerous for anyone with any brains in their heads. Just stay home and be content, that's my take on it all."

The grin on Alden's face widened, as he listened to Ryan's speech with obvious admiration.

"Well..." Ryan stubbed out the joint and threw the butt into the wastebasket. *The jerk bought it, hook and sinker.* "Let's say we go to the Memorial Mass to pay our respects to Kate. They'll have a luncheon afterwards, someplace nice in Springfield or the outskirts." He began to laugh.

"What? What's so funny?"

"I just had a brilliant idea. The Lakeside Inn, here in Mill Pond," Ryan said. "Is that name familiar to you?"

"That fancy place out by the lake? I've never been there. I tend to go to that bar in town if I'm eating out—"

Ryan didn't try to hide a satisfied smile. "That's the place where the sixty-one massacre took place. If we could get them to have the luncheon there..."

Alden still looked confused. Slowly, he ground out his cigarette butt in the ashtray on Ryan's desk and sat back.

Ryan spread his hands to show Alden how obvious it all was. "Hell, I went to school with Father Murphy, the priest at St. Mark's where Kate's service is going to be held. I'll call him and offer to pay for the luncheon, anonymously, of course, in honor of Kate's memory. She's a Mill Pond girl. It's only right that the luncheon be out here."

"I don't know," Alden protested. "I wouldn't feel right in a place like that, and Molly will be there, I expect."

"Oh, right. You wouldn't want Molly hurt. You're going to come out of this with half a million dollars, and you could get her back, easy. Women and money, you know how that goes.'"

"Half a mil? I am?"

"Oh, yeah, Al. That's how I'm going to reward you for helping me pull this off—or am I helping *you* pull this off?"

"*You're* helping *me*." Alden grinned, sat back, and asked, "But what are we going to do, and how will we get away without being nabbed for it?"

Ryan winked. "You just leave that to me. I'll make sure Molly's safe, and I'll provide believable alibis for you and me. When it's all over, the people we hate will be dead, you and I will walk away scot-free, and you'll be a rich man with Molly and your kids back with you."

"Okay!" Alden extended his hand to Ryan over the desk. "You work it all out, and I'm in, one hundred and fifty percent. Now, I guess I better get back to work."

"Good idea, partner." Ryan showed him out with a smile.

Left alone in his office, he began to laugh. Everything was falling into place, and working out so well. He thumbed through the phone directory looking for the number of St. Mark's Catholic Church. He dialed the number, and his old high school friend, Patrick Joseph Murphy, answered. That taken care of, he took the diary from the drawer and resumed reading.

I took a baby present over to Francie. Whoo-hoo! That's Forrest's brat, I'd bet my life on it. He looks like Jane-Michelle did when he was a baby—same dark eyes, round face, and tufts of sandy hair. They named him Ryan Donald. I wanted to suggest they name him Ryan Forrest, but that would have just been too cruel, wouldn't it? I almost said it when Donnie left the room to get us some sodas, but I checked myself at the last moment. I don't mind hurting Francie, but I might need her some day. The more people who owe me favors, the better for me. I'm going to write that book some day. Peyton Place is nothing compared to this town!

I did go downtown to Willow's to get a frosting, though. I can't believe I already have a little gray showing through, so early, just like my mother. I mentioned baby Ryan to her and how I thought he looked at lot like Jane-Michelle had. She sort of laughed it off and said, "Oh, all babies look alike."

I let myself smile a little knowing smile and let it go.

My eyes lit on the stupid watercolor Janie did of her house—like that's any castle, or anything—that she threw away in art class that Forrest dug out to give to Willow, knowing about her hopeless crush on Janie. Everyone in school—everyone in Mill Pond—knew about that crush—and it took a long time before she could go anywhere without people snickering at her, or asking her some supposedly innocent question about Janie. I was surprised Willow didn't move out of town after Janie went to college and never came back—especially after her parents moved away, but Willow just had the baby, named it after Jane-Michelle, opened her shop, and just kept on keeping on. I have to give her credit. She has more guts than anyone else in this God-forsaken town.

Ryan, who had been interrupted in his reading when Alden came in, laid the book on his desk and cupped his chin in his hands. Sure, he had grown up with the rumors, the behind-his-back gossip, the taunts thrown at him by a few of the more daring boys. But after he'd knocked two teeth out of Kenny Flynn's big mouth and given Les Kane a black eye, the taunts had stopped. That meant he was probably Jane-Michelle's cousin, as Forrest was Willow's sister. Maybe that's why he had always felt drawn to her.

Something foreign, a strange kind of feeling interrupted his reverie. What the hell? Something or someone was invading his mind, and it felt like a mouse poking into the corners, almost an itch, definitely a mouse he didn't want crawling around in there.

Skye's sharply planed face gradually formed into an image in his mind—so real that he might well have been looking at her in person. Her blue eyes stared at him, and he felt her presence beside him. He shivered. This had never happened before. He was always the one who invaded other people's thoughts, pretty much at will. He felt an icy coldness and sensed the power of her dislike for him.

He tried to push her away with the force of his will, but she was too strong. She smiled, but it was a smile that sent a chill all through him. Her words formed in his mind, as hard as he tried to put up a mental wall to stop them.

"Ryan, we have to talk."

He pushed back at her with all the strength of his will. "Forget it, bitch. Soon you're going to die—all over again."

Forty-one

Jaime waited on pins and needles for Evan's return from the hastily called Board of Ed meeting, but the hours dragged on until well after lunchtime. She called his cell a number of times, but he never answered. Jack and Josh appeared to have picked up on her anxiety, racing around the house, up and down the stairs, chasing each other and yelling at the top of their lungs. Finally, at the end of her patience, she banished them from the house.

"Okay, you two. I can't take this anymore. Out you go. Ride your bikes up and down the sidewalks, play basketball out back—I don't care. Just take your noise outside."

The June day was cool, but the boys ran out the back door willingly. Jaime, fighting a headache, heard them as clearly as if they had still been in the house. She brewed a fresh pot of coffee, and when it was done, poured herself a steaming mug of it and wandered into the living room. Pulling aside the draperies, she watched the boys race up and down the length of the hedge separating their house from Jane-Michelle's and wondered what game they were playing. She took the phone off the phone stand and put it down on the coffee table, on top of *Architectural Digest*, and sank down on the sofa. Why hadn't Evan called? It must be bad news. She sighed in frustration. She had grown to love this little town that had seemed so familiar from the first day, and she loved her friends. The kids were happy and seemed to her to have a new sense of freedom—not that they needed any more freedom—and now what? After only one year, they would have to move and start all over again?

The phone rang, startling her. She reached for the receiver in such a hurry some of the hot coffee splashed on her hand.

"Ouch! Evan—why didn't you call—?"

"Sorry, Jaime. It's Skye."

Jaime's feelings of anxiety increased. "What is it, Skye? Have you heard anything about the Board meeting—from Francisca, or *anyone?"*

"Yes. Dane called and said it was almost over, and he'd be home soon. But—I need to talk to you about something else. I'm back at Francesca's, and Molly is still here from our get-together this morning."

Jaime felt a flicker of jealousy. Francesca had invited Molly and her kids to stay and not her and the boys? Well, her kids *could* be loud and obnoxious. Francesca was probably glad to get them out of her house. She pushed the feelings down as unworthy of herself. Francesca had been *such* a good friend over the past year, and Molly *was* a lovely person. *Shades of Barbara and Janie—it never ends, does it? Same story over and over.*

"Jaime—-?"

"Yes, I'm here, Skye. What is it?"

"We think you ought to come back over here. Francesca asked Dane to bring Evan with him, and we are going to call Willow and Jane-Michelle as well. Things are really boiling to a head, and we have to get everyone on the same page."

Jaime caught her breath. "This sounds as if something else has happened since this morning, Skye. Did you have the meeting about the funeral mass?"

"Why don't you just get the kids and come over?" Skye insisted. "We'll lay it all out when everyone's here. Oh—" There was a pause, then Skye resumed. "There's Dane's car now, and Evan's with him. Come over as soon as you can."

"Ten minutes."

~ * ~

Francesca fed everyone for the second time that day, putting out sandwiches cut in fourths: turkey, tuna-salad, and peanut butter and jelly for the kids. There were also plates of deviled eggs, baskets of chips and pretzels, and a dish of cut-up fruit.

"Notice how *they* don't have a pink table." Josh glared Jaime as the women settled the kids in the kitchen. "They have a real table, just brown wood."

"Ours *is* a real table," Jaime retorted, not amused for once. "And I painted it hot pink, and I like it, and it's going to stay there."

"Then we're never eating in the kitchen again," Jack put in. "We'll come over here for breakfast."

Jaime and Francesca left the kids in the care of the teenagers, who seemed to still have plenty of energy left to deal with them, and joined the rest of the crowd in the Summers' spacious living room. In addition to the pale green damask sofa and loveseat, several pale pink and green tapestry occasional chairs circled the glass and wrought iron coffee table. Francesca removed the exquisite bonsai, a living miniature cherry tree with actual pink flowers, from the table and replaced it with wine glasses, a bottle of red and a bottle of white, and an ice bucket with ice cubes and tongs. She went back to the kitchen and returned with a tray bearing several individual bottles of beer and a few frosty mugs.

Francesca looked around the group and gestured for everyone to help themselves. She sat next to Jaime and smiled at her. "We should be fortified for whatever. Please take whatever you want."

Jaime, Francesca, and Molly poured themselves glasses of the crystal clear pinot grigio, and Skye selected merlot. Evan and Dane filled mugs with the cold beer. Willow and Jane-Michelle declined anything to drink.

Jaime was gratified to see that Willow and Jane-Michelle had shown up. Although Willow looked tense and tight-lipped, as if she disapproved in advance of whatever was going to happen, and Jane-Michelle appeared decidedly on edge, it had probably been difficult to refuse Skye's insistence that they come. Jaime smiled at them both. Willow looked away, and Jane-Michelle nodded but did not return the smile.

As several people leaned forward to take up Francesca's invitation, Jaime caught Evan's eye. In all the confusion, she hadn't had even a minute to speak to him, but she noticed, with relief, that he seemed much more relaxed than she'd thought he would be. He smiled and nodded at her, putting his thumb and index finger together in an 'okay' sign.

She smiled back, but her anxiety remained. They couldn't have decided to let him keep his job, could they, with all the dissention his policies had caused this year?

Evan cleared his throat. "I guess you all want to know what happened at the meeting."

There was a chorus of assents and nodding heads.

"I think Dane saved my aa—my job." Molly stifled a giggle. "Most of the board was supportive, actually, of the things I've been trying to do this year. The Bauer Brothers have been very vocal, giving negative statements to the papers, and such, which has made it sound like there has been a lot of opposition."

Dane held up a finger. "Which there hasn't really been. And the entire board was appalled at what happened to your house."

"So what does that all that mean?" Jaime's heart was in her mouth. "You mean Evan gets to keep his job?"

Evan nodded at her. "I hate to compromise on what I truly believe in, but maybe it's necessary to take it a little slower around here."

"What does that mean, exactly?" Willow looked directly at Evan for the first time. "I know I haven't been out there cheering in public, Dr. Reid, but in general I've approved of the changes you've been making."

Jane-Michelle looked at him and nodded too. "So have I. I've done a lot of thinking about this lately, and about all the things that have been happening. It's about time someone dragged this place into the twenty-first century."

There was a stunned silence. "I never knew you felt that way, Janie." Willow raised her eyebrows in surprise at her daughter.

"Well, how would *you* feel, Mom, if everybody knew—" She broke off, embarrassed, and bit her lip. She turned back to Evan. "What restrictions are they putting on your program, Dr. Reid"

"First of all, among friends, and I consider everyone here a friend, I'm Evan."

Willow and Jane-Michelle nodded.

"Second of all, I can agree to these restrictions for a year or two, but not much longer. If the town isn't willing to move forward for the sake of its children, I'll have to move on."

Dane lifted a finger to get the floor, and everyone fell silent. "Evan needs to soft-pedal the black history program. As ridiculous as it sounds, there are still people here who don't want to give African Americans credit for doing anything to contribute to building this country."

Skye bit her lip. "I might be able to help with that. Boston is very liberal, and we might be able to get something through the state legislature that mandates such a program. I could introduce such a bill."

"Oh, that's a wonderful idea." Francesca clapped her hands as Evan and Dane, looking pleased, nodded in agreement.

"And what else?" Jaime asked.

"Cut back on the arts programs." Evan held up his fingers in sequence. "Eliminate a couple of the art teachers and schedule art once every other week instead of twice a week. No portfolio class in high school. No dance or creative writing classes. Band and chorus are all right, but no music history."

"Whew." Molly let out a long breath. "I used to just live for art class in high school."

"Well, that's the way the cookie crumbles." Evan grinned at his use of such a cliché phrase. "But I'll gradually put it all back."

"They also want to mandate an appreciation-of-rural-life sort of overview in the schools," Evan continued. "Starting in kindergarten and going all the way through high school, an emphasis on small town life in America and what's good about it."

"Actually, I like that idea." Jaime looked around the circle. "I've grown to appreciate small town life in the year we've been here, and I hope we're here for a long time."

"You heard it from the horse's mouth," Evan teased. "I never thought to hear than from Jaime."

"I think we can work with all that." Dane raised his beer mug in Evan's direction. "Anyway, Evan has his job, on probation, for another year. Little by little, we think we can get where we need to go."

Evan finished off his beer and helped himself to another. "Now..." He gestured in Skye's direction. "You've heard what we have to say. Suppose you fill us in on why we're here, meeting with all of you, in the first place. What's the so-called crisis, as you put it?" He sat back, watching her.

"I suggest you all listen for a change, don't change the subject, don't blow us off, and pay attention." Jaime couldn't help but admire the woman's poise and tone of authority. She suspected that Skye was about to suggest to them an absolutely preposterous situation—-and she expected them to take her very, very seriously.

"If we don't do something about it," Skye continued, "we'll all be dead by next weekend."

Skye, aided by Jaime and Francesca, reviewed everything that they had experienced during the past year. Dane listened with interest, but Evan fidgeted, obviously impatient with the whole subject.

"I just think your imaginations have run away with all of you." Evan sat back with his hands in his pockets and gave them a tired smile. "Ryan is a respected businessman in town, and Alden—well, he doesn't have the intelligence or the guts to pull off something like that."

Willow spoke up unexpectedly. "Ryan is Forrest Brown's son. I have known him since he was a baby, and his father was my brother. He was an evil man, and I believe that genes for that can be passed down. Ryan has had an 'attitude' all his life. Not many people see it. They remember Francie and Donnie, who were good people, but Ryan is not Donnie's son. He is perfectly capable of something like you're describing."

"On what do you base your conclusions?" Evan sounded like the academic he was.

Jane-Michelle took a deep breath and put her hand on her mother's knee. "I can probably answer that better than she can. He's a few years younger than I am, but I have always known that he was, most likely, my cousin. Forrest was my uncle."

Willow stared straight ahead, her face reddening a little. "Balls raped me. I was young and naïve, and so lonely. It wasn't the same with Francie. She went out with Forrest willingly, and was pregnant when Donnie came back from the Marines and married her. It makes a difference. Jane-Michelle isn't anything like Ryan. Or Balls."

"Of course not—" Jaime began, but stopped as Jane-Michelle cut in.

"Ryan was a few years behind me in school. We look alike— same eyes and nose, same coloring. But he was mean, sneaky mean. I saw him pinch girls until they cried. He was always hanging around when we lived down by the river, and I had several dogs and two beautiful cats who all died by mysterious means. We always found them dead on our front porch. After Annie, my long-haired calico, died, we never had any more pets."

"That doesn't prove he did it." Evan's voice carried a 'now, let's be reasonable' undertone that Jaime knew well.

"I got to know a couple of the girls he dated, after high school." Jane-Michelle bit her thumbnail before she continued. "They both said he roughed them up, was inconsiderate with sex with them, and one of them, Patty Blaine, said he told her he thought killing a whole bunch of people, like Forrest and Brass did, must be the most exciting thing in the world to do, even if you lost your own life while doing it."

The group was quiet as they digested this information.

"I *feel* it in him," Jane-Michelle persisted. "There's just something in him that's pushing to be unleashed, to be set free. The last time I spent any time with him was when he brought my tiles over, and had coffee with me. The way he looked at me made me feel really scared." She looked at Jaime, tears in her yes. "And I'm so sorry, Jaime, that I told him that you had Kathy's diary. I had no intention of doing that, and I don't know why I did it."

"But you did see him go into our back door and run out again a few minutes later, right?" asked Evan.

She nodded and wiped her eyes with a cocktail napkin. "I *know* he is capable of killing us all, at the church or at the Inn later. I just don't know how we're going to stop him."

"One thing we can do..." Molly said, no longer sounding as timid as she had, "is not sit together at church. If we spread out, he can't get at us all at once."

"I think he's more likely to do something at the Inn." Francesca's voice carried a thoughtful note. "And we've been assigned to one table there. We have to sit together." She looked around the group. "Who picked out the Lakeside Inn for the luncheon anyway? It's the same place the sixty-one massacre happened, and..." She shivered. "It's almost the same date. How could that have happened?"

"Don't you know who arranged that?" Skye gave her a wry smile. "Ryan did. He called up his old friend, Father Murphy, and offered to put the luncheon on at his own expense. I objected—of course—because she was *my* cousin, but I was away in Boston, and Ryan and Father Murphy made the arrangements and put out the publicity before I could stop it. Ryan told the priest that he had asked my permission and that I was okay with it. Kate was well known, and people are coming from all over for this. We can't change the place at this late date."

"I still can't—" Evan began, but Skye, with an unusual show of anger, cut him off, gesturing at him with her forefinger. "Mr. doubting Thomas! What is it going to take? Do you want a demonstration?"

Evan stared at her. "Demonstration? What do you mean?"

"Okay! I swore I'd never do this, but there are people here who need to be convinced beyond anything I can say." She held out both hands. "Everyone join hands, please." As Willow, Dane, and Evan hesitated, Skye became more insistent. "Just do it! You wanted proof—I'm going to give it to you."

Evan, with a sheepish look, took Jaime's hand on one side and Skye's on the other. Willow hesitated a moment, then took Dane's hand and Jane-Michelle's. Jaime suspected that Evan was about to make a wisecrack about covens or new age, and pushed her foot against his in warning.

"Now," Skye said, "just think about Ryan Barrett. Try to picture him in your mind. If you find yourself thinking about your golf game or the Sunday roast, push it out of your mind. Close your eyes and think about Ryan."

Evan muttered something under his breath until Jaime squeezed his hand hard. With a sigh, he fell quiet, and silence reigned over the group. For several minutes nothing happened, and Jaime began to doubt that anything would. What was Skye trying to do anyway? She opened her eyes, looked at Skye, and froze. Skye was as pale as snow, and somehow her skin had become translucent, as if someone else lurked behind it.

"Close your eyes, Jaime."

Jaime was glad to obey.

A few more minutes passed, and Jaime knew that Evan would not be able to go on with what he considered a charade much longer. True to form, he dropped her hand and began to stand up. "Okay, enough of this. I have things to attend to—*oh my God!*" As his matter-of-fact tone turned to a horrified exclamation, everyone opened their eyes and saw what Evan saw.

A ghostly figure hovered in the air over their heads. It was Ryan Barrett, without a doubt, but a Ryan Barrett none of them had ever seen before. The translucent figure wavered in murky shades of brown and gray, and the pale late afternoon light from the windows shone right through him. Ryan's face seemed elongated, as if something invisible tugged at it, pulling it downward, and his eyes burned with hatred as he glared at them. For no more than twenty seconds or so, they all stared at the vision, transfixed. Then the apparition shattered silently, like glass raining down on the coffee table and disappeared.

"That's what I've seen for years," Skye told them in a world-weary tone. "That's what I've been trying to tell you, and that's how I know."

~ * ~

Molly collected her kids, and Jaime rounded up the boys as they prepared to leave. Although the mood of the group was subdued, it seemed to Jaime that there was also now a ray of hope. The men had seen the Ryan's apparition, and his evil had been evident to them as it had been to everyone else. Willow and Jane-Michelle were now also on board, and their chilliness toward Jaime had thawed.

As they all bid each other goodbye, Jaime drew Willow aside. "I told Evan this morning, but I wanted you to be the second to know." She raised herself on tiptoe and whispered a few words in Willow's ear. "We're not ready to tell everyone yet, though."

"I'm flattered you told me," Willow said, looking mystified, "but why would you tell me before you tell your friends—Francesca, Molly?"

Jaime whispered into Willow's ear again. The look that came over Willow's lined face was all that Jaime could have hoped for. It was as if the pain of untold years and humiliation melted away as she watched.

"Thank you." Willow wiped her fingers over her eyes.

"What is it I'm not supposed to hear yet?" Francesca asked, coming up behind them.

Jaime turned to her and grinned. "That I'm pregnant, and if I have a girl, I'm going to name her Willow."

Forty-two

Jaime sat with Evan in the middle of the large, ornate church. St Mark's was a landmark in Springfield, and the diocese, as well as the well-heeled congregation, had seen to it that the church was well taken care of, its Corinthian pillars kept in good repair, the gold-trimmed altar and pulpit untarnished, the rich, dark red pew cushions and kneelers re-covered when necessary, the stone floor scrubbed and polished. It was a beautiful church, with the niches that held statues of Jesus, Mary, and the saints unblemished by time or vandals as well.

Evan poked Jaime when Ryan Barrett and his wife came in, genuflected to the crucifix, and took their seats near the front of the church. Even Alden Snyder made an appearance, sitting several rows behind Molly, and actually looked somewhat respectable in a well-worn tweed jacket, his unruly hair oiled smoothly down. All during the service, he stared at Molly, never taking his eyes off her.

"They don't look like they intend to kill anyone today," Evan whispered to her.

Jaime moved closer to him, seeking his strength. She had trembled all through the service, and now it was nearly over, Father Murphy speaking his last prayers. They were all there, Francesca and Dane, Willow, Jane-Michelle, and Skye, seated in the second row. They had agreed to spread out, just to make it more difficult for Ryan, or whoever it was who intended a mass murder, no pun intended, to kill them all sitting together. Evan, although he still did not accept their reincarnation theory, had been sufficiently shaken by the apparition at Francesca's house to admit the possibility that Ryan might have murder in his heart.

There were other people whom Jaime recognized from the community and the school system who also attended the service. There were the Bauer Brothers, looking grumpy as usual; Mack Blake, the president of the Board of Education; the boys' perky kindergarten teacher, Sandy Gleason, and her handsome husband; and sitting with them, Matt Thompson, the spacey fifth grade teacher, accompanied by his significant other. Matt was attired rather conservatively, for him, wearing a gray Glen plaid suit, a yellow shirt, and purple tie.

Father Murphy pronounced the blessing and invited everyone to attend the luncheon at the Lakeside Inn an hour from then. The congregation began to file out of the church.

"Dr. Reid," said a voice behind them, as Jaime and Evan moved down the aisle. "Did my men do a satisfactory painting job for you?"

Jaime felt herself pale, and she grabbed the end of the pew to steady herself. But Ryan Barrett didn't look anything like the vision they had seen. He looked like the amiable young man who had tended bar at her cocktail party, months ago.

"Perfect, thank you." Evan kept his voice even. "Can't see any of those words anymore."

Ryan smiled. "Glad to hear it. There won't be any charge for that, Dr. Reid. It's reprehensible that anyone would do that to our superintendent's home."

Evan began to protest, but Ryan waved him away. "Nothing to thank me for, Dr, Reid. See you at the luncheon." He moved past them, and as he reached the front door he was joined by Alden, who had made no attempt to follow Molly's flight out the side door near where she sat.

Ryan and Alden stood on the portico outside the front doors, and as Jaime and Evan moved past them, she could not avoid hearing Ryan say, "Alden, I'm afraid you won't be able to go to the luncheon. There's a problem back at the plant that needs your expertise, and I have already told the guys you're on your way back to help them."

He meant us to hear that. He wants us to think Alden won't be there, if anything happens. Alden now has an alibi.

~ * ~

Jaime, wondering if it would be an inexcusable thing to plead a headache and insist that Evan take her home, waited near one of the windows while Evan went to the bar to get them drinks. The lake sparkled outside the inn. It was a beautiful June day. *Too bad you're all going to die.* She shivered as Ryan's voice went through her. She looked around and searched the milling crowd, but he was nowhere in sight.

"Jaime." It was Matt Thompson with a younger, slightly built man by his side. "I wonder if I could ask a favor of you?"

"Certainly. What is it, Matt?"

"This is Bobby Shane. He's been substituting in English over at Sand Hill High and will probably have a full time position in the fall. Bobby, Jaime Reid, the super's wife."

"That's wonderful. Congratulations." Jaime wondered how the pale-faced young man who looked as if he would run if challenged by a rabbit could control a classroom.

"I wondered if Bobby could hang out with you for just a little while? I got a call on my cell from my sister. It seems my mother fell, nothing serious I guess, but I need to run over there to make sure things are under control. Sis tends to get a bit hysterical over minor things."

"Oh, I hope everything will be okay." Jaime smiled at the nervous young man. "He'll be fine with us until you get back,"

"Just introduce Bobby to a few people." Matt patted Bobby's shoulder. "He doesn't know anybody here, and..."

"Certainly, Matt, I'll be glad to." Jaime was relieved to have something to do while Evan procured the drinks and greeted all the people who wanted to speak to him.

"I'll be back in less than an hour, well before they put out the buffet." Matt squeezed Bobby's arm and hurried out, his suit jacket flapping behind him.

Skye edged out of the crowd and came over to them, accompanied by a short, slim woman dressed in an exquisite—and obviously expensive-black silk suit.

"Jaime, this is Suzanne White, the fashion editor of the Springfield Register. I think you remember that we mentioned that she was a close friend of Kate's."

Suki, back with the rest of us, just in time to be murdered.

"But I've had such a hectic schedule I just never had time to get together with the rest of you." Suzanne fluttered her fingers at Jaime. Flawless complexion, perfect teeth, beautiful hair, completely put together in a display of impeccable good taste.

Jaime introduced them to shy Bobby, who was quite obviously in awe of the tall, beautiful, well-known Skye and the overwhelming fashion icon Suzanne.

"I don't see Ryan anywhere." Skye spoke in a hushed voice. "I don't like it that he's not here. Nor is Alden."

"I heard Ryan tell Alden there was something he wanted him to do at the lumber company," Jaime told her. "Ryan sent him over there."

Skye threw Jaime a skeptical look. "So he said. Oh, here comes Evan. Everyone has been trying to talk to him, and mostly it seems to be supportive."

Evan did seem more relaxed than he had been, as he smiled at Jaime and greeted Skye and Bobby, whom he already seemed to know. He handed Jaime a glass of Chardonnay. "There you are, my lady."

A waiter wearing black pants and a white shirt appeared with a tray and offered them assorted canapés. He centered his attention on Bobby. "Would you like me to get you something from the bar, sir? I can bring it on my next go-around."

Bobby gratefully accepted, opting for a vodka and tonic. He took a phyllo dough-wrapped tidbit from the tray and nibbled at it as he gazed up at Skye, who towered a good six inches over him.

Dane and Francesca wandered over toward them, and Jaime introduced them. Dane, in his genial, interested-in-everyone way, inquired if Bobby, being new to the area, had been told about the priceless collection of antique books displayed in a special case on the second floor of the inn.

Bobby suddenly came to life and lit up like a Christmas tree. "Why no, sir. Nobody ever mentioned that, and I'd love to see them. Is it possible to go up there now?"

"Certainly." Dane motioned toward the exit. "We won't be eating for some time. Why don't I take you up and show you right now?"

"Oh, would you? I would really like to see them."

The two men headed toward one of the winding staircases. There was one on each side of the room that led to the second floor. Jaime turned back to the window and, looking out, noticed that the sky, which had been clear and blue, had clouded over. Hints of gray streaked across it from the west.

Jaime looked around in surprise. "Is it supposed to storm?"

"I didn't think so." Evan closed the distance between them to stand beside her.

Francesca gestured toward the window with her wine glass. A few drops splashed on her dress. "Whoops. Clumsy me. There is a change in the air. You can almost feel it, can't you?" She swiped at the damp spot with her napkin.

Skye shivered. "It does feel as if the temperature has dropped. I wouldn't be surprised if we do have a storm. I'm glad I wore a jacket."

As if to prove her point, a rumble of thunder sounded, and the sky visibly darkened as they stared out over the lake. The wind picked up, and the surface of the water began to ripple.

Uncomfortable, the group moved away from the window. People began to notice the change in the weather and congregated more in the center of the room. Many found their tables and sat where the name cards indicated. Several bellboys in green and gold uniforms ran around, untied the cords from the draperies, and let the heavy fabric fall over the windows and conceal the changing weather outside.

"This is our table." Francesca moved toward a round table at the far side of the room, just a dozen feet or so from the other staircase to the second floor.

Jaime felt a strange, lightheaded sensation overtake her, and it was only Evan's firm arm around her that kept her steady.

"Take it easy, Jaime," he whispered to her. "Ryan's not even here."

"That's what I'm worried about."

They took seats around the table, saving seats for Dane, Matt, and Bobby.

It's déjà vu, déjà vu, not memories of how we sat here fifty years ago, same Lakeside Inn, same time of year... it just can't be.

The entire atmosphere of the room had changed. Although the occasion was a sad one, there had been the usual light chatter of people coming together who hadn't seen each other in some time, accompanied by a feeling of closeness and affection for Kate, who had been loved and respected and met her end in such a tragic way. People shivered, and those who had sweaters or jackets put them on. The thunder continued to rumble outside, and Jaime heard a light rain begin to patter on the stone patio and pathways.

Barbara, Paul, Donnie, Janie, Sylvia, Francie, Kathy, Suki, Marc...

Molly, Evan, Dane, Jaime, Skye, Francesca, Kate, Suzanne, Matt...

Jaime's headache throbbed. There were cruets of wine, both red and white, on the table, but Jaime, being pregnant, settled for ginger ale. She watched with envy as Francesca drained her glass and refilled it from the fancy flask in front of her.

A sudden gust of wind whipped through a window that must have been inadvertently left open, and several crystal goblets few off a nearby table and splintered all over the hardwood floor. Two waiters rushed over, and it took both of them together to wrestle the window shut.

"I don't like this at all," Skye murmured to Jaime. "Ryan isn't here. This does not bode well."

"Dane isn't here either. Nothing can happen until we're all together."

"Let's hope they stay upstairs for a long time," Skye quipped.

Then—Ryan was there. They all turned toward the podium placed in the forefront of the room. Father Murphy stood there with Ryan. Conversation died down as the priest began to speak.

"...and we all have Ryan Barrett, one of Mill Pond's leading businessmen and outstanding citizen of this wonderful community, to thank for this luncheon reception in honor of Kate Knight. Although I was her pastor, I didn't know her nearly as well as I'm sure the citizens of her own home town must have, so now I'd like to allow Ryan to say a few words."

There was a round of applause for Ryan, but Skye glared at him without moving a finger, and Jaime followed her example,

Suzanne leaned in toward the others. "Kate didn't even know Ryan very well, if at all. I didn't go to Mill Pond, but I never heard Kate mention him. Now he's pretending he was a dear friend. He was at least five or six years ahead of her in school. Did you know him, Skye?"

"If you remember, although my parents were from here, my father was in the service, and we lived all over the world until they came back when I was in high school. So—no, I never knew him."

Jaime focused on her glass of ginger ale. *You knew him better than all the rest of us did, even if it was in a very unusual way.* "It begins to sound like nobody knew the real Ryan."

She looked up as Ryan began to speak, although she could barely endure the sight of him.

He went on to laud Kate's achievements, the awards she had won for the Springfield paper, her numerous friendships, her long connection to Mill Pond. As he spoke, Jaime forced herself to watch him. Against her will, she saw again the murky vision of him they had all experienced at Francesca's place. It settled like a mist over him, the dirty colors just pale enough for his actual face to show through.

Ryan, winding up his talk, met her eyes. Abruptly she jumped up from the table, unable to bear the triumphant evil she saw there. She grabbed her purse.

"Ladies' room." She gasped, and fled.

Jaime ran into Matt in the hallway. He struggled for breath, puffing hard, and wet in spite of his umbrella. Pellets of water ran over his forehead, and his suit was soaked. In the hand without the umbrella, he clutched a plastic bag. "It's brutal out there. I knew I'd never make it dry, so I brought along a change of clothing. Where's Bobby? Is everyone finished eating?"

"No, we haven't started. Bobby's upstairs with Dane, looking at the old book collection. They've been there for an hour. Matt—I'm so worried. I can—"

He didn't seem to hear her. "There are several unused little rooms up there. I'll just run up and change, and I'll bring the guys back down with me." Before she could protest, he dashed up the stairs, which, considering his bulk, must have taken considerable effort.

Jaime sensed the tension in the air as the storm began in earnest, and the throbbing in her head became almost unbearable. She leaned against the wall for support. The flight to the ladies' room was an excuse. She needed to breathe air not contaminated by Ryan's presence and the evil she felt emanating from him. She noticed the spatter of raindrops Matt had left on the staircase like the breadcrumbs in that old fairy tale. Hardly knowing what she was doing, she turned and followed the trail upstairs.

~ * ~

The landing on the second floor of the Lakeside Inn gave way to a spacious room that had never been redecorated and wasn't used for much of anything. Faded yellow floral wallpaper was water-stained in places, and the elegant crown molding had lost its gleam years ago. Several small rooms, still used for occasional meetings, lined the far wall. At the front, tall small-paned windows looked over the velvety lawn. Between the windows were the cases of rare books that had lured Dane and Bobby upstairs.

Dane turned and smiled at Jaime as she reached the landing. "I guess you came to summon us for dinner."

Bobby looked up as she approached. He straightened up with obvious reluctance and backed away from the case of books he was perusing.

She joined them and stood very close to Dane, soaking up reassurance from him. "No, we're not ready yet. I just needed a break."

One of the small doors opened, and Matt came out. He padded across the floor and joined them. Jaime regarded him in amusement. He sported a dry outfit consisting of a bright blue sports jacket, pale blue pants, lavender shirt, and a kelly green tie with some sort of college crest on it.

Dane gestured toward the stairs. "We'd better go down and join the others. I'm sure Francesca's wondering where I am. I hope we didn't miss anything important."

Jaime shook her head. "Just the invocation, and Ryan's tribute to Kate." She paused. "And I can't vouch for how sincere that was."

Dane took Jaime's arm, and Bobby fell into step beside Matt. Jaime stopped short, startled, as the door nearest the landing flew open. Two men, dressed all in black and wearing ski masks confronted them, guns drawn.

"Hold it right there, you slimy bastards."

Jaime immediately recognized the voice. *Ryan.*

Dane reared back. "What the hell—?"

Jaime tightened her grip on his arm. *He still doesn't get it. After everything Francesca, Skye, and I told him, he still doesn't know what's happening.*

The other man, taller than Ryan, waved his gun at them. "Move, you creeps. We're going down the other staircase so you can join your classmates, and you can all die together... again."

Jaime knew his voice, too: Alden Snyder.

Dane didn't move. "Classmates? What are you talking about? Who are you?"

Jaime squeezed his arm. "It's Ryan Barrett and Alden Snyder. Remember what we told you, Dane?" *Donnie and I, dying together again.*

'Oh." Suddenly he chuckled. "Okay, you guys, I get it—a reunion joke, but not in very good taste, I must say. Now, enough is—"

"Not a joke." Ryan raised his gun and struck Dane across the face. He gestured toward the far end of the room. *"I said move."*

Jaime flinched as if she had been the one he hit. Dane looked as if he didn't believe what just happened. He touched his hand to his face, then stared at his open palm covered with blood. In slow motion he fished a handkerchief from his pocket and wiped his face.

Jaime tugged at his arm and nudged him toward the opposite end of the room. "We'd better do as they say."

He looked down at her as if nothing had happened and they had all the time in the world. Tenderly he touched the necklace at her throat. "You wore the necklace, the silver *J*."

"Move it!" Alden turned to Ryan. "Hit him again."

Jaime tugged at Dane's arm, and the group began to walk across the floor ever so slowly. Jaime glanced back as she heard Bobby whimpering. He jumped as thunder crashed outside and lightning flashed through the windows.

All of a sudden Matt stopped short. He planted his feet on the floor and refused to move. "And what are you going to do if we don't go over there. Are you going to shoot us all right here? That would alert everyone downstairs."

Alden snorted. "We'll start with sissy-boy here. I'll stuff your faggy tie in his mouth and have a little fun with him." He pulled an ugly-looking knife from his pants pocket and pantomimed a slashing motion across his throat.

Bobby began to shake. His voice came out like the whine of a whimpering dog. "Don't hurt me. I never did anything to you."

Ryan gestured with his gun. "You're Matt's boyfriend. That's reason enough."

Jaime released Dane's arm and thrust herself between Ryan and Bobby. "Don't hurt him. We'll do what you tell us." She nudged Dane and the group moved forward again.

Jaime's emotions swirled, alternating between fear and disbelief. Then she understood, as clearly as she had ever known anything. This is why fate brought her and Evan back to Mill Pond. This is what the whole thing was about. It was going to happen all over again.

Dane dropped his bloody handkerchief on the floor. "Matt," he said, without turning around, "do you remember *Geronimo*?" His voice was calm and deliberate, as if asking whether or not Matt liked his new tie.

Jaime risked a glance at his face. *He remembers.* She felt a flicker of hope. If anyone could figure a way out of this, it would be Dane.

Matt didn't answer, and Jaime's heart took a dip. *He doesn't remember.*

"Ouch!" She flinched as one of the gunmen jabbed the gun in her back, none too gently either. "Move it, bitch. There ain't no way outta this."

As they reached the top of the stairs, Dane wheeled around to face Ryan and Alden. "Look, what do you want, money? Why do you have to murder innocent people?"

"Karma." Ryan's laugh made Jaime shiver. "Don't you remember, *Donnie?"*

Matt spoke up out of his confusion. "His name isn't Donnie, it's Dane. You have us mixed up with other people." Beside him, Bobby sobbed.

Dane stared at Ryan, holding his eyes. "Yes, but you don't have to carry out this vendetta. Let it end here. Now."

"My father would want me to." Ryan spoke with real pride. "Forrest Brown. He's watching somewhere and rejoicing. Toasting me, his bastard son, with a really good beer."

Alden waved his gun around. "I don't know about any of this crap, but let's get 'em down there. And we're getting Molly outta there first, right?"

Ryan chuckled. "Right." He jabbed Jaime in the back again. "Let's go. Let's join the rest of your too-good-for-this-earth friends downstairs. You first, Janie, little cat-eyed Janie." He shoved her with his hand, hard enough to throw her off balance. She stumbled back against Dane.

Jaime took the first step down. She clutched the old railing, which seemed to stay in place by pure faith, as it was broken in several places, and sagged in others. She felt Dane pressed up close behind her. She risked a quick glance back and saw Bobby, supported by Matt, with Ryan and Alden close behind.

"Stop at the first landing." That was Ryan's voice.

Jaime stopped on the landing, just before the staircase turned. There was a window there, and she put her hand on the sill to help balance herself. She noticed that several of the windowpanes were cracked. Outside, the storm raged, and the original Lakeside Inn sign swung on one chain, repeatedly banging against the side of the building.

Another jab with the gun, and Alden's voice this time. "Move on down, slowly."

Jaime took several more steps, followed by the others. All at once a strong gust of wind hit the sign, and the remaining chain broke. Like a swing given a mighty push, the heavy sign crashed through the window, scattering splintering wood and glass everywhere.

Jaime screamed as a sliver of glass scraped her arm. She plastered herself up against the wall of the staircase, her hands protecting her eyes... Hearing the howls of pain, she dared to look up. Everyone seemed to have taken some kind of blow, and there was blood everywhere. Dane, Matt, and Bobby looked dazed, but were still on their feet. The sign had smashed into Ryan and Alden, knocking them down, and one of the guns now lay at Bobby's feet.

No one, least of all Jaime, expected Bobby to act the hero. He grabbed the gun, turned like a ballet dancer, and fired, plugging a bullet into Ryan's chest.

"Geronimo!"

Jaime watched open-mouthed as Dane and Matt acted in unison. *Just the way they used to coordinate at the basketball games.*

Ryan, already badly wounded, had no fight left, and Dane dragged him past Jaime and hurled him down the rest of the stairs. He crashed through the flimsy door at the bottom and slid onto the polished floor of the banquet room. Matt threw himself at Alden's legs, trying to throw him off balance. Alden clung to the banister with one hand. He waved his gun around and fired several wild shots into the air. Dane tackled him, but the man hung on with amazing strength. Dane tugged at the railing. A foot-long piece of it broke free, and Dane used it like a club. After several hard blows to the head, Alden let go. He fell forward down the stairs and hit his head on one of the steps. He catapulted down the rest of the steps, landing on top of Ryan, his arms over his head as if in surrender. The old Lakeside Inn sign tumbled down the steps after him.

Jaime, shaking, climbed down the rest of the stairs, followed by the others. A crowd had already gathered, trying to figure out what happened.

Two waiters extended their hands to Jaime and lifted her over the bodies. Several others, seeing that there were more people in the stairway, dragged the two bodies out of the way. The same waiter who had circulated with the drinks at the start of the evening approached her. "Are you hurt, ma'am?"

"No... no, it's just... just blood." She couldn't stop shaking. She didn't know for sure if she were hurt or not

Evan was there, a familiar source of strength surrounding her with love. "Jaime, Jaime, are you all right?"

She fell into his arms. At that moment she didn't care about anything except Evan and that she was safe with him.

The crowd of onlookers grew. Francesca shoved people aside to rush into Dane's arms.

"It's over," Jaime said to her. "It's over."

~ * ~

Police sirens screamed outside the Inn.

Evan greeted the policeman. "Well, Sergeant Foster, for once I'm glad to see you."

The cop stared down at the two masked men. "Who are they?" He bent down and pulled the masks off their faces. "Alden Snyder, well that's no big surprise. But—Ryan Barrett?" He pushed back his cap and scratched his head. "That I don't get at all." He turned to Dane. "What the hell's been going on here?"

"It-it was a hold-up." Dane gestured to Jaime, Matt and Bobby. "The four of us were upstairs looking at the antique books, and these two tried to hold us up. I thought it was a joke at first."

Seth looked doubtful. "Ryan didn't need to hold anyone up. He owns an entire lumber company, or half of it, anyway."

How are we going to explain this and not come off as totally nuts? Jaime, from the safety of Evan's arms looked at Seth. "Ryan Barrett wasn't the good man everyone thought he was. He and Alden had a lot in common."

Seth turned to her with a face etched with doubt. "And after just one year living in Mill Pond, how would you know that, Mrs. Reid?"

She bristled. "I've had enough contact with both of them to know."

Dane backed her up as he pointed to his face. "See this? Ryan bashed me with his gun, then forced us down the back staircase here. He—well, who knows what he intended to do?"

Seth looked around as if wondering what to do next. He gestured to one of the younger policemen. "Take Matt and the other guy somewhere else and get their statements. I'll try to figure out what went on here."

Jaime watched as Matt and Bobby in their blood-spattered clothing were escorted out of the room. She gazed around the elegant room, the buffet table abandoned, and back at all the people staring at them. It was such a shame that Kate's memorial dinner had been ruined by two men who now lay dead at her feet.

Seth gave his head another scratch and regarded her and Evan, Dane and Francesca with a sour look. "You four have provided me with more excitement this year than I ever needed. I see your wife is pretty shaken up, Dr. Reid. Why don't you take her home? I'll be in touch with you all later to get the details down on this... what looks to me like an attempted robbery, which I don't at all understand, but..." His voice trailed off. He bent down and picked something up from the floor. "Is this yours, Mrs. Reid? It looks like somebody's necklace."

Jaime took the necklace and examined it. It was worn and tarnished, a silver *J* with rhinestones, some of them missing. She turned it over in her hand. Something stirred in her mind, as if an old memory were pushing at the surface. She couldn't pin it down. She shrugged and handed it back to him. "Not mine. I have no idea where it came from."

Evan took her hand and squeezed it. "The storm's over. Come on, Jaime. Let's go home.

"Home." Jaime glanced back at the wreckage, the broken door swinging on one hinge, the Lakeside Inn sign in splinters on the floor. She turned back and smiled up at Evan. "Home. I don't think I've heard a more beautiful word."

Meet

Joan Conning Afman

Joan Conning Afman grew up in New England and Central New York state. It was always a choice between English and art—but ultimately she majored in art and has been a retail commercial artist and copywriter, a public school art teacher, and a college adjunct instructor. Now retired in Florida, she blends her two major interests by painting and exhibiting her work, and expressing her ideas in writing. She has a son and three daughters, and six beautiful grandchildren